THE
SINNER
AND ✝ THE
SCHOLAR

THE
SINNER
AND THE
SCHOLAR

A SINNER SISTERHOOD NOVEL

LANA PECHERCZYK

Paperback ISBN: 978-1-922989-11-6

www.lanapecherczyk.com

PROLOGUE

Rain drizzles in Cardinal City.

Gloom bathes the streets, but citizens still go about their day,
ducking and weaving around a lone figure ringing a bell and
wearing a signboard with the words *Judgment is Nigh* written
in shaky handwriting.

A hoarse voice shouts to anyone and everyone, "The lambs are
breaking the seals! First, Pestilence will bring disease. Second,
War will spread dissent and revenge. Third, Famine will unfurl
starvation. Fourth, Death will ride a white horse and cleave a
path so that Fifth, the Antichrist will rise to claim the earth for
the Sixth, when the Heavens fall."

The lone figure turns, revealing the back of the sign:

Have you made peace with your sins?

ONE
THEA

Across the street from a nightclub called Purgatory, I check my cell phone and confirm my location. Yes. Right place, right time, but the wrong outfit.

I glance down at my black dress. The neckline is too high, and the hem is too long. It's almost midnight, and the club is pumping. I unclip my dagger from my thigh holster and use it to shear off a good two feet of fabric. Then I slice down from the center of the neckline, freeing my breasts from captivity. Well, almost. A lace bra stops me from completely exposing the world.

Once satisfied with my alterations, I sheath my weapon and fluff up my hair. Lastly, I poke the silver crucifix on a necklace deep into my bra.

Business time.

Walking like I live in stilettos, I strut across the street, tossing my long dark hair and swaying my hips.

As predicted, the bouncers are too busy checking out my goods to bother with ID or, I don't know, the fact that I just cut the line. The trick is to look like you're expected and unhappy about being late.

Once inside, I hold that persona and move down a rabbit hole with thumping music vibrating the walls. Cigar smoke keeps what happens inside the seedy club hidden. I crest the foyer and take a moment to gather my bearings.

High-class women in skimpy clothing tend a bar to the right. A sunken dance floor is perfect for lusty voyeurism from wealthy businessmen sprawled in booths around it. I have no doubt the women dancing between lascivious men are hookers or wannabe sugar babies. I continue hunting until I find what I need—the man with the fattest ego, copious women on his arms, and men groveling at his feet. He's bald, wears a gold chain, and sits on a throne with a vantage point of the entrance.

He's not my guy. He's just in my way.

With my eyes on the prize, I stalk toward him, chin high and shoulders straight. As I pass the bar, a handsome man widens his eyes and opens his mouth. He takes a step toward me.

"No." I hold my right hand near his face and keep walking.

He shuts his mouth and slinks back to the bar. I don't have time to play tonight. Besides, ignoring every other man making eyes at me right now is part of the plan. Never once removing my gaze from the target, I walk across the dance floor. Perhaps it's my confident carriage, devilish outfit, or

God-given good looks, but dancers part like the red sea. When I hit the opposite end of the floor, I feel my target's eyes groping me.

I climb the steps and stop at his table.

His gaze deliberately walks across my body, lighting up with every inch he covers. The women on either side of him pout. Their need to scratch my eyes out is like a hot poker in my side. They probably think I want to snort the two lines of cocaine racked up just for them. A few empty shot glasses, a Benjamin, and a credit card are also scattered across the table.

Pipe down, ladies. I'm not here for you.

The bald man licks his lips and states, "There's a line, honey."

I don't know if he's offering me a line or if he's talking about the women waiting to be with him. *Gross.* Either way, I don't smile, blink, or even glance at the smoldering cigar wobbling on his lip.

"I'm not here for the line," I reply.

"Oh yeah?" He chuckles.

His big belly squashes against the table with each heaving breath. Two men behind him make a deliberate move to ensure I see the firearms holstered under their arms. Glocks.

I refocus on the kingpin. "You're in my seat."

At first, they laugh. The girls are cackling hyenas, and the men are weasels. The kingpin eventually slows his chuckle and glares at me. He's smarter than I pegged him for because he seems to have recognized the death in my fearless eyes.

Only three types of people would look at him the way I am —fools, psychopaths, or someone more dangerous than both.

He gives a negligent wave of pudgy fingers, and his two henchmen skirt the booth and come at me—one from either side.

Game on. My hands whip out and grab a handful of henchman testicles. Thumping music drowns out their cries of agony as I squeeze, wrench, and damn near castrate.

They double over, conveniently bringing their chests within range. *Don't mind if I do.* Removing their weapons is like taking candy from a baby. Once I have their guns, I push the magazine release on each, remove the live rounds, then toss the empty hunks of metal.

I do all this with my eyes glued to the kingpin.

"Psycho bitch." He jumps up, but his fat belly knocks his table, sending cocaine flying. He's too big, half-cut, and concerned with cigar ash now smoldering on his shirt.

I climb on the table and push the lit cigar past his gaping lips. Then I hold my hand over his mouth to keep that burning fucker inside until smoke puffs from his nose. Finally, his survival instincts knock out his shock, and he reaches for me. It's no use. I've already drawn his pistol and have it pointed at his head. This one, I leave fully loaded.

"You're in my seat," I repeat.

The girls scramble out, allowing me space to sit next to the man and let go of his mouth. He coughs, spits out the smoldering, soggy cigar, and it lands in one of the empty shot glasses. His cheeks tremble with rage as he turns toward me.

A slow sigh releases from my lips. Now it's going to get messy. The moment his hand leaves that table and heads my way, I smash the butt of his gun into his nose. Blood spurts.

"You had to keep pushing, didn't you?" I grumble.

He covers his face and whimpers.

"Fucking bitch," he spits at me. "*Whore.*"

I grin wildly. "Say it again. I dare you."

His eyes widen. "You're insane."

"Close, but no"—I glance at the brown stub in the shot glass—"cigar."

"What?"

"I'm impatient, asshole. That's what I am. Now get out."

He scrambles his sweaty, awkward, and blood-stained body out of the booth. I set his gun on the table and sweep the club with my gaze. As expected, eyes dart away. Whether security is afraid, ignorant, or biding their time, I don't care. My real target will be here any minute.

The kingpin blabbers something about me paying for what I've done.

"Blah, blah. I'm going to hell." I shoo him away. Just in time, too, because the man I'm after walks into the club.

Tall, dark, and possibly demon-possessed. Outwardly, he looks like your everyday Wall Street wanker. Inwardly, he's swarming with evil and sin. I glance at a picture on my cell phone and confirm he matches my mark. He has the same appearance, give or take the dark circles under his eyes.

Last week the Hildegard Sisterhood received a complaint from a wife concerned about her husband's change in behavior. Her local church ignored her, the local diocese ignored her, so she found us.

Only because we wanted to be found. Our supernatural ghost-hunting team ad in the paper is a front for our secret, centuries-old organization. We get a few nut jobs calling in, but occasionally, we get something worthwhile. They don't need to know we've only just discovered demons are real.

With the pistol on the table and my bag next to it, I nab the hundred-dollar bill and stuff it into my bra. Then I stretch my arms lengthwise along the back of the booth and study my mark. I need to work out if he's genuinely possessed or if this is a false alarm so I can return to my regular assassin's schedule.

He goes to the bar and orders a drink he doesn't touch. It's not long before he notices everyone in the club is looking at me. Dark eyes take me in, see me in my skimpy and lonesome glory, and then he makes tracks my way.

Some poor fool tries to warn him about me, but he ignores them and snakes through the dance floor. The dancers don't part. For a moment, he's lost in the teeming, writhing bodies. It's exactly what I imagine hell would look like—when I eventually end up there. If I squint, it's easy to pretend they're not smiling but screaming. That's not desire in their eyes but agony. They climb over each other to escape but go nowhere, doomed to suffer an eternity in this cesspit.

I shake off the notion just as my mark resurfaces on my side of the sunken dance floor. Something is wrong. He moves jerkily as though unfamiliar with his body. His shirt buttons are mismatched, his tie is stained, and sweat darkens his collar.

If he's what I think he is, the pistol will be useless, so I leave it behind, pick up my clutch and meet him before my stolen throne.

"Let's take this outside." I force a come-hither smile and drag my fingers down his chest. A sour and sickly scent wafts into the air.

I walk toward the bathrooms, where an emergency exit leads to an alley. The unique stench of his perfume stays with me, so I assume he follows.

I'm not a nervous person. I haven't been since the Sisterhood whipped it out of me almost two decades ago. I don't startle, and I don't balk. But the instant I find myself alone with him in the dark alley, my pulse quickens.

What am I doing here?

I've been trained to deal with dangerous, wicked men, but this... this is not a man. I feel it in my bones. But I have to be sure.

Keeping that grin on my lips, I back up until I hit a wall next to the exit door. To my right, an overflowing dumpster blocks the way to the street. To my left, a cat urinates on a crate stacked against a dead-end brick wall. The cat hisses and arches its back, then quickly darts away.

"I've been waiting for you." I crook my finger.

The lack of surprise in his eyes is unnerving. Surely this is just another bored, seedy stockbroker with too much cash in his pocket. He's not possessed. Demons aren't real. Because if they are, then hell is too. That's the last thing I want.

The thought makes me stand straighter.

This will end up as just another job. I can imagine the conversation with my superior now. *"Sorry, Reverend Mother. No dice. Just another cheating husband accused of possession."*

Suddenly he lurches and reaches for my neck. Because I know I must test this, I steel myself and let him pull my dress down to expose my breasts... and the blessed silver crucifix.

He hisses. Blinks. And his eyes turn completely black—no white shows. No color. Nothing but pure evil looks out at me. There is a moment of us weighing each other, a split second of him wondering about his opponent, and then he realizes I know what he is. Words spill from his mouth and sound like they're scripted in hell. His voice is deep, guttural, and full of vile insults that would make any sinner blush.

Evil.

It's in every atom, every particle, every breath I take.

I freeze.

It's real. Hell is real.

If Hell is real, then so is Heaven. Prayers sling from my lips. Every word is like a hit to him. He flinches and snarls. But he doesn't stop pawing at me. The heel of my palm flies up and hits his nose. His head snaps back. He stares at the starless sky for so long that I think I've broken his neck. But then he slowly returns his gaze to me, oblivious to blood gushing from his nose. His hand circles my throat, and he tries to steal a kiss from me. I whimper.

The smell. It's so bad.

Panic grows in my chest like vines squeezing my heart. I

don't know what to do. This is wrong. So wrong. But I know I'm not ready to die.

Not if hell is real. Not if I'm going to end up there.

And that's precisely what will happen if that man gets his mouth on me. I have no idea how I know that or if it's true, but the fear is real. I pull the blessed dagger from my thigh sheath and shove the blade into his chest.

He vomits on me, but that's not the worst of it. A dark, invisible presence flows from the wound. I *feel* it brush over me like an arctic breeze. Goosebumps break out across my skin, and my soul quakes.

Then it's gone, and the man collapses. His hands fall by his head, and I glimpse a strange tattoo beneath his sleeve. I tug it up for a better look. Ooh. *That's not good.*

TWO

THEA

The taxi driver's eyes dart to the rearview mirror, again checking on me in the back seat. He has questions.

Is this lady for real?

Should I go to the police?

Will I ever get that smell out of my upholstery?

I stare back to mess with him. His gaze flicks away, and he flexes the thick fingers of his left hand. He hasn't kicked me out yet, so I guess that's a win.

He probably thought this would be an easy, well-paying job with a scenic route. He maybe thought I was leaving a Halloween party, except... it's July, and this isn't a costume.

I crack the window. Air tasting like mist and pine gushes in. We're headed upstate. Dawn peeks over the forest on either side of us, just enough to show deer grazing and wandering onto the road. They see us coming, freeze, and then bound away.

The driver's eyes slide to me in the mirror again. This time, they hold an edge of fear. Maybe the deer have spiked his pulse. Or maybe the severed hand is starting to smell more than the pea soup vomit. He's probably wondering if I'll go all Urban Legend on his ass, lure him into the woods, and mate with him wearing a stag skull before eating his curly bits.

He's lucky the limb hasn't started to decompose because that smell, accompanied by the rest of the demon's special sauce, would be impossible to ignore.

"Just up there, thanks." I tap the window to my right. We're approaching a gravel driveway that cuts into the forest.

His exhale is audible, but his eyes narrow. He must know that only one place exists down that way. He opens his mouth, shuts it, and then opens it again before finally saying, "Are you sure, Miss?"

"Yes, thank you. This is me."

His brows lift, but he turns the car down the crunching gravel road until trees make way for a picture-perfect fairytale setting. The Hildegard Sisterhood Abbey is on a large, sprawling country estate between mountains. Drizzle never fails to fall from the sky. Pretty, poisonous plants fill the walled garden. Roosters crow in the coup. Ghosts haunt the old gothic church. It's a regular wonderland.

He pulls up curbside and stares through the wrought iron gates at the estate. "You're not going to prank them, are you?"

He hasn't noticed the barbed wire running along the top of the limestone boundary walls.

"Nope. This is home."

I pull that crumpled Benjamin from my bra and dangle it over his shoulder. Having his gaze still frozen on the abbey, he jolts when my hand snakes by his face. For a moment, he's paralyzed, but then he takes the money.

I slide out of the cab, and because I can't help myself, I shoot him my best beatific smile and say, "Peace be with you."

I wave goodbye, intending to close the door, but the damned severed limb is so heavy and sweaty that I fumble and almost drop it. Tires spin, and he speeds off. The car hits the hand in passing, and congealed blood smears along the yellow quarter panel.

"Whoops."

I want to care, but I'm exhausted and need a shower. I lift my chin to the camera over the gate. Within moments it buzzes open, just like it should. They know not to leave a Sinner out here. No one wants to have *that* conversation if the public catch a blood-covered assassin welcomed at the gates of a nunnery, even in this isolated place.

The walk down the driveway is long. I cross a bridge over the lake and pass a decommissioned Gatling gun left from the Civil War.

Some time ago, this place was built by an aristocrat from England. The story goes that he came here for a better life, but his wife died of dysentery. He created a mausoleum beneath the oak trees for her, and the gothic church has angels instead of gargoyles as a sign of his love. Eventually, he went mad and deserted the place.

That's when the Sisterhood moved in and brought it back to its former glory.

My legs ache, my back protests, and dried blood and vomit itches like a motherfucker. Cracking my neck releases tension, but it's not enough. It's never enough. All I want is to remove my contact lenses, complete my penance, and then study the pages of the latest holy manuscript pulled from the archives. It arrived a few weeks ago with a crate of other relics from a dwindling Sisterhood chapter in Spain.

I sigh as the morning sun crests the enormous wood and stone abbey. This may be my little corner of hell, but it sure looks pretty. It's home.

I take the large stone steps two at a time and shoulder through the carved cedar and stained-glass doors. A Magpie almost knocks me over. Sister Margaret. The plump nun gasps and clutches her rosary beads before gathering her composure. She makes a hasty sign of the cross, squeezes my shoulder as if to say, "Welcome home," and then continues out the door. Her black robes rustle like the wings of an angel.

The energy to grin leaves me.

Due to the nature and secrecy of the Hildegard Sisterhood, the nuns in this chapter lead a monastic life. Apart from us Sinners, the Reverend Mother and the priest, all here have taken a vow of silence to protect the secrets inside these gates. They protect us, the Sinners—the secret sanctioned assassins, seductresses, and general bad-doers of the Sisterhood.

All in the name of a better life for women.

All in the name of God and the Mother Mary.

When Beyonce said, "Girls run the world," she didn't know the half of it. We do. From Joan of Arc to Margaret Thatcher. A clever woman is behind much of history, or a man who's made history.

We put them there.

Sinners.

I should go straight to the Rev to debrief, but a niggling feeling sends me up the creaky staircase to the third-level dormitory. It's eerily quiet in this wing of the house. Sinners should be awake and on their way to training.

At the landing, I take in the hallway and draw on every instinct drilled into me since my teenage years. Cold stone floors. Closed wooden doors on either side. No sounds.

Yet the prickling on the back of my neck increases. Maybe I'm still jittery from earlier, but... *A Sinner must always trust her instincts*, my crotchety old teacher would say. *Evil lurks in the wings.*

Unlike the pure, chaste nuns flapping through the abbey, Sinners go straight to hell. Unless we repent and purge our souls through pain and prayer... and I'm not sure if my body can keep up with my sins anymore. We break commandments weekly, and there's no sugarcoating that.

The severed hand is clammy, squishy, and cold. I have to get rid of it. But first, I need to check on my things. My monastic cell is on the left. I hesitate with my hand on the doorknob. Why am I feeling like this? Is it simply the after-effects of my mission?

I shut my eyes against the memory—the demonic voice. Spittle flies from his mouth. The strange mark on his hand. The foul and obscene gestures he made... and finally, how he'd just... erupted.

I shake it off, hold my breath, and open my door.

A simple, small room. The cot is made. The bedding is clean. Wood is polished to shine on a one-person pew. A small, closed window reveals manicured gardens three levels below and a sprinkler *tik-tik-ticks* as water sprays rhythmically. But the room is empty. And that's the problem.

Where were my things?

Sweat breaks out on my brow. I rush to the next room, rap on the door, and then yank it open. Clean. Empty. The next room is the same. Every door on the left side of the hallway opens to an empty cell, cleaned out as though the Sinners never existed.

My worst nightmare has come true. Invalidation. Eradication. Erasure.

They're finally getting rid of us despite the Rev's promise to have our back. *Always.* Maybe Sinner Alice had the right idea—maybe I should get out now while I can... go and join her and the Deadly Seven fighting crime in Cardinal City.

Voices have me spinning—*the other side of the hallway.* Someone is still here. I thump on the first door and burst through, almost sobbing in relief to see the blond, American Pie sweetheart Sinner reclining on her bed, listening to the collection of Nina Simone records Alice left her. Tawny smiles at me and tugs her large retro headphones off.

"Oh, hey, Thea." Her smile drops. She waves her hand across her pale, freckled nose. "Gosh, no offense, but you smell awful."

"Where's my stuff?"

"Your stuff?" Her nose wrinkles again.

I gesture down the hall. "My manuscript, my belongings, *my stuff!*"

"Oh, your *stuff*." She bites her lip. "Yeah, everyone on that side has had their things moved to this side, and we're sharing now."

Only then do I notice another cot squished into her tiny room. I blink. Stare. Someone's belongings have been piled onto that cot. Leather, torture devices, and crumpled cigarette boxes. Probably Raven's.

Tawny puts her headphones back on, pops a Cheeto into her mouth, and closes her eyes as she bops her feet to the beat. She acts like this move doesn't affect her, but I know her. Another empty Cheetos packet is on the floor. *Stress eating for breakfast.* And sleeping in. Inside her peaches and cream complexion lays a vicious viper coiled tight. Tawny hates letting it loose. I've never met a Sinner with as many inner demons as that one right there.

She reluctantly holds out her Cheetos packet to me.

With a frustrated growl, I walk next door and knock. "Where's my stuff?"

No answer.

I open the door but freeze as a Smith & Wesson barrel touches my forehead. Leila glares at me, her nostrils flaring.

"I'm not in the mood, Leila."

"Then don't get me started," she replies.

The stunning Chinese-American brunette puts her gun away, flops onto her squeaky cot, and resumes tossing a tennis ball at the peeling wallpaper ahead. If Tawny is stress-eating, I'm surprised Leila's not outside running laps of the estate.

The second cot isn't mine. It seems to belong to a Sinner on an extended mission—Hannah. She's heavily infiltrated the Pentagon. We might not see her for another year. I glare at Leila—lucky bitch. This room is like having no roommate at all. And Leila will use force to keep it that way.

I step outside, close my eyes, and rub my temples. *Please don't let me be with Mercy. Please don't let me be with Mercy.*

She's our team leader, but for heaven's sake, she's a nightmare to live with. Gingerly, I knock at her door. No answer. I press my ear to the wood and hear talking. I open and then immediately close. The sight of a top naked, buxom redhead pouting and making sex sounds at a laptop screen is burned into my retinas.

And I didn't even see what was on her other cot.

Fuck it.

I steel myself and open the door again. Mercy shouts and pitches a long, purple, vibrating dildo at my head.

THREE
THEA

"Hey!" Mercy shouts, scowling at me through thick lashes. "Some of us are trying to orgasm here!"

I clench my jaw and point at her. "Don't you throw your vibrator at me."

"Don't you point your severed hand at me!"

"You're testing my patience, Mercy."

"Yeah, well, join the club, missy." Mercy sighs in defeat and blows a kiss at the screen. "Laters, babe."

After slamming the laptop lid shut, she glares at me. I expect a lecture. Everyone knows Mercy needs her *alone time*, but we all have our crosses to bear. Her overactive sex drive is why she was handpicked from foster care at fourteen to come here and train. Who knew she'd excel and become one of our best assassins?

No one came to claim her.

No one came for any of us.

A little nervous, I focus on the cot and sigh in relief at the small collection of trashy magazines, clothes, and bubblegum. Not mine. Thank Christ.

Mercy rolls her eyes. "Don't get too excited."

She covers her creamy skin with a lacy bra and pink satin robe she ties at the waist. The robe slides from her shoulder. One more inch, and we'd be graced with the shadow of nipple through the lace.

She mumbles, "We're all in the same boat with this new sharing arrangement. Why do you think I was getting in my last hurrah? Jasmine will be back at the abbey in no time."

"Jasmine?" An itch has me glancing down at my hand. Vomit has crusted over my skin. Seriously, pea soup? I suppose I'm lucky there are no carrots. There are always carrots.

"Yes, but she just left to visit the European Chapter to swap notes on demonology."

Since no one in the history of our organization has seen demonic activity of this magnitude, we are ill-equipped to handle it.

Sure, they've made movies about possession. Sure, the Vatican claims they have a few exorcists running about with their secret service boogeymen. But the unholy truth is that faith has been nothing but conjecture and belief for the past two thousand years. No one had *proof*. All the relics, manuscripts, and books in the archives are just stories.

Until a few months ago when strange things started happening. Abnormal animal activity was caught on camera, swarms of bugs in the cities, new contagious diseases filling hospitals, and an explosion of psychotic crime.

While we've been scrambling to catch up, a family of genetically modified heroes in Cardinal City has been doing all the dirty work. And so they should. They caused a rift between our world and a hell dimension. It's closed now, but we aren't sure why mystical anomalies keep cropping up.

Is hell about to be unleashed?

Deep down, every Sinner hopes it doesn't exist. It's a fate we were all too glad to ignore. But apparently, it takes evil to fight evil.

That's why Sinners were created.

Now we are the world's only hope. The only ones dark enough, bad enough, and lethal enough to deal with the devil himself. To wine, dine, and sixty-nine him—and then spit him out like yesterday's dinner.

Mercy shrugs, slips on feathered slippers and plumps her coppery hair like she's going on a date. "The Rev told us to meet on the front steps at eight."

I check my watch. "That's five minutes away."

"I suppose it's good you interrupted me, then." She lifts her robe and scowls at a chain cilice pinching her upper thigh. Bruises blemish her creamy skin. Any tighter, and she'd bleed. "I don't fancy being sent to the Sin Bin today."

So, if I'm not sharing with Tawny, Raven, Leila, or Mercy, that leaves only one option. The oldest Sinner here, Prudence Cane. Mid-forties, grumpy as hell, a recent assault survivor, and in no way, shape, or form a person I can stay up reading with all night.

She deserves peace.

I open the final door, and sure enough, my things are packed neatly on the cot. But no manuscript and no Prudence. She's probably at the indoor pool doing laps. That woman works out like clockwork. Dedication to her role is the reason she is the oldest active Sinner. Being captured and tortured by the Cartel hasn't slowed her down. Most Sinners either perish in the line of duty or, if they're lucky, they're one of the two who escaped.

I glare across the hallway at my old cell. Fury bubbles over, and I almost throw the severed hand. God help the person who lost that manuscript.

Slipper kitten heels click as Mercy comes to stand by me.

"It could have been worse." Her eyes meet mine. "You could be sharing with Raven."

I open my mouth, but a cane slamming rhythmically stops my reply. Mercy stills. Under her breath, she whispers, "The Reverend Mother."

I face the hallway just in time to see the Rev storming toward us, using her cane for support. Her black robes swish like the wings of death herself. Two years ago, the elderly woman took over the top role at the Sisterhood. Round eyes, a hook nose, and flat lips. She looks like a wrinkled old prune and acts like she needs one, but she's grown on us.

She's the only Rev who hasn't treated us like lost causes.

"Chop-chop, girls," she barks, voice ragged with age. Her

face twists in confusion when she sees Mercy's robe and my filthy state.

"What on earth happened to you?" the Rev asks me, blinking.

"The mark exploded in my face," I reply with a scoff of disbelief. "Here's his hand. Strange tattoo on the wrist. It seems new but looks archaic. Could mean something."

A secret smirk lurks in the Rev's pale eyes. I know that look. It's her plotting face. I last saw it when Father McBride, the only male on-premises, said he knew better about *punishing* us girls because he is ordained and she's not. Father somehow missed out on his laundry being cleaned that week. The Rev never admitted anything, but I saw her afterward in the church saying her Hail Marys at an alarming rate.

The Rev says, "There's no time to change now. They might as well see what they're in for from the moment they arrive. Saves us trouble later."

They?

"Can I at least dump this hand at the archives? It's starting to go squishy."

"No time. Bring it with you."

She continues down the hall and smacks her cane on the wall, rousing anyone within earshot. Like troops following their drill sergeant, we walk down the stairs and out the front door. We line up on the landing and wait, staring at the front gates in the mist-covered distance.

Mutters of dissent rumble out of us. I'm the worst. This is

ridiculous. After my night, I want to get rid of the damned hand, shower, and fall into bed.

"Who are they?" I mumble, but no one replies.

Tawny and Leila are the only Sinners wearing their prescribed uniform—something akin to hooded, black yoga attire and a blood-red scarf pooled around the neck. But no weapons.

Mercy fixes her disheveled robe. And by fix, I mean she makes the shoulder fall more. That's when I realize she knows exactly who's coming, and this is her rebellion. She straightens her spine, pushes out her ample breasts, and then arches a manicured brow at me.

Prudence arrives from somewhere with a bagel in her hand. From the dampness of her slick brown ponytail, I was right about laps in the pool. Only one Sinner is absent. Raven.

"Why are we here?" I ask, blinking widely to ease the irritation from my contact lenses. "And why have half our rooms been cleared out?"

The Reverend Mother shares a knowing glance with Mercy and then faces the front. "I suppose there's no hiding it from you now."

She opens her mouth to say more, but a roar fills the air. A black limousine pulls up at the gates simultaneously with a leather-clad rider on a black Suzuki motorcycle. Raven's rainbow ponytail swishes from the back of her shiny black helmet.

Both vehicles won't fit through the gate at the same time. Raven doesn't care. She angles her visor at the limo driver. She revs the engine in warning. Once. Twice. The instant the gates open, the limo goes in first. My eyes widen. Raven won't like that. She revs harder, spins her back wheel, and spits gravel. Then she rips up the curved driveway, speeding to catch up with the limo. Side by side, they approach the one-lane bridge across the lake. You'd think Raven would overtake, but she holds steady next to the limo, daring them to a silent game of chicken.

Unlike the limo driver, we're not concerned. At the last moment, Raven zooms ahead and cuts them off to take the bridge first. She stalls the bike at the base of the abbey steps.

The Reverend Mother clutches rosary beads secured to her belt. "Heaven help us."

As the limo completes its coast along the drive, Raven removes her helmet and shakes out her ponytail: black at the roots with rainbow tips. The Latino woman lights a cigarette and squints kohl-lined eyes at the vehicle. She's probably seen the guests arrive in one of her prophetic visions.

"Fall in line, Raven," the Reverend Mother says. "They're here."

"Who's they?" I ask, exasperated that I am the last to know.

The Reverend Mother stares at the limo. "Team Saint."

My stomach bottoms out. "As in, *the* Saints?"

The Vatican's male versions of us? They're even more covert than their secret service, The Entity.

"One and the same," she grinds out.

The plump male driver exits and moves to the rear

passenger door, but someone inside opens it first. I snort. Of course, they would. A Saint never lets *anyone* do the work for him. The fucking sycophants of God are so holier than thou. They can do no wrong. They allegedly do the same morally grey things as us, but because they each have a cock and balls, they're lauded as Saints.

Leila spits near her feet and shoots daggers at them.

When I look at my sisters, their faces are unreadable, but I know what they're thinking. The cells are cleaned out, and we have to share, all so men can swoop in and save the day. Fury of untold proportions rattles my bones. *How dare they?*

Wait.

My head snaps to the Rev. I wondered why she didn't care about mine or Mercy's appearance. Now I know. She wants us to be seen in all our sinning glory. I grin. This is a shakedown.

Fuck the Saints.

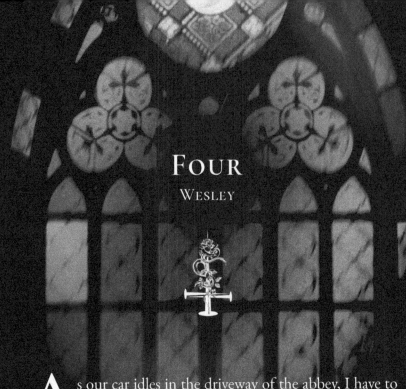

Four

WESLEY

As our car idles in the driveway of the abbey, I have to repress my disgust. It's not from the faceless motorcyclist who tailgated us. It's the sinking feeling that I'll have to work in close quarters with these... women.

I force my gaze to remain steady on each Sinner standing on the front steps. We can't let them see our distrust. They're killers, whores, the scum of the earth. They'll find out what they can about us and then use it to manipulate. They think we're here to teach them about demonology, but we're here for one thing... maybe five things, and then we will dismantle their organization.

"Fuck me," Zeke blurts, craning his neck. "They're all hot."

I shoot him a warning look. "Keep your todger where it belongs."

"It belongs in them."

"Potrebbero avere una malattia," Dominic mumbles in Italian, meaning they could have a disease.

Cisco gives Zeke a priestly warning look of guidance but it doesn't work.

Zeke mumbles, "You all need to get laid."

His words cause a fit of wet coughing. It's worsened since we landed. As stupid as it sounds, I can't help thinking his condition is my fault. But people get sick around me. Pets die. Not even goldfish live long in my vicinity. Before I dwell too long, I hand him a handkerchief from my pocket.

We all want to snap a retort at his cheeky insult, but something holds us back. He has a point. The only company I've kept lately is Team Saint on our demon-hunting trips across Europe. And that's purely platonic. Prior to that, I spent decades working for the Vatican with my nose in a book. Dominic is an actual Saint. I've never seen him romantically with a woman, man, or anyone. Cisco is... well, a priest. The Monsignor is an old white geezer who's been ordained his entire, long life.

On the other hand, Zeke has only been with us for a few short years investigating demonic activity. He's not like us in the sense that we've been called to this holy life. He was dragged into it, kicking, screaming, and drenched in his baby sister's blood.

He has plenty of reasons to turn his back on the cause, especially in his condition, but he stays. He even allowed Cisco to baptize him. I like to think that we're rubbing off on him, but then he goes and makes comments like those.

"You've worked hard to get to where you are," I remind him. "We all have."

"Wesley is right," Cisco says in his thick Italian accent, taking charge as usual. "We stick to the plan, no?"

I catch my reflection in the window. Hard face, spectacles, and shaggy hair that won't stay put no matter how much gunk I put in it. I nonetheless run my fingers through it and catch the tiny scar beneath my eye. Zeke's not the only one who's seen tragedy. My uncle might have been hauled to hell decades ago, but it was enough to shape my future. Enough for me to realize there is no negotiating with evil. There is no forgiving sin, no matter what these women have been told.

Then why are you here? Asks a small voice from the back of my mind. *Why come here based on the words of a hidden gospel the Vatican discredits?*

Rather than answer my conscience, I return my gaze to the group on the abbey steps. I see stern faces and defensive postures. They're as uncomfortable about this merger as we are. They should get used to it. Soon it will be a hostile takeover.

I frown—one is covered in blood and something dreadfully gory. But I can't say I'm surprised.

My gaze tracks from her feet to her head. Like all the Sinners here, she's beautiful. It's as though the devil himself reached into his bag of tricks and pulled her out for one purpose only—to tempt and corrupt me. She has smooth brown skin and dark, luscious hair hastily tied at the nape. I'm sure her big eyes have made lesser men fall to their knees. Her dress is torn in places that tease her femininity. She has a bold look about her—something that's so magnetic I have difficulty pulling away. It's enough to make me wonder what she looks like clean.

Cisco clears his throat, returning my attention to his watchful gaze.

"Remember the plan," he repeats.

Zeke and I share a look. Then I open the door.

FIVE

THEA

While Team Saint removes suitcases and trunks from their limousine, I am both underwhelmed and intrigued. I thought Saints would be scarier. More... holy? But they're five ordinary men. One old priest, one younger priest, two in suits—one well-built and the other wearing spectacles—and a man wearing torn jeans and a well-loved Rolling Stones T-shirt.

These are our male equivalents. I screw up my face and glance at Mercy, expecting a similar reaction, but her eyes are full of heat as she twirls her coppery hair.

"Now," she says huskily. "A man with lips like that has no business being a priest."

"You better not be talking about the old timer," Leila says.

"They're *both* ordained!" I exclaim a little too loudly. Ew. The men glance over.

Raven takes a puff of her cigarette. "When has that ever stopped her?"

Tawny snorts. Prudence scoffs. Mercy shrugs. Her robe falls another inch off her shoulder. *Nipple.* There it is. I roll my eyes.

"Ladies." The Rev's mumbled warning has zero effect. We all start talking over each other, trading teases and insults.

"Put your tits away," Leila mumbles to Mercy.

"I just want to go back to bed." Tawny yawns. "It's too early."

"Like you haven't slept all morning?" Mercy scowls at her.

Tawny pokes out her tongue. "At least I know how to use the bed properly."

"You know how to get lazy," Leila adds. "That's what you know."

Tawny's mouth widens to an O of shock. Push the sweetheart's buttons, and the viper springs free. Tawny's eyes flash, and she steps past me toward Leila.

To stop the coming fight, I point the severed hand and say, "I can't believe none of you told me about Team Saint." The hand accidentally slaps Tawny in the face, distracting her. She swats it and I almost drop it. "Seriously. Don't ask me any favors."

Raven pinches her nose. "Like what, don't do our laundry in the same load as yours?"

"Maybe I'll rub your face in it instead." I step down with the hand poised to strike, but Prudence captures my wrist and shakes her head. Our eyes meet. *Poker face,* she used to tell me during training. *Don't let them see your cards.*

I return to my position. The girls begrudgingly follow suit. We all make our expressions blank, much to the Rev's relief. By the time the men walk up to the base of our steps, our tension is sufficiently released, and we can turn the smoldering remnants of our fury toward the five men without killing them. The... Saints? I'm still not understanding. They look like a ragtag circus.

The older priest struggles to move his frail body up the steps. The Rev stays put on the landing and looks down as she balances on her cane.

"Monsignor," she greets. "Welcome to the Hildegard Sisterhood. I trust you and your men had a comfortable flight across the Atlantic."

There is a bite to the Rev's tone. So much so that we pause. Tension zings. I want to laugh but hold it in. Raven doesn't.

"*Roasted,*" she snarks, flicking her cigarette butt. It arcs through the air and lands on a shiny designer loafer belonging to the handsome brown-skinned man in a tailored suit. Square jaw, hard eyes, shaved head. His nostrils flare as he glances at Raven, probably because she's right. This is *Team Saint,* and yet they arrived in an expensive limo. They probably flew First Class. He wears frickin' Versace, for Christ's sake, but damn, he makes it look good.

As he bends forward, I glimpse a crucifix branded on the back of his scalp. That had to hurt. A thin layer of shaved hair grows everywhere except that scar. His fist swallows the smoldering butt and shoves it deep into his pants pocket. Raven glares at him. He ignores her.

I take back my earlier comment. Anyone who can ignore Raven *is* a Saint.

The Monsignor nods to the Rev and speaks with an Italian accent. "Our journey is, ah, very pleasant and, ah... how you say... we are most humble to be sharing these accommodations with you."

He pats his sweaty forehead with a handkerchief.

My gaze darts between the men. None of them speak English. Good. Then I can ignore them, too. They don't need to know Sinners are multilingual. Easier to garner state secrets and assassinate that way.

The Monsignor and the Rev continue polite chit-chat. I tune out in favor of studying the guests, as I am sure my sisters are doing. We like to get the lay of the land before it lays us.

The man in torn jeans has brown, medium-length hair. Olive skin—perhaps Mediterranean or Turkish in his heritage from the cut of his features. He could pass as a supermodel if it weren't for the smudges beneath his eyes. He looks rough... the kind of rough that comes from experiencing hardship. He moves like a panther as he wheels a heavy suitcase made of metal. Knuckles are scarred. He'd be a dirty, unpredictable fighter.

Proceed with caution, my subconscious warns.

The other Suit can't be older than thirty-something, yet his attire screams stuffy old professor. White. Messy blond hair. Ray Ban spectacles. His vest is crumpled. A pocket watch on a chain. He'd be attractive if he weren't sucking on a sour lemon as he looks at us. I catch distaste when his gaze flicks toward me, and immediately I want to shove this severed hand down his throat. That arrogant mouth looks like a great place to rest it.

I shift my attention to the younger priest. He is also in his thirties... but maybe a touch older than the others. Brown hair, tanned skin, tall, clean-shaven, and wearing his clerics—white roman collar and black shirt. My eyes say priest, but my gut says something about him is unsuitable for sermons on humility and turning the other cheek. It's how he fills out that shirt, how his broad shoulders stretch the seams, and how it hugs his trim waist like a glove. A scar runs across his upper lip, and I swear there is a hint of tattoo at his collar and wrist. Mercy is right. Those lips are made for kissing, but those hands are made for choking.

Apart from the old priest, they are all in their prime, fit and handsome. Even the scowling scholarly type.

Each Sinner is plucked from orphanages and foster care homes because of her looks first and grit second. All the better for us to lay honey traps. Can the Vatican possibly use its Saints the same way as the Sisterhood uses us?

Maybe they're not so pious after all.

"Let me introduce our Sinners." The Rev's voice filters back in, and I flinch. She points at each of us and says our names. The men watch with veiled curiosity behind their wariness. The Saint lingers on Raven, the blood over my body, and the severed hand in my grip.

The professor-type coughs when Mercy curtseys and flashes boob. The younger priest hastily looks away, which makes Mercy virtually preen.

The Monsignor points at the torn jeans guy. "Zeke is our gunman, yes?"

Zeke lifts his chin in greeting. I sense Leila stiffen beside me. She's probably feeling the pinch of competition as our weapons expert.

"Next is man who turns pages of books, yes. He is, ah, how you say—our... ah..."

"My name is Wesley," says the blond with spectacles. Liverpool hints in his crisp, British accent. Not Italian. Interesting. The hint is almost too thin to detect. It's like he's tried hard to erase his roots. He gives the Monsignor a tight smile. "Perhaps I can finish the introductions?"

Gratitude washes over the old man. He pats his forehead and nods.

"Right," Wesley says swiftly, all business. "I'm Wes, the occult and demonology scholar. You met Zeke, our weapons specialist. This is Father Angelotti, our exorcist. And that well-dressed chap at the end is Saint Dominic. I think the name explains itself. Nice to meet you all." He adjusts his spectacles with a finger. "A point of note, I'm the only one fluent in English."

Right. How convenient for them. So the game is afoot

already. Perhaps that's what prompts me to drawl, "Only one Saint? I thought there'd be more."

Raven snickers. Dominic's gaze snaps to her, then to me. As do the rest of them. Oh yeah, they understand, all right.

The Monsignor clears his throat.

"*Si*," he says and glances at Wesley for help. "One. There is... ah..."

Wesley finishes for him. "What he's trying to say is that there aren't many saintly souls left in the world." His finger returns to his spectacles at the bridge. A nervous habit, I realize. Or perhaps tell of a lie. "But I suspect you know that already."

"Welcome inside." The Rev seizes control of the conversation. "The girls will show you to your cells and around the abbey. Dinner is at six, lunch is at noon, and breakfast is at seven. I suggest we meet in the archives tomorrow morning to begin our merger discussions and education."

Merger!

Sinners' eyes snap to the Rev, who studiously ignores us. This is why she kept the details secret. She knows we would never allow men—the word leaves a bitter taste in my mouth —*five* men—to come into *our* home and tell us how to run the place. We can't even stand needing a man to absolve us during confession.

Five?

She gives us a look that says we'll discuss it later. We know better than to challenge her authority in front of interlopers.

Prudence leaves without a backward glance. Like the

switch being flipped, everyone follows. All playfulness destroyed, Mercy casts a disparaging look at the men before hugging her robe tight and heading back inside. Tawny kindly offers to show them to their rooms. Leila begrudgingly collects the Monsignor's bags. Wesley is last up the steps, lugging a heavy, ornate wooden trunk on wheels.

I could offer to help.

He makes it to my step, pauses, glances down at me, and his upper lip curls. He smells like aftershave, sweat, and something else I recognize more than my own scent—ink and books.

He points at the severed limb dangling in my hand.

"Interesting symbol," he remarks dryly. "Ancient Sumerian?"

I give him nothing.

"Right, then." He stares. "I'll just... head inside."

I stare back.

He moves, hesitates, then points at my jawline. "You have something there."

He reaches with a grimace. I catch his wrist before he connects. Our eyes clash, and my stomach flutters at the impact. It must be my lack of sleep stopping me from looking away. Thick lashes surround honey eyes with lids that droop on the outside. Just a little bit. He's like a puppy I want to pet. A puppy won't complain about me reading all night. It will give me unconditional love and endless cuddles. But puppies don't look at you like you're made of dirt.

I deepen my scowl.

His jaw tightens as he forces his hand and plucks something sticky off me. He eases out of my hold with a slow wrist twist before holding it before my face. "Seems rather like brain matter, wouldn't you say?"

Is that supposed to mean he has our number as much as we have his? It's not like I was hiding the blood on my body. For once, I'm grateful I still have the cold, sweaty severed limb in my hand. I use it to give his head a patronizing pat.

"Top marks for the scholar. You want a gold star?" I ignore his glower and turn to the Rev. "I'm going to get cleaned up now, and I'll drop this off at the archives."

"Aren't you forgetting something, Thea?" She raises her brows.

"Confession." My stomach rolls.

"Father McBride will be waiting for you in the chapel. Best not to keep him waiting."

I slap the hand into the Rev's palm and then head toward the Sin Bin, completely thrilled to find out what penance I'm due after the day I've had.

Six

Thea

As I head toward the back of the gothic church, my steps echo across the wooden floor and high, arched ceiling. It's empty here, but I hear shuffling in the sacristy—the small room near the altar. Father McBride must be waiting inside. He's an Irish import in his fifties and the third priest we've gone through in as many months.

The sacristy has been converted into a room dedicated to the penance of Sinners. All vestments and supplies have been removed in favor of what we girls liked to call a necessary evil —the tools that help purge the sin from our souls. Torture devices, whips, flogs, cilices, and coarse hessian robes, just to name a few. Two walls are lined with them. Some are ancient and outdated, but we keep them out of respect for the Sinners who came before us.

Pushed against one torture wall is a table covered in

weapons Father blessed—daggers, swords, bullets. Against the second wall is a table with prayer candles just for Sinners. And at the third wall, an uncomfortable kneeling pew and vintage wooden confessional under the watchful gaze of a wooden crucifix.

They say this devotional room is for our privacy and because we'd clog up the main confessional with all our sinning, but it feels more like a dirty little secret.

The Sin Bin: where shame and secrets are locked away beneath mortified flesh. Where the devil is told, not today. And our sins are absolved.

We hope.

I can't wholly blame this establishment for the pain inflicted in this room. I can't even blame myself. Part of it is cathartic. Every wince or stab of agony releases something dark within me, cleansing the grimy feeling nipping at my heels.

Each Sinner has a different relationship with this room.

The bright purple penance stole draped around Father's neck flickers gold as he adjusts the prayer candles. Sweat glistens on his freckled skin. His fingers tremble on the aluminum candle bases, making them tinkle. Usually, he's inside the confessional if he knows one of us is due. But I've kept him waiting.

It's a good thing he's out. I need his help with this one.

I clear my throat.

He jolts and faces me. Pity enters me at the fear in his eyes. He hears the worst from us and still has to find a way to sleep at night. I give him another week before he packs it in and returns to the local diocese for sanctuary.

"Dorothea," he greets with a crack in his voice.

"Father."

"You look troubled, child." His complexion pales.

"You know what that means."

Father gestures at the single one-person pew facing the wall.

Right. Assume the position.

He offers, "Perhaps a few extra hours in the kitchen will suffice for penance?"

"Not this time." I pluck the scourge from a hook on the wall and place it in his shaking hands. "Thank you."

He hesitates. This is where we lose most of them. They try to go easy on us, but easy is for the weak. It's not enough. It's never enough. He gives a resigned nod.

I could do it myself. Some of us do. But I need someone else to do it for me, or I'll make up some excuse and procrastinate. I need him to witness my efforts, to make it real.

I take a deep breath and remove my clothes until I'm in a bra, panties, blood, vomit, and a crucifix around my neck. I kneel, clasp my hands together and close my eyes to pray.

A rasp sounds behind me as he runs his fingers along the whip.

"Forgive me, Father," I murmur. "For I have sinned. It has been one day since my last confession. And these are my sins."

HOT WATER SPRAYS MY FACE, numbing any feeling left after penance. I rest my forehead on the cool tiles, my lack of sleep catching up.

Disturbing images flicker behind my eyes. Sounds. Smells. The possessed man. The kingpin. The nightclub I'd found them in. The using myself as bait despite the bile rising in my gullet. His greasy hands ripping at my dress in the dark alley, and the hiss of rancid breath when he exposed my breasts... and the blessed crucifix I'd tucked there.

I'm still struggling to describe what happened next. It was a feeling. A vibration in the air... a knowing. Pure to the bone, evil stared at me from out of those soulless eyes. A flash of the demon himself before the unintelligible vitriol spewed forth. The weird, guttural voice sounded more like it came from a cloven-footed beast than a man. I can't believe I froze in fear.

Two for flinching. Prudence's voice floats from my memories. After arriving at the abbey, she spent a year following me around, jump-scaring me and then punching me twice in the arm—*hard*—if I flinched.

Sinners *never* freeze in battle. We're too hardened. Too seasoned. But I did. When that demon looked at me, I goddamn froze. I stabbed a sanctified dagger deep into his chest, and he exploded.

Father tried to tell me not to be so hard on myself, that the man I killed was possessed, but he was still a man. Someone loved him enough to answer the ad we put in the paper. There might have been a way to save him.

The shower goes cold. I turn off the faucet and step into the tiny bathroom—the only one we share on this level, which is hard enough with all the women living on this floor. Now we have to add five men. Perhaps four if the Monsignor sleeps downstairs where the Magpies and the Rev stay. Far away from the tainted chaos of us Sinners.

I wrap myself in a threadbare towel, put on my spectacles, and wipe condensation from the mirror. The reflection staring back at me is as foreign as she was this morning. Brown skin. Thick dark lashes. Brown, empty eyes. Dark long hair plastered to my face and shoulders. I often wonder if I'd look the same without the Sisterhood. Would those lines bracketing my lips be there? Would that hardness exist beyond the pretty smile? It's impossible to be sure.

Who are my family? Would they want me if they saw me today? Would they care that I sacrifice my soul for a better world? Did they even care in the first place, or are they all dead?

I hate not knowing where I come from. It's like I'm constantly floating, with nothing to ground me.

All I have are vague memories of playing between the legs of a family near a well-stocked party table. My family were giants to my small body. Other children played with me. We must have been doing something naughty because we ran outside after being scolded. I remember the smell of spicy, sweet, and salty food, and then there's some sport on TV. I don't know which sport, only that the drone of the commentator's voice was so familiar it felt comforting. That's all I have of my past—fleeting memories, feelings, and deja vu.

In my reflection, I glimpse welts on my back and wince as my raw skin pulls tight. No blood was drawn this time, but there is something else—a scratch. I frown and crane further. It's more than a scratch. It looks like a strange symbol carved into me with a crude blade... but I never put it there, and Father McBride certainly didn't. The carved circle has six lines dissecting, kind of like the symbol on the severed hand. Maybe it's the same. I should take a picture.

A clatter at the window stops me. I look up and see a crow on the sill, pecking at the glass, its beady eyes watching me.

Tap. Tap. Caw.

"Shoo." I wave my hand.

Its beak taps incessantly at the glass.

"I said, *shoo.*"

Tap. Tap. Caw.

Another crow lands on the sill. It pecks until a hairline crack in the glass webs out. My pulse quickens. Another lands. And another. Soon a sea of black feathers block out the sun. The temperature turns icy—hairs on the back of my neck lift. I search for my crucifix pendant. It's buried somewhere beneath my dirty dress. I don't know if it will help against an army of crows, but I left the dagger in my room. Maybe I can smother them with the shower curtain. Or lock them inside the bathroom and leave.

Tap. Tap. Caw.

A knock comes at the door. "You all right in there?"

It is one of the men... Wesley, going by the accent.

"I'm fine," I shout, finding the crucifix and holding it at the window. "It's just a few crazy birds trying to get in."

The window shatters. Darkness pours in at the same time as the door opens. Wesley's arm bands around my front and yanks me against his body. He throws something bright, like a ball of light. Gunpowder or firecrackers explode. A silent sonic boom whooshes past my face. Time stands still. I hold my breath. My heart thuds. Then the birds squawk and shriek. Wings flap, and the darkness dissipates.

The crows are gone, but a smoldering white card remains, floating to the tiled floor.

Wesley still holds me, his warm breath tickling my ear. With every breath, his cotton shirt grazes my sensitive, flogged skin. An odd tingling sensation causes me to glance down. A large male hand grasps my right breast, with only a threadbare towel separating his palm from my nipple.

I stare at his hand, feel the warmth of his touch, and become all too aware that he's a man and I'm a woman. And it's been a very long time since someone touched me there. My body reacts before my brain catches up. Then I recall his look of disgust when we spoke on the steps. The crows that tried to eat me. His bursting in like I couldn't protect myself.

I grit my teeth.

Don't kill him. That would be overreacting. *Just think of the penance you'll have to endure.* I pry his hand away before rounding on him with a calm, indignantly arched brow.

"Sorry." He raises his palms defensively.

"You're not sorry."

"I believed you were in danger."

"Fuck off. I can take care of myself."

"I see that." He takes in my disheveled state with a mocking tone.

Don't kill him.

I survey the destruction, the broken glass, the feathers, and the blood spatter. An errant breeze lifts the edge of the smoldering white card on the tiled floor.

That bright light he'd thrown.

His breath hitches. I spin to find him staring at my back. Darkness settles over his expression as he grinds out, "Who hurt you?"

I consider my response. That symbol could be important. Do I want him to know, to ask for his help, or should I change the subject? At my silence, lightning flashes in his gaze, his jaw clenches, and his hands flex like he's trying to hold in his anger. At me, or my wounds? The movement draws my attention to his rolled shirt sleeves and surprisingly muscular forearms covered in occult tattoos.

Scars slashing his skin remind me of knife wounds, but I don't think they're self-inflicted—thinner scars thread over his hands. Come to think of it, when he showed me his palms earlier, I glimpsed scars there too.

An odd feeling churns in my chest. It confuses me. I don't like knowing he's suffered. It makes it harder to hate him. He's probably thinking the same thing about me. But it still doesn't give him the right to get up in my private business.

"I don't know what the symbol on my shoulder is." I dismiss him to study that smoldering card warily.

"There's no symbol," he retorts as if I'm being deliberately obtuse. "I'm talking about the welts."

Unexpected heat hits my cheeks at the realization he's talking about my sins. But if I let him know I care, I'm... I just can't. I hug my towel and pick up the card.

"What's this?" I hold it up. "How did you... What *did* you do?"

He rubs his jaw, looking at me in a way that says he's not done making demands, but he points at the card. "It's the arcane arts. Geomancy. We draw symbols to invoke the powers of the cosmos and—"

I hold up my hand, cutting him off. If he is going to make up circus bullshit, I don't need to hear it. "Forget I asked."

He blinks, visibly taken aback. I get the sense that might be a rare thing. "You don't believe me."

"That a magic card saved me from a bunch of rabid birds? No." But then again, I'm still processing the demonic possession from earlier. "You must have put gunpowder in there or something."

"No, I didn't. As I've just demonstrated, geomancy works. John Dee's books have a lot more—"

"John Dee!" I laugh. "He's an insane alchemist who pretended to talk to angels, all so he had an excuse to swap wives with his buddy. Even the Vatican denounced him." I scoff. "It's like, just own your depraved shit. Why spend a life-time inventing an angelic language all so you can send secret messages to your mistress."

His eyes flash. "He was denounced *before* demonic activity woke from a long, dormant sleep. The Vatican has been known to reverse previous statements when new evidence comes to light."

"Hmmm. You mean like how they branded Mary Magdalene a whore—Jesus' only female apostle—then spent centuries hunting down opinionated women and called them witches, *then* changed their mind and said, oh no, sorry, we might have got the whore bit wrong. We actually don't know what Mary was, but we won't mention the thousands of women we killed. You mean like that statement?"

"What has that got to do with anything?"

"It has everything to do with everything."

He puts his hands on his hips. "While you women were here, meddling in the affairs of men, we've been hunting demons across Europe."

My blood boils. *Meddling in the affairs of men?* This is the same kind of sexist horseshit that led to the creation of the Sisterhood. A switch flips inside my head.

Every hormone, emotion, and cell in my body explodes uncontrollably. One second, I'm standing there, seeing red. The next, my fists grip his collar and shove up beneath his jaw, like I'm a hairline away from choking him out. I'm so close I could bite off his nose.

"You think what we do here is a child's game?" I shoot

heat from my eyes as if I can burn him alive and save the devil a job. "You think the murderers, rapists, and psychopaths we kill should be allowed to live, to have power? You think they have a right to abuse the weaker sex? You think predators should be free to roam the streets and group homes where little girls are vulnerable?"

I hadn't meant to say that last one. It triggers a paralyzing squeeze of anxiety in my chest, flooding old memories to the surface. The foster care group home I lived in was a long-term orphanage.

"Take it," the janitor says, handing me my first Harlequin romance book. "I've got plenty more."

"I'm not supposed to read these. They're for grownups."

"Pah." He waves his hand. "It can be our little secret. I've marked my favorite chapter. Read it and tell me what you think."

It wasn't until I was older, at the Sisterhood, and in charge of my own body that I realized this man had been grooming me, using my loneliness and yearning for love to earn my trust. If I hadn't been found with those books under my bed, if I hadn't been so vicious about protecting my right to read whatever the fuck I wanted, the Sisterhood would never have found me, and I'd have suffered worse than the attention of a slimy man.

Many never get so lucky.

I expect disgust and disdain on Wesley's face, but I don't expect the tenderness in his gaze. It's uncomfortable, like a brush of fire against my skin.

I could end his life. He knows this. But he's not afraid.

Why?

He can't possibly think he can beat me. He *knows* what I am. He saw the blood, vomit, and brain matter. He should be permanently disgusted. So why?

Who hurt you?

Unbidden, my fists relax on his collar. My hands splay out, flattening the crumpled mess I made until his shirt is smooth again. But I can't pull my hands away. I'm stuck, suddenly aware of the breadth of his broad chest, sharp jaw, and flared nostrils. It's funny how a startled reaction born of fear can mimic arousal. The heart rate elevates. The pupils dilate. Breathing becomes stilted. Suddenly, I'm not grasping a stuffy, arrogant scholar but a man looking at me like no one has before.

Too close.

I shove off and readjust my towel.

What had we been talking about? Increasing demonic activity.

"How could you have been investigating demonic activity," I say, "when the rift to the hell dimension was closed a few months ago."

My words break whatever spell had frozen him. "Bloody hell, Thea. This activity has been increasing for years. That rift wasn't the first."

Something stills inside me. Something dark, insidious, and afraid. I lock it away.

"So why come here then?" I flash my eyes. "Why not stay where you're wanted?"

His long lashes lower, shadowing his eyes. A flash of defiance is all I get before he shuts down his expression. He pauses at the doorway and looks back. "I'll see you for tomorrow's class."

"I thought we were discussing the merger."

"It's already done. We begin teaching you everything we've learned. And you're welcome." He gestures at the window, to the black feathers caught in the broken glass.

I have nothing to throw, so I flip up my middle finger.

Emotion dances in his eyes. I can't tell if it's humor or a challenge. Like he's about to attack me to prove he can dominate after all. Something about that thought shoots heat into my lower belly, and I'd love him to try.

"Miss Thea." His respectful goodbye nod is contrary to the sarcasm in his tone.

I slam the door after he leaves, hating what passed between us. He pushed my buttons, and I lost control. He invited himself in and now probably thinks he saved the day. I would have been fine on my own. I always am. A frustrated sound rips out of my throat, and I stomp to the mirror to check my shoulder.

He's right. The symbol. It's definitely gone.

SEVEN

THEA

Dressed in black activewear, spectacles on, and still exhausted, I board up the bathroom window. Once done, I notify our custodian to organize repairs. The nuns residing here are multitalented. They cook, clean, garden, heal, and fix shit. We help them when we do our penance... if we have time. If we don't, we choose the faster, more painful route in the Sin Bin.

When I'm done, I head straight to the archives to confront the Reverend Mother.

The archives take up most of the level. If it's not bookcases filled with ancient tomes and manuscripts, it's tables set out for reading them. The reliquary on one side is where we lock away artifacts entrusted to the Sisterhood over generations and from around the world, dating back to medieval times. Next to the reliquary are rooms used for meetings and classes. The frosted windows are dark and dormant because we haven't

taken on a new generation of Sinners since the current Rev
came on board.

Activity surrounds a single archive table located in a vast
space between two sets of stacks. It seems like the others had
the same idea as me. They surround the Reverend Mother and
the severed hand, now in a sealed plastic bag. Other strange
items, books, and relics are there too.

I pass a cart with items needing to be shelved. Among
them is my lost manuscript. I snatch it up, still bristling from
my encounter with Wesley, and hug it to my chest.

Whoever cleaned my room should have left the book with
my belongings. I'm not done studying the half-empty pages.
They don't make sense. Who would create pages half filled
with an unknown language?

I meet the Sinners at the table and slam my manuscript
down. The only person who jumps is the Rev. The rest probably sensed my arrival when I stepped onto this floor.

The Rev removes her spectacles and uses them to point at
the symbol on the hand, then looks at me.

"He's right," she says. "It's ancient Sumerian."

I ground my teeth. "*He* also burst into the bathroom—
uninvited—and threw this at a bunch of damned crows trying
to peck their way in."

I toss the scorched white card, which bounces off the hand
and lands on the table.

"Ah, yes." The Rev puts her spectacles back on and
inspects the card. "I believe this is what one of the classes will
be about tomorrow."

"Classes?" Leila balks. "As in academic?"

Raven folds her arms. "Fuck that bullshit."

Tawny agrees. As does Mercy, now in decent clothes. I search the floor—Prudence isn't here. She's been distant since she was rescued from the Cartel a few months ago. Understandably so. We still have hope that she will recover. In the meantime, we give her as much space as we can, but I'm wondering if there's more I can do. I miss her sassy prankster side.

"Need I remind you, girls," the Rev points out, "that we've been floundering since demonic activity began? We're taking stabs in the dark. Nothing we do works. And it's getting worse."

We don't reply because we know it is true. It still doesn't help our pride to say it out loud. Something big is coming, and we're powerless to stop it.

We've been trained to use men, overcome them, and be better than them. Now we have to lie down and show our bellies to them. It's not in our blood to submit.

"The Vatican has selected this group to support our systems already in place. I've been assured they will not replace us." The Rev lifts her chin. "Believe me when I say they will dance to the beat of *our* drum, not the other way around. But first, we must learn. We must be smart. We must ask questions." She stands slowly, her old bones creaking, and she points at the ancient mark. "This is how we learn. Let's begin our research. Look for anything similar in the old Sumerian texts. Scatter."

I stare at her for a moment longer than necessary, wondering how she became so wise. What's her story? What brought her to this life?

She waves her hand, and the Sinners move, each taking a corner of the archives to scour while I remain.

The Rev meets my steady gaze. "Now, what's this about crows?"

The fight leaves my body. I frown, remembering my eerie feeling, the birds, the symbol that was there and then wasn't. It's possible I hallucinated it in my exhaustion, maybe a little PTSD. But the crows... they were real. Wesley saw them.

"Crows," I reply. "A murder of them pecked the bathroom window until it broke."

She picks up the scorched card with arthritic fingers. "And this?"

"Wesley threw it at the birds. A bright light exploded like a firecracker, and then the crows left."

"Probably some kind of gunpowder," Leila suggests as she returns with a book.

I throw up my hands. "Right? That's what I said."

The Rev inspects other items on the table. None of them I recognize. New books and new relics. I shift a tiny wax stick labeled with arcane symbols.

"This is their stuff," I note, a slow smile stretching my face. "You're snooping."

"Well..." She sniffs with a shrug. "They leave their things there for all to see."

When I walked up the stairs, I missed the boxes, trunks,

and suitcases on the landing. A used lock pick set is on the carpet by an open trunk that's been dragged halfway to this table. *Right... left for all to see.*

"Anything interesting?"

"Plenty," she replies. "Only we don't know what it means."

My shoulders slump. "So, we really need them."

Intelligent eyes study me. "You tell me. What happened on your mission with the unholy one? Why was his blood all over you?"

I shake my head, going cold with the memory. "He looked normal. Gross, seedy, lecherous... but normal. When he saw the crucifix, he hissed and then... and then I saw it"—I swallow—"the demon. It's... so *evil*. A suffocating presence." I pause, trying not to let the terror enter me, and realize all other Sinners are back at the table listening. "If Father McBride hadn't blessed that table of weapons before I'd gone, I don't know what would have happened. I stabbed the demon with a sanctified dagger, and his chest exploded. The presence burst out."

"You think the blessing exorcised him?"

"Not sure. It seems a little too convenient. I don't think exodus from a knife wound is normal. I think I got lucky." The man... not so much.

"The sooner we accept the olive branch from Team Saint, the better for all of us," the Rev says.

"I know." I rub my temples. "I know."

"I need to meet with the Monsignor and Father McBride."

She touches me gently on the shoulder, her eyes softening. "Will you be okay?"

The compassion this Rev shows us is astounding. No other in my history here has been as forgiving, kind, and equally determined. It's rare. If I'm honest with myself, it's purely because of her that I haven't followed in Alice's footsteps and left the Sisterhood altogether. She found a loophole to escape despite the death sentence decreed for any deserter. I'm sure I can too.

But I wouldn't know what to do with myself. Reading books and sipping wine from a porch with a puppy running about seems like a good fantasy until I think about how utterly alone I would be.

Our organization has remained in the shadows since the Middle Ages. The Vatican itself only discovered us a few years ago. The larger world has no idea we—or Team Saint—exist. It's not like I'd have skills I could transfer to another job.

I nod and give the Rev an empty smile. She leaves, hobbling on her cane, with one last worried glance tossed over her shoulder at me.

When she's gone, I peek inside Wesley's trunk. Manuscripts, more wax sticks, books, relics... I shift a leather tome out of the way but then run my fingers over it. I'm drawn to it.

"That looks familiar," Tawny says from over my shoulder.

Raven, Leila, and Mercy also watch curiously.

"Shouldn't you be reading Sumerian texts?" I mumble.

Raven snorts. "You're not."

"True."

We stare at the off-limits treasure trove.

"It's like porn for an occult nerd," Mercy comments.

Tawny pulls out the old tome.

I narrow my eyes. "It *does* look familiar."

Rushing to the table where the Rev had sat, I collect my half-blank manuscript and hold it next to the one in Tawny's hands. Same leather binding. Same thickness. Same paper.

"It feels weird." Tawny's nose scrunches. "I don't like it."

I take it from her. The halves move together but repel simultaneously. The weight wobbles in my hand.

"Help me," I urge.

Raven, Leila, and Mercy each grab a corner and push.

"It's like a magnet," Mercy notes. "It wants to be reunited but doesn't."

Vibrations tingle up my arms.

"Push," I demand. "Push the halves together."

We muster strength in our hands and push. We heave. We force. We pray.

Tawny finally caves and slaps her hand on the book. She is the last puzzle piece. The two halves snap together. Bright light fills our vision, blinding us.

I WAKE on the carpeted floor of the archives with my cheek smashed to my palm and little bright dots swimming in my vision. Sitting up, I wince at the dizziness and grasp my forehead.

"Thank the Lord, you're awake," Tawny says, her eyes glistening.

"What happened?" I rasp, still groggy.

"The manuscript blinded us."

Vague recollections come back to me. "It exploded."

She shook her head. "No. It's in one piece."

To my right, Mercy is on her back, eyes closed. Raven is on her side, facing away. Leila is curled in a fetal position. The distinct smell of burned parchment is in the air.

"They passed out," Tawny explains, rubbing her eyes. "Just as you did."

I crawl to the manuscript and open it, shock crashing into me like a wave. No longer half empty, words and symbols cover every page. That strange language has also morphed into something I partly recognize—Ancient Greek.

"Oh my God," I breathe. "Can you see this?"

Or is it another hallucination?

"*¡Dios mío!* I see it," Raven's husky voice comes from over my shoulder. Groaning and moaning, Leila and Mercy also straighten, rubbing their temples. "What the hell happened?"

"I don't know." I shake my head. "But these words weren't here before. Hardly any of it was."

A new inscription has been scorched into the leather cover. I run my finger over it, astounded as I translate. "*The Good News of Mary Magdalene.* Shit. It's her gospel—the full unredacted gospel."

"No shit," Raven blurts, scrambling closer.

"Are you serious?" Mercy joins us.

There it is, plain as day. The lost Gospel of the Apostle of Apostles, the only female in Jesus' disciples. The same female the male Apostles distrusted, the same female they said had seven demons driven out of her, and the same female that Pope Gregory decided was a whore in 591. As if a woman couldn't be the most trusted confidant of Christ, so she must have been a liar and a whore.

I'd only just been talking to Wesley about her hours ago.

"This can't be a coincidence," I say. "I mean, what are the chances it turns up now? That it shows itself to us—to women."

We're also liars, sinners, and arguably whores. She might not have been any of those things. It could have been lies from the papacy to discredit and denigrate her. The fact is, no one really knows.

Until now. With this book.

"I agree," Mercy says solemnly. "It means something."

"If you told me three years ago that a book would magic itself together, I would have laughed in your face." I'd never heard of such a thing. The only other explanation is that this is a mass hysteria, or maybe toxic mold is hidden behind the stacks. But as I try to rationalize it, I know I'm grasping at straws.

Leila paces, biting her thumb. "I've never believed in demons. Or even the devil. Or hell. But, shit... that was *not* normal."

The weight of the changing world settles on us. We'd always known that a level of mysticism existed. Raven is psychic. Before her, the Sisterhood had other psychics. But there's been no solid evidence of hell. No sorcery. No angels talking back to us. No God answering our prayers.

Now we have real demonic possessions. Unseen spiritual energy. Evil incarnate. Magic fucking cards and shining books.

"Quick." I point at a white cloth used to protect another tome. "Hand me that."

Leila tosses it to me. I use it to wrap the book and then heave it onto the table. It is so old that I worry my natural oils will ruin the pages. We gather to read. I glance at Leila and say, "Keep watch."

She nods but barely lifts her gaze. Like me, everyone is drawn to the book, to the new dark words written in a feminine scrawl. It feels as though it's been made for our eyes. Like fate.

"This can't be it," Raven mumbles. "Can it? I mean, it's in great condition."

I see what she means. "The parchment should be disintegrating in our fingers."

"So it's a fake," Tawny blurts.

"I didn't say that. It could be protected by the same mystical energy that united it."

They all study me, deferring to my expertise.

Raven holds her hand over the top and flinches. "There's an energy to it. It feels the way I feel when I have a vision."

I meet her kohl-lined eyes. "It feels good. Joyful. Holy."

We reverently study the first page.

"Definitely Ancient Greek," I note. The found pages in the Berlin Codex were said to be translated from Greek about the time Constantine converted Rome to Christianity and decided what went in the gnostic scriptures. "They say Mary's gospel only has nineteen pages and is missing the rest. But this is an entire book. This tome is filled with so much more. This is... wow."

We're all lost for words until Raven scoffs, "*They* talk a lot of shit."

"*They* usually have a penis," Leila adds dryly.

"It's long been surmised the Savior had secret conversations with Mary Magdalene," I point out. "They even hint at a marriage between them. There's only a *hint* of this in the codex. But this..." I flip the pages, scanning the recounts. "This is proof. This is..."

"Probably worth a shit-ton of money," Raven points out.

"Probably going to get us killed," Mercy adds. "I mean, this changes everything, right?"

I see what she means. The simple fact this gospel exists proves that Christ treated women as equally as men. No, more than that. It proves his highest of confidants was female. Today, this would mean the church should allow women into the seminary. It proves that the backbone of their male-dominated institution was built on lies. Scandal. Sin.

I pause at a paragraph recounting Mary's visions and glance at Raven.

"She's psychic. Like you."

Her eyes harden. "So what does this mean?"

"I don't think this is just a gospel. I think this is a prophecy. Look." I point at a page set apart from the usual recounts of her talks with the Teacher. "Her visions."

Five points of the star will make
Five cracks in the brave so that
Five relics of the divine borne by
Five sinners of saints to mend
Five heralding horses

The first is the last
The enemy is within
To sin is human
To forgive is blest

One heart to bleed
One body to heal
One soul to sacrifice
One broken exile
One stone freed

It shall be on this day when one crack becomes
many, and many become one, the disagreeing savior
shall usher forth an age of sin.

"I'm a little rusty. I don't think I have that right," I

mumble, losing the translation. *Disagreeing* sounds like the wrong word. And divine might be holy or heavenly. Blest could be the archaic form of blessed or something else. There is more, but I lose the flow.

"Yeah, that's weird." Tawny nods.

The prophecy goes on for multiple verses. Some of it looks like the inner workings of a mad woman's mind. It doesn't make sense, but the fact that it mentions both sinners and saints makes my skin crawl. This means something to us *today*.

But it's gibberish until I can translate the entire book.

"We can't let them know about this," I announce. "We found it first. Men discredited Mary."

"Fuck them," Raven spits. "They come here all high and saintly, thinking they know better than us."

"We're the ones sacrificing our eternal souls." Tawny scowls.

Mercy folds her arms. "I won't let them take the glory."

"Then it's decided." I close the tome and wrap it in a cloth. "I'll keep studying it in secret, minus Team Saint."

"Saint," Raven snarls the word. "What exactly can he do, anyway? Act all devout and scare the demons with his bulging muscles?"

We chuckle.

"The priest, I get," Leila adds. "He can exorcise them. But is the Saint even ordained? What's the deal with that? And the weapons expert—" She cuts herself off with a frown.

"Who gives a shit? They're all sexy." Mercy smirks. "Father Angel-hottie can take my confession any day."

"Team Saint," Raven considers. "Only *one* is righteous enough to hold that title. And that goody-two-shoes won't be able to get the job done. No way. This is dirty work. It's why they need us."

"Goddamned virgins, the lot of them." Mercy folds her arms, completely serious. "You can't trust them."

"They're up to something." Leila cracks her neck. "I'm not giving anything away."

"I give them a week," I say, despite what Wesley told me about them having already worked around Europe. I shake my head, laughing under my breath. "One Saint. Four supporting him." Another snort. "How many men does it take to support a Saint?"

"How many to change a lightbulb?"

"How many monkeys to give his banana a—" Mercy cuts off mid-sentence.

"A peel?" I finish with a chortle.

No one answers. When I glance up, they all exude stillness from their bones, except for Tawny, who blushes and glances over my shoulder toward the stairs.

"They're behind me, aren't they?" I tense.

Raven gives a curt nod.

Fuck.

EIGHT

THEA

I slowly turn, keeping the cloth-wrapped manuscript hidden behind me. Four men stare at us from the landing of the archive's staircase.

Zeke in his worn clothing. Wesley with his wrinkled suit. Father Angelotti in clerics. And Saint Dominic, venerable in Versace. They sicken us.

From the looks on their faces, the feeling is mutual.

Oh, it's on.

Wesley's eyes snag on his open trunk, and then he glares at me—*me*, no one else. Me, like he assumes I'm the worst thief of us all. "You've been snooping through our privates?"

Mercy opens her mouth to, no doubt, let out smutty innu-endo, but Raven steps forward. That's all she does, and the world holds its breath. I'd run away screaming if I didn't know her and met her in a dark alley. She has this look in her eyes: a glint, the spark of a maniac. You never know which way she's going to move. Will a switchblade materialize in her hands or a cigarette lighter? The rainbow streaks in her hair are the only bright thing about her. I sometimes wonder if it's her cry for help, the hand waving above water before she drowns and disappears altogether.

I wonder this because I sometimes feel the same, except I am too cowardly to stick up my hand. Instead, I tell people to fuck off and that I can take care of myself.

Holding Raven's stare, the Saint casually walks toward her. Their boots go toe to toe as they meet in the middle by the open trunk. He might be a head taller and twice as broad across the shoulders, but Raven doesn't cower. Her stature comes from someplace deep within that I envy. I might pretend to be confident, but I take my lead from these women. She reminds me a little of Mary Lazarus, the Sinner who rescued children created in a lab to sense deadly sin. She sacrificed everything to raise them as her own, teaching them how to fight and love. Those children are now the heroes and saviors of Cardinal City: the Deadly Seven.

My fingers twitch for a dagger, a weapon, *something*... and then Dominic leans over and shuts the trunk lid.

Wesley touches his spectacles and strides over, a challenge in his eyes. I had wondered if that touch was a nervous tick, but I think it might remind him to keep his scholar's disguise in place because I no longer believe that's all he is. It's just what they want us to see.

"I never thought nuns were thieves," he says, tone scornful.

"We're not nuns," I reply. "We're not married to Christ. We lie. We screw. We steal. We kill. And we're unapologetic as fuck about it. We're Sinners, Wesley." I cock my head. "Or did you forget that when you had your hand on my breast?"

He blanches.

Tawny swallows a giggle.

Mercy twirls a lock of her copper hair, eyeing them, especially the priest. "I'd be happy to remind them."

The pulse of every man in the room lifts. It's not because they probably just shot their load at the sultry promise dripping from her tone, but because of the murderous intent in her eyes. Mercy can take them all on with one hand tied behind her back, whichever way she wants. We all can.

And they all understand, despite their charade of not speaking English.

As soon as the thought hits, I see no threat. They are nothing to us. Boys playing with cards and religion. We are the real deal. I shift Mary Magdalene's gospel to my chest. Wesley's whispered words follow me as I walk out.

"I would have shared if you'd asked."

THE FOLLOWING DAY, I walk into the archives bleary-eyed from staying up half the night studying the gospel. Most of the words, like the prophecy, are in Ancient Greek. But some words seem to be in another language, after all. I have a grating suspicion Wesley would understand them. But since our classes start today, I squish the book beneath my thin cot mattress and then mess up my blanket to hide the bulk.

Strolling into the classroom, I'm surprised to see the girls already in attendance, all wearing their Sinner uniform—black from head to toe—while I opted for a little silent protest by wearing my sweats. I even leave my contacts out and wear my spectacles. At the front, Wesley stands before a chalkboard he's scrounged up from an ancient storeroom. The chipped wood looks like it might be infested with termites. The smell is musty and stale in here.

I walk toward Leila at the end of the long boardroom table. Cleaning a variety of daggers before her, she's not the only one multitasking. Mercy brought nail polish. Tawny and Prudence brought food. Raven... a notebook?

"You're late," Wesley clips, checking his pocket watch before shoving it back into his three-piece suit vest.

I sink into the seat and pick up one of Leila's daggers. It's more like a hunting knife with its curved blade and serrated edge.

"Right, then." Wesley gives a tight smile. "I was just explaining to the rest of the class what geomancy is and how it works. Does anyone want to fill in Dorothea?"

He called me Thea before, but now it's *Dorothea*.

Silence is his answer.

Crickets.

My lips twitch, and I stab the wooden table, then carve lines.

"You ladies are making me work for it," he mutters.

I can't help the pull between my brows. It's not as though we dislike being taught. We suffered years of brutal training in the Art of War from martial arts experts worldwide.

It's just that they're *men*. Know-it-alls. Something about reading the derogatory and snide comments from the other Apostles toward Mary has put me on edge. The worst part is that Mary's account was still so... I struggle to think of the word... she wasn't naïve, but impervious. Tolerant. Hopeful. Vulnerable. Prey. The derision is picked up between the lines —it's what's *not* said as much as what *is*. Mary's not even angry over how the men spoke to her, and I wanted her to be. I wanted her to stand up for herself. To punch them in the junk.

There was no more perfect example of turning the other cheek than her. It makes complete sense why she was the preferred disciple. It had nothing to do with the fact that she was a woman or possibly Jesus' wife. It had to do with her understanding him in a way no one else did.

That kind of connection is special, and I'm furious it was hidden from the world for so long.

A sigh punctuates rustling, so I glance up. Wesley clears his throat, shucks off his jacket, and hangs it on the back of the chair at the table. Then he proceeds to roll up his shirtsleeves. His fingers mesmerize me. Long, competent, and deft. I imagine them turning the pages of books in the late-night hours—fingers smudged with ink, just like mine. Without the bulky jacket, his trim body is on display.

Tattooed forearms are such an odd part of him that it

throws me off. What kind of Vatican scholar looks like that beneath his clothes?

He scrubs the back of his neck, disheveling blond hair before going to the chalkboard and drawing circles with arcane symbols at varying points. Every time he lifts his arm, the outline of his appealing physique teases me through his clothes. Muscles roll in his back. Biceps flex.

"Girl, I see that look in your eye." Mercy leans toward me with a quiet smirk.

I shake my head. There is no way I'd ever go down that road. Wesley is attractive, but Team Saint is here peddling rubbish the Vatican discredited decades ago. I'm not a fool. If the situation is so dire here, they would have sent more than one Saint. There must be something else going on. It's no coincidence this merger has been forced on us under the guise of aid.

Unless saintly people really are in short supply.

Doesn't matter. The point is the rest of the team are ring-ins. What help can they possibly offer except parlor tricks? An exploding card won't save me from a demon. Unless we're ordained and can conduct our own exorcisms, we have to find alternatives. What happened the other morning was a fluke. I don't expect another demon to suddenly expel itself again.

"He's not bad to look at," Leila chimes in absently.

"Fuck off," I growl and carve some more.

Wesley turns from his chalkboard. "Pardon?"

Leila laughs at my scowl and goes back to cleaning, but

this time she rubs the cloth over her blade with lewd intentions, waggling her brows at me and mouthing, *Enjoy the ride.*

In other words, get my kicks in before I get to hell.

Heat licks up my neck from Wesley's impatient gaze. Fine wrinkles appear at the edges of his eyes as they narrow. Call me crazy, but I like seeing the beginnings of those crow's feet. They remind me he's a man who's lived. Someone up for a challenge. Someone who won't buckle under pressure.

I glance down at the table. Wait... What the hell? I stand, knocking the chair back. My dagger clatters to the floor. The symbol I'd carved is the same one that was on my shoulder.

"Thea?" Tawny asks, and suddenly the weight of a thousand eyes lands on me. She leans across the table to inspect. "That looks kinda like—"

But I don't stick around to hear more. I mumble an excuse and leave.

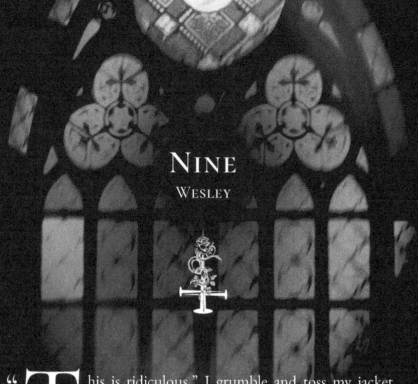

NINE
WESLEY

"This is ridiculous," I grumble and toss my jacket onto the cot in Cisco's room. Dom and Zeke have also squeezed in.

"I agree," Zeke mutters, his lip curling as he surveys the tiny room. "Living here will drive us nuts."

"You have a warm bed, clothes on your back, and food," Cisco reminds him. "We've all had worse."

I sense the eye roll coming from Zeke, but he holds it in.

"I meant that working with these infuriating women is ridiculous." I clench my jaw and force myself to relax. "I've tried being their friend. I've tried offering help. I spent the morning teaching them, but only the psychic seemed to care. The rest spent the class joking. One cleaned knives, and another walked out."

They distrust us. I can't blame them. We are, after all, here to eventually dismantle them. But first, we're supposed to learn everything, including their processes and history. On top of that, there's the other reason for being here. Only Zeke knows how I orchestrated events for our team to be picked to come here. If Dom and Cisco learn I've manipulated them, they won't be happy, but I hope the end justifies the means, and once we get there, I'll be absolved.

"*Si*. Something is *molto* wrong in this place," Dom says.

Their disdain for Sinners is palpable. But after catching the scars on Thea's back and hearing her words when she shoved me against the bathroom wall... I can't help thinking there's more to these women than we were led to believe.

You think predators should be free to roam the streets and group homes where little girls are vulnerable?

She haunts me. I replayed that moment all night, tossing and turning on my lumpy cot. The tremor in her tone. The pain in her eyes. The desperation. Maybe I'm making it up, but I couldn't get past the notion she was talking about herself. A part of me sympathized with her pain. A demon influenced me in the asylum and tried to get me to do things... evil things.

That fleeting, lost look in her eyes was the first moment of truth I've had from her, or any of the Sinners. That was... until she shuttered it all behind a cold facade and told me to fuck off.

It's not like I expected these deadly women to welcome us with open arms or to blurt out all their secrets. It's just that none of this is what I expected. I was prepared for evil sinners —an easy target to ruin—but I wasn't prepared to see the toll of those sins or the righteous reasons for making them.

Her back had fresh flogging marks. I was there on the steps when the Reverend Mother reminded her about penance. Thea left to see the resident priest, which meant he was the one who hurt her. My gut twists when I visualize a man bringing down a leather cord, marking her skin, and her flinching beneath the judgment.

I consider confiding in Cisco, but I don't want to betray Thea's trust for some reason. Those desperate brown eyes flash in my mind again.

I rub my hands and clear my throat.

Dom claps my shoulder and squeezes. "*Pazienza*, Wesley. Patience."

"Easy for you to say," I grumble.

Something flickers in his eyes, and he lets go of me before looking outside the window.

"How can we get them to trust us?" I ask. "Without being obvious, because the current methods are taking too long. The Entity wants more information, and all we have to give now is that they broke into our supply trunk and refused to take lessons."

I know they have the missing manuscript. I'd hoped Thea would come to me for help by now, but I'm still on the outside.

Cisco raises his brows. "Find common ground."

"With assassins?"

"With women," he corrects. "With people. Humans. They have hopes and dreams like all of us."

"Do they?" Zeke reclines on the cot and digs into his jeans. Deep in thought, he pulls out a cigarette and taps it on the packet. "Actually, Wes and the bookish one both talk in nerd. Try her."

"She's the one who walked out of class," I remind him as I take the cigarette. He should know better.

Zeke gives me a dry smile. "That means you're under her skin. Keep pushing. Or let me fuck one of them and learn their secrets that way. Women say things in bed."

I ignore him, as do Cisco and Dom. We're used to his crude methods by now. Sometimes we need that risky wildness in the group, or we'll never get anything done. But sometimes, Zeke's death wish makes my skin crawl.

Especially with... I open my hand to look at the crushed cigarette. The paper is torn, and its innards have spilled onto my skin in a sickly reminder of what we're facing. I confiscate Zeke's cigarette pack, smack him over the head, and then hand it to Dom, who I know will dispose of it properly.

Zeke's brows join in the middle, but he says nothing.

"What's one thing," he once asked me. "One thing you would change if you could turn back time?"

It was about four years ago. We'd just met. I was in the States on a research trip—studying the mystical leylines and reporting back to the Entity about the authenticity of it all when a possessed man in a subway attacked me. Zeke happened to be there, lurking about in a hoodie and hiding his face. He was the last person on that platform I expected to come to my rescue, but he did.

I was in a chokehold when a bullet whizzed by my cheek and hit my attacker between the eyes. At first, I thought it was a lucky hit, but Zeke had a knack for hitting his mark—he still does. The bullet didn't kill the demon, but it slowed him down.

It gave us time to escape. Zeke took me through a network of hidden tunnels to emerge back topside amid a busy city. I offered to buy him a drink. He accepted.

It turned out Zeke was a wanted man. What he did for me put him at risk of being discovered by the authorities. I couldn't leave him—he saved my life—so I convinced the Entity to bring him into the fold.

"One thing."

"I have too many things," I replied to Zeke as he downed his beer. "But maybe I'd find a way to..."

"What?" he asked, a wry smirk on his face. "Don't go shy on me now."

I studied the foamy residue in my empty glass, and thought how worse it appeared without the beer to prop it up.

"I'd find a way to bring someone back that I lost," I confessed.

"Who?"

"Anyone. So I don't have to be alone."

So I can break the cycle of people dying around me.

I found Zeke staring at his empty glass, much like I had

looked at mine. On the way to the bar, he'd told me about his baby sister. The blood on his hands. His self-made mission to hunt things that went bump in the night, in particular, any demon that used fire. His failure at finding peace. But there was something else... or rather, someone else.

"What's your one thing?" I prompted.

He slid me a smirk. "Smaller dick."

I chuckled and rolled my eyes. We both knew it was a lie. But voicing his one thing must hurt him, so I didn't push it.

"Seriously," Zeke said, doubling down. "It's too big."

"Right." I paid the bill. "Whatever you say, mate. Come on. Let's see about a fake passport."

Zeke grew ill after joining Team Saint and becoming my friend. He wasn't even a smoker until after the diagnosis. Now his mysterious one thing is forever out of reach, and it's probably my fault.

My mind turns back to Thea, and I think Zeke is wrong in his assessment of her. She might like reading, and she might like books, but she's not like me. I have no problem talking to beautiful, confident women like her. I can be cool and calm. Okay, fine. That's a lie. Admittedly, occasionally I have to channel my inner Zeke to get by. But around Thea, I feel like an imposter. Like I'm a clumsy teenager with two left feet. She sees right through my act, and it makes my anger rise. I haven't felt this tumultuous since the days I tried to convince everyone that demons were real and one had dragged my uncle to hell.

The days no one believed me.

The days I was on my own.

But I found Team Saint. These men have unique skills that elevated them to this team. We have the potential to use them for good. I refuse to let the cracks in this team get any bigger... even if one of those cracks is because of me.

"Fine," I say. "I'll work on Thea."

TEN
THEA

I avoid class for the next few days. Instead, I spend my time in the archives, squirreled away at a desk in a gloomy corner, studying the prophecy. The Rev must be busy with the Monsignor and other merger business because she never sent for me. I also haven't seen Father McBride around, and remember the Rev telling me she was meeting with him. He's probably long gone by now.

I take it as a sign to keep working on the translation.

But I keep to a dark, quiet spot. The floor-to-ceiling stacks are bookshelves on rollers that move to accommodate the small space. I pushed all the stacks to this side, so I'm extra hidden behind a giant wall of shelves. You'd have to know I'm here to find me. Apart from passing the moody interlopers in the hall or when I'm due to help in the kitchen, gardens, or chicken coup, I rarely see them.

Sooner or later, Team Saint will figure out that their

manuscript is missing. Hell, they probably already know and are biding their time to use it against us. Last night I copied as many pages as possible while Prue was sleeping, just in case the book was confiscated. Prue never glanced at me before sliding onto her cot and passing out from exhaustion. Leila, our biggest gym junkie, said she'd not worked out once this past week without Prue doing the same.

I worry about Prue.

I want to confide in her about what happened to the five of us, but I'm unsure how she'll respond. The old Prue was one hundred percent on our side. She was lively, a prankster, and solid rock. This new one who spends days exercising her demons—literally *exercising* them out—can't deal with an unknown danger in her life. She might tell the Rev about our discovery. And then, the Rev will make us share it with Team Saint, and they'll claim it belongs to them. No, we should keep this to the original five.

I can support and protect Prue better if I figure out where the danger lies.

Five is a recurrent number in the prophecy. It's significant. I have to trust my gut. Instincts are everything to Sinners. They are the hairline difference between life and death.

I sketch the symbol from the demon's wrist on the note papers. I searched every ancient Sumerian text but came up short of an exact match. We know it's Sumerian because of the style of glyphs, but not what this arrangement means.

Voices from a dismissed class filter over the stacks. Frustration is a hammer in my head. *Nothing!* I shove the latest book away. I've come up with *nothing* definitive and can't even claim I've skipped class for a valuable reason. The moment the Rev discovers my truancy, there will be consequences, like... Sin Bin consequences. I shudder at the thought. As far as the Sisterhood is concerned, the way out of this demon infestation is through Team Saint. But I can't help my gut pointing me toward Mary Magdalene. There are too many worrying words in the prophecy. Words like horsemen. Like, the enemy is within. And an age of sin.

And then there's this:

On that fateful time, the wise woman shall usher forth an age of sin, and the sinners shall corrupt the saintly to reshape the light of truth from lies and deceit. Yet, in this time of darkness and despair, a glimmer of hope shall shine forth, for there are those among us who have been shunned by society and cast out into the wilderness. These outcasts shall rise up to challenge belief, embracing their true desires and the power of love. And though others may label them as sinners and cast them out, their paths lead to salvation. For who are we to judge what is right and wrong when the very fabric of society has been torn asunder? Let us not be so quick to cast stones at those who walk a different path, for they may be the ones who hold the key to unlocking the secrets of the universe. And let us remember that the divine relics, though

powerful, are only tools in the hands of those who
wield them. True strength lies in accepting the
darkness within and forging a path of love and
compassion, even in the face of adversity.
So let us embrace the outcasts and the sinners, for
they may hold the key to unlocking the mysteries of
the divine. And let us question what others call sin,
for there is no sin but what you who make sin do.
The path to salvation lies in embracing our true
desires, returning to our roots, and accepting all
through the power of love.

It's clearly referencing us. We're the outcasts and sinners. It all sounds like the end of days, but I don't want to worry anyone if I can't crack this code. At the moment, it's still gibberish. The newly appeared parts don't match the verses the world knows about, but I can see why her gospel being discredited was so palatable for people. To them, Mary was a woman, a sinner, a harlot who stole Jesus' time and said things like 'there is no sin.' But to me, she's an incredible beacon of kindness, compassion, and tolerance. She's questioning the status quo. She's saying that we're all made of the same stuff. She's wondering who has the right to judge when, at our very hearts, we're all flawed.

There's more prophecy. I'm sure one passage refers to mass genocide by a queen of terror, of Venus reigning, and volcanic fire erupting from middle earth. It sounds remarkably similar to something Nostradamus wrote... only Mary's reference is to the feminine. Her gospel clearly predates the French Seer's written works. It's almost as if Nostradamus found this manuscript and changed events to suit the patriarchy and their oppression of anyone not cis male. Almost as if this gospel had been reunited once before.

I pull off my spectacles and rub my tired eyes. I need more time.

Footsteps approach.

I shuffle papers and close books. Someone blurry turns the corner. I pop my spectacles back on and see Wesley. No jacket. No vest. Just in his button-down shirt he rolled up at the forearms. His hair is messy, like he's run his hands through it all day. His fingers are stained with chalk. For a moment, I think, *What a coincidence.* He's searching the archives and has stumbled across me, but he makes a beeline for my desk and gives me a tight-lipped smile. "You weren't in class."

I stare as if to say, *Yeah, and... your point?*

"Again," he adds dryly.

Rage simmers in my blood. My spectacles slip down my nose, but I refuse to push them up. He breaks eye contact first and inspects my work.

I cover the papers. "Is there something you need?"

A muscle ticks in his jaw. He looks me squarely in the eyes. "There are things I can teach you. If you let me."

Maybe it's Mary's words telling me we're all made of the same stuff, or maybe it's the ease I feel around books, but his deep, cultured voice messes with my mood. I'm transported to that moment in the bathroom, to when his hands flexed on my hips and his scent permeated my lungs.

There are things I can teach you.

Suddenly, I'm not thinking about books and scholarly papers. I'm not even thinking he's the last person I want lessons from. I'm thinking about his mouth and how it would feel against my lips. Which is wrong. So wrong.

I clear my throat and feign interest in a book at my table. "No, thank you. I'm good."

He drags over a chair from another desk and sits.

"Sure," I drawl. "Take a seat. Why not?"

He smirks at my sarcasm, which makes my insides boil. The lamp blinks, and he knocks it until it settles. The man makes himself at home at my desk. I shouldn't be surprised. It's what they're all doing in the abbey.

Dom has taken over specific machines in the gym—setting all the weights to his liking. Cisco has moved furniture in the sacristy and snooped in the reliquary. Zeke is more secretive, but he's in the kitchen daily, chatting up the nuns and trying to get them to break their vow of silence. When Mercy told me that last one, I grew particularly peeved.

Team Saint shouldn't cause trouble. They're supposed to be the good guys, but they're thorns in our crowns.

"Right," Wesley says, returning his attention to me. "I know what you're probably thinking. These incredibly attractive lads are swooping in to steal your thunder, but I think we got off on the wrong foot."

"Incredibly attractive? I wouldn't go that far."

"But..." His long lashes lift, and he meets my gaze. This close to him, I feel the impact in my chest. I want to gasp, hold my breath, and force my heart to slow down. It takes everything I have to pretend the way he's looking at me has no effect. "The last thing we want to do is step on anyone's toes. Believe me, we want to learn from you as much as teach you. We're not the enemy, Thea. The demons are. Souls and lives are at stake."

Great.

Now I feel like a bitch.

My shoulder itches, and I rub it. I don't realize what I'm doing until Wesley's attention lands there. It's the spot that was marked. I snatch my hand back and tap my thumb on the leather binding of a book.

"If you'd joined us today," he continues, "I would have explained the meaning of that mark you carved."

"The mark on the severed hand? Or the one I carved?"

"Both."

They were similar but not quite the same.

Did I want his help? No.

Did I need it? Maybe.

Those stupid honey eyes look at me expectantly. I can't exactly spend weeks combing through the library when one conversation with him will be faster.

Fine. I need him.

"What is it?"

"You... actually want to know?" His voice cracks in surprise.

"Don't overthink it." I squirm in my seat.

Wesley springs up and rushes off. His long legs make short work of the library floor. I think I've offended him for a moment, but he moves a few stacks until he finds a particular row and pulls out a book. He's already flicking through the pages when he returns.

"There." He puts the book down and points to a page with a similar symbol. "That's it."

I lean closer to read the inscription. "The mark of Lilith. As in, the demon?"

"The *Mother* of Demons," he corrects, puffing up with self-pride, and damn it, he looks better than hot. Blistering. Again, I shouldn't be thinking about his looks. This is becoming quite an annoying habit of mine.

While Sinners are allowed to have sex, we find partners outside the abbey estate out of respect. Even the nuns are safe here, and with Mercy around, that's saying a lot. But he's an attractive man. He smells nice. And he confuses me with his willingness to help.

Wesley stands behind me and rests one hand on my seat while the other reaches around me to point at the page. "Lilith is the first wife of Adam... but also rumored to be Lucifer's wife and, here—"

He turns a few pages and then places his palm beside the book. The heat of his body buzzes along my back, making me feel like I'm standing before a warm fire on a cold day. It distracts the fuck out of me.

"I know who Lilith is," I clip, shifting in my seat. "She rebelled against the very first mansplainer."

He doesn't take the hint. So I scowl and refocus on the book, specifically the passage about Lilith and the color plate illustration beside it—a familiar figure with long red locks, a voluptuous body, and a temptress portrayal. She reminds me of Mercy.

A sick feeling rolls in my gut, and I itch to reread the prophecy in case this likeness makes a difference. But Wesley launches into an explanation of the levels of hell and demonology. I find myself reluctantly listening. His passion for history is like mine. Admiration creeps in. He's not just a handsome face. The man knows his stuff.

It's sexy.

It makes me want to forget I'm a Sinner, forget about the world ending, and play a game called I belong in a romance novel starring Wesley as my book boyfriend. It would start with a stolen kiss between the stacks and end with me corrupting his delicate sensibilities... just like Mary predicted.

And the sinners shall corrupt the saintly to reshape the light of truth from lies and deceit.

Before I know it, my traitorous body is on fire. The girls would tell me to just fuck him. Get him out of my system. Enjoy the ride. But it would be a game. Distraction. Torture. More trouble than it's worth.

I've heard most of his lecture before, so I zone out and flip through the book about Lilith. There are many sketches and lithographs of her with others. There is Satan, or Lucifer. Samael, the fallen angel. According to whoever is telling the story, high-level demons were decreed as kings or princes of hell. One demon steals my attention. Asmodeus is a handsome devil who carouses and peddles lust and gambling, but that's not what grabs me. He's named the king of earthly spirits, of lust, war, and revenge... or... I tap the word on the page and interrupt Wesley.

"Do you know that word?"

He squints at it and leans closer, bringing the scent of his citrus aftershave so close that I can taste it.

"*Sakhr*. Islamic, I believe. Something like the rock, or I think I've seen it as the—"

"Stony One," I finish for him. "*Sakhr* means rock or something."

"If you can translate it, why did you ask me?"

"I wasn't a hundred percent sure," I mumble.

Wasn't there something in the prophecy about a stone?

Wesley says, "Asmodeus is sometimes known as a benefi-cent demon. Perhaps even a friend to man, if you will. He's frequently mentioned in the *Kabbalah* and even invoked for spells and incantations. I think there's a copy of the *Malleus Maleficarum* somewhere. I could check to see if there's more information for you."

"No." I close the book. "It's fine, thank you."

I stand, essentially pushing him out of the way. Gathering

my things, I go to leave, but Wesley blocks me. "I haven't finished telling you about the mark of Lilith."

"That's because you were wrong."

He blinks. "I beg your pardon?"

I reopen the book and point to the mark he showed me. "It's not the exact mark. The one I carved had bits in these places. So, thank you for your time, but I don't need to know anything else."

"With respect, love, yes, you do." He blocks me again, getting into my space.

It's hard to breathe. Hard to think. I can deal with violence, but names of endearment, even if they're common throwaways, are not something I'm used to.

I hate it.

"What's so important then?" Irritation bleeds into my voice.

"The mark is a sign of possession... the Mother claiming the vessel."

Cold fingers trail down my spine. I had that mark on my body. Does that mean I'm...?

His perceptive gaze is on my face, watching for my reaction. I shake off the feeling and push him aside. He jogs after me as I stalk down the aisle between the row of stacks he separated, where he has the gall to block me again.

"Wesley," I grind out. "You're walking a dangerous line."

He holds up a hand to stop me. "You didn't wait to hear about the second mark."

"So?"

He pauses, and a look of hate-filled reluctance flashes over his expression. It's almost as if he doesn't want to share the words on the tip of his tongue. Obviously, now I *must* know what they are, so I stand up straighter, harden my tone, and deliver my bait.

"Just what I thought." I let my eyes rake down his body with disdain. "You don't know any more than I do."

His gaze smolders at my challenge. I sense an insult coming. Go on. Say it. Call me a spiteful bitch. Call me a whore. A sinner. A coward.

"It's the mark of the demon Vepar," he reveals. "Except... it's also of Pestilence."

My heart stops. "The horseman?"

He shrugs. "Or an affinity with it. Vepar spreads pestilence. It could mean an allegiance with the horseman. The marks seem to be some kind of symbol of—"

"Cooperation," I finish. "Like an army or cohort."

The horsemen were in the prophecy, but I dismissed it because Mary wrote about five of them, not four as the book of revelations states. Wesley might have actually helped.

My heart starts again, my blood thrumming with the thrill of discovery. I see it in Wesley's eyes. It's like he gets off on this shit, too. If he wasn't my enemy, I think I'd like him. I hug the notes to my chest, which draws his attention. *Stupid.*

"What are you hiding?" His eyes narrow.

"Nothing."

"Thea," he says my name like I'm twelve. "You skip classes and burrow here, poring over books and papers. You're clearly keeping secrets, and I just showed you mine, so now it's your turn."

"Burrow?" I scoff, even though it was precisely what I did.

His lips flatten. His nostrils flare.

Oh, you poor stupid fool. You don't even know what you're up against. He telegraphs his impending attack like an amateur. I deftly dart out of the way as he reaches for my notes.

"Really?" I drawl.

I'm too busy gloating and assuming he knows jack shit about close combat because he's a scholar. I didn't realize he distracted me like a magician. I find myself with my back against a stack. The books wobble around me, threatening to topple. His hands grip the shelf on either side of my face.

He lowers until we're nose to nose. "What secrets are you hiding, Thea?"

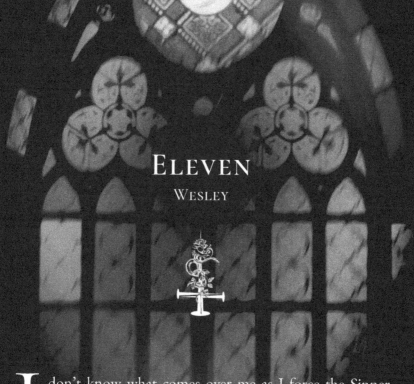

ELEVEN
WESLEY

I don't know what comes over me as I force the Sinner against the stack and cage her in my arms. She keeps testing me, resisting every effort I make to gain her trust. Something about her defiance challenges every base male instinct I own. I want to force her to pay attention to me.

It's part desperation, part need, part wicked want.

My hands grip the shelf so hard; I fear I'll break something with my anger... and... there's this other infuriating sense riding my system. She smells good. Too good. It's making my head light.

Secrets. Lies. Taunts.

She still hugs those papers like she's hiding something. Warm brown eyes flick up to mine and dance with humor. Like me, she has spectacles on, but they don't hide her ego. I don't think I'll ever prove myself worthy enough to earn an invitation behind that wall she's built around herself.

Just give me the gospel—lead us to the relic.

I flatten my lips as she smirks up at me. I should take it from her. But that would make me as bad as she is. I'm already flirting with damnation with what I've done to bring us here. Now every minute in her presence brings me closer to a temptation I can't afford.

Push off. Leave. Let her come to you in her own time.

But somehow, I stand there, caught in a snare that begins somewhere in her scent and ends around her plump lips. I don't want to kiss them. I want to bite them.

She brazenly rolls her hips into mine as if she senses my thoughts and can't resist deploying her filthy Sinner tactics. Contact sparks a frenzy of sensation in my body. Pleasure skips up my spine. But it's not my mouth that releases a moan of appreciation. It's hers, along with a flutter of her lashes and a lick of her lips.

Inside my body, a holy war wages in my blood. Half rushes south, hot on the heels of temptation, while the rest prays to remain in control. God, give me the strength to resist this woman. She's a devil who will bring me to my knees. She'll veer me from my path of redemption, and I simply cannot.

I cannot.

"What wicked things will you teach me, Wesley?"

Arousal bleeds through her husky voice. She rocks into me again, but this time, it's more of a lover's maneuver, a way to close the gap she's longed to obliterate. It shocks me. Throws me into an alternate reality where she's not my enemy but the woman I've been searching for my entire life. The one who will fill the empty hole in my heart, the one who will be strong enough to stay by my side... to resist whatever curse inevitably kills everyone I care about. Another roll of her hips into mine, another bite of her lip, and I swallow a groan in my throat.

Stop. This is too far. This is beyond a game. This is the edge of the cliff. *Remind her that the promise of sex won't buy you. Remind her of what she is.*

"Flexing your filthy Sinner skills, I see," I whisper darkly. "To distract me? It's only making me think whatever you're hiding must be valuable."

I know I've made a mistake when her eyes flash with spite.

"If I'm a filthy whore, then you're a dirty man."

To prove her point, she rubs her hip bone into my groin. Hot pleasure threatens to undo me, but I won't give in. I won't let her win this battle.

Step away. End this now.

I press closer, trapping her with my body, keeping my expression passive. She is soft and hard at once. Feminine but toned. A contradiction my body welcomes.

"I'd bet you'd love it, wouldn't you?" she continues softly. "You'd love to take me here, make me beg, and then scold me for not keeping quiet."

My lungs seize. She just described a fantasy of mine so accurately it's like she's wrenched it from my dreams. When I was young, working late and in the library alone, the gaping hole in my heart grew bigger. Oh, how I would prop my chin on my hand and watch the pretty librarian meander about, shelving the books. I was too shy to act on my crush. Too afraid.

I want to think Thea's manipulating me. That she's somehow guessed my desires, but instead, I think we're just the same. Zeke was right.

Wes and the bookish one both talk in nerd. Try her.

The fact that I'm still crowding her, pushing harder against her, proves we want similar things. She whimpers with what sounds like need.

Chase it, my body urges. *Roll in it. Tease it open. Make her yours.*

This is no longer a distraction to her. She's testing me, pushing me to my limits, and wanting me to submit as she is. Wanting us to fall together. Perhaps that's what throws me off the most. Her reaction to me is genuine. Her pupils dilate, she pants, her cheeks flush with stunning color. This isn't an act. I arouse her.

If we want similar things, perhaps we're fighting the same inner war.

That last thought floors me. I lose the battle in my blood. It all rushes south. My cock grows hard, achingly so. Instead of making me feel lost, I feel like I belong. On the next undulation of her hips, I thrust against her. We clash. Gasp. Her eyelashes flutter. She sees the change in me. The satisfaction, the thrill, the raw longing. It's like I'm staring at a reflection of my soul.

No more.

Yes, once more.

I grind against her, and she does the same. I glance at her lips—my mouth waters. My mind wanders into a dream, remembering a part of the gospel I'm asking her to relinquish —sinners deserve a second chance—everyone does.

I'm no fool. Bad people did everything possible to ensure the gospel never saw the light of day. I'd assumed it was to stop a dangerous prophecy from leading sinners to holy relics of power, but now I'm unsure.

Now I fear I've been blindsided.

Maybe the prize is this letting go of hate, this division between our genders, because the tiny kernel of warmth in my heart seems to grow despite my excuses. It's as though that part of me knows something my mind doesn't.

Thea's vulnerability is beneath the hard exterior, and I worry about it. I worry about what made it hide far away and what's keeping it there.

We hear male voices filter from somewhere close. Zeke. Cisco. Dom. I'm instantly reminded of what I'm here for, and it's not love. Lust. Whatever this is.

I'm here to save the life of someone I care for. And to dismantle this organization. An unwanted sense of grime slices through me, but I ignore it. I'm not alone in this mission. Although it pains me, and every cell in my body screams for me to do the opposite, I step away from her.

She almost had me there. *Almost.*

I adjust my erection so it's not tenting my slacks and catch a genuine glimmer of disappointment in her eyes. Something about this moment begs to be savored, studied and understood.

Another time. In another life.

I have to do something drastic to gain her trust without being manipulated. Before I can talk myself out of this incredibly foolish move, I dig beneath my collar and tug out a charm I haven't removed in years.

"I have something for you."

"What?"

"A gift. Here." I show her the small colored stones linked by a silver wire and threaded onto the leather. "It's a good luck charm."

"Luck is for the lazy," she blurts, then shuts her mouth. "It's what the Rev always says. But frankly, she's right. Sinners can't hope for a strike of fortune or the hand of God to bail us out. We make our own luck."

She's blabbering, trying to throw up one last defense. I find it strangely endearing. It makes me think she's as confused about her feelings as I am. I remove the charm and belligerently lean toward her. Her breath hitches as I get close. My hands pause at her neck, my face beside hers. I want to give her time to decline, to say no, but her lips angle toward me. Despite everything, I have a surreal moment of thinking she wants me to kiss her.

Tie the cord. Don't blow this, Wes.

My senses catch fire when I brush her skin with my knuckles. I push her hair aside and knot the cord, barely suppressing a shiver.

When I'm done, I linger and stare into her eyes. I find something that wraps around my chest and squeezes. Bloody hell, it rocks me to my core. It's not hate. Nor is it defiance or derision. It's the earth-moving realization that I've done something meaningful for her. She doesn't even know the full power of this gift, but she accepts it.

Because I gave it to her.

I want to feel triumphant. I want to know that I've won this round. But instead, I feel humbled. I clear my throat and step back. "It's wise to always wear it, even when you sleep."

She frowns at the tiny charm. A million thoughts cascade through her mind, none of which I'm privy to, but I sense her hesitation. If I tell her the truth about that charm, she'll take it off. I know it.

"Don't overthink it, Thea." I echo her words from earlier. "It's a peace offering and for lucky dreams."

Then I adjust my spectacles, shove my hands in my pockets, and walk away.

Something big is happening between us. Big enough to destroy my world... or finally mend it. If only I knew which one.

TWELVE

THEA

I spend the following evening in my cell, avoiding responsibilities, resisting the call of my vibrator, and knowing consequences are coming for my behavior. But I don't seem to care. I'm stuck in a weird mental space. Wesley has me tied in all sorts of knots. I'm on the verge of hunting him down, tossing him against a wall, and screwing his brains out.

To get it out of my system.

I don't know how Mercy does it. She's a sex junkie, but she manages to control her impulses every minute of the day while here I am, positively dripping and panting after a close encounter with a man I hardly know.

It's because he's unexpected. I'm used to men working against us and not living with us—occupying our safe space and being kind and shit. He's swiftly taking over my thoughts; I can't have that, and it's distracting.

He gave me a gift. Right?

I mean, it wasn't a joke.

My hand closes around the charm. It's pretty—small stones of different colors are wrapped in wire and linked on a cord. Such a weird gift. The kind you give your teenage crush on Valentine's Day. The kind the Viscount gave his new Governess in the last Harlequin novel I read... right before he kissed her and set her world on fire.

What would Wesley's lips feel like against mine? What would his hands do if given free access to my body? What would have happened if things had gone a different way? The questions are there, and they won't leave.

And they won't stop heating my blood.

At least Prue isn't here, so I have privacy to gather my thoughts... and vagina. Ultimately, I cave and take my vibrating bullet from my bedside drawer, use it, orgasm immediately because I'm so wound up, and then swear like a sailor. Unsatisfied and still on edge, I toss the vibrating traitor into my drawer and close it.

Get a grip, Thea.

Think about the marks he helped you identify, not him.

Don't overthink it.

But that's exactly what I'm doing, and the bastard probably knows.

Don't overthink it.

Prue said that to me the first time I killed a person. She took me deep into the slums of a nameless city, taught me how to use my innocence to bait a known sex offender, then helped me follow through with the kill when I balked.

I close my eyes and feel her steady hand wrap around my trembling one as it gripped the dagger. The blade was already against his throat. He was unconscious—that part was easy. He tried to assault me. But now he was just a sad man lying on the cold concrete and smelling like piss. Big nose. Short. Stained shirt open at the collar to reveal a hairy chest.

And a vein that pulsed in his neck.

"Don't overthink it," Prue said as she gripped my hand. "That will get you killed."

We sliced.

"Harder," she said. "Through the tendons."

The man's eyes opened and saw the two of us. He didn't realize the blade was already in his throat. I increased the pressure. Felt something hot and wet slide over my cold fist. Panicked, I closed my eyes.

Prue touched my back and quietly said, "Open your eyes. Witness his death. Give his life meaning."

"But..."

"Make sure Elvis has left the building, Thea."

I forced my eyes open, forced them to watch his life ebbing, and came face to face with my sin. He was the old janitor from my foster care home who groomed me. I got away before the damage was done, but he continued to offend. I had enough time to stumble to a steaming drain before my lunch was violently ejected.

Prudence was behind me instantly, holding back my hair

and prying the murder weapon from my shaking fingers before I cut myself.

"Shh. You're okay," she murmured. "You're safe."

But I couldn't breathe. Couldn't stop my diaphragm from convulsing. Maybe I'd just saved more children. Maybe I didn't. How would I ever know?

"We won't let anything happen to you again." Prue smooths my hair. "You're one of us now. We protect our own."

"But..."

"Don't overthink it, Thea."

Coming back to myself, I scowl at the memory. Thinking is what I do. It's what I've always done. I pull out Mary's manuscript and open it to a new page. Everything happening is connected. I feel it in my bones. From the likeness of Lilith reminding me of Mercy, to the disappearing mark on my shoulder, to the *Stoney One* being similar to the *one stone freed,* to five of us needed to reunite the gospel. A woman wrote it, and we are an organization run by women—one wise woman, like in the prophecy.

Maybe I'm jumping to conclusions because I want to be more relevant than Team Saint. But I can't help the inescapable feeling that Mary chose us. We Sinners are her new disciples, her messengers. And the men... they're... I don't know. All I know for sure is that I can't trust them, and I want to fuck Wesley.

And that bugs me on both accounts.

After a while, I find the words blending and head down to

the training room, where I belt out a few minutes against the boxing bag chained to the ceiling. I'm not the only one in the gym. Prue is here, as expected. I consider joining her, but she's running on that treadmill like the devil is nipping at her heels.

I hope she's just distracted by the mockingbirds flittering outside the window she's facing. She used to walk in the garden and follow them. I'm sure she had a bird-watching diary somewhere. She would be so angry at me if I interrupted her and frightened them away. I asked her once why they enamor her.

"You ever read To Kill a Mockingbird?" she asked.

I shook my head.

"They're a symbol of innocence."

I wasn't too sure. They're also the state bird of Memphis, and she loves her Elvis.

Zeke walks in from one direction and Leila from another. I pick up my towel. The look they give each other reminds me of the burning distrust I feel for Wesley... or did. Do. Definitely still do. I'm not in the mood to play referee between them. Not in the mood to encourage a fight, either. I head to the indoor pool attached to the gym, but Tawny and Mercy are swimming. So I make a fast break, exit the room, and walk outside to the lake.

Mist drizzles. Perfect.

I remove my sweats and drape them over a lookout bench beneath the beech tree. Left in my one-piece Speedo, I wade into the lake. The water is cold, but it's exactly the kind of thing I need to take my mind off things. Within minutes of swimming, all I'm thinking about is my breath, my heartbeat, and the pattern of my strokes. Soon I forget that Team Saint and a pair of honey eyes exist.

When I emerge, thoroughly worked out, I find Sister Margaret sitting on the bench. The last time she saw me, I was covered in blood and vomit. I plan to leave, but her look of serenity captures my attention. Rosy cheeks and a wistful smile are her makeup. The sun breaks through clouds and shines on her closed eyes. I almost feel bad crunching over gravel to retrieve my sweats. Disturbing her is the last thing I want... but somehow, I don't silence my feet.

She sees me and broadens her smile. The allure of her contentment has me sitting next to her after I dress. Sniffing, I stare at the lake and worry my bottom lip with my teeth.

We sit in silence.

But while she's seemingly comfortable, my nerves and anxiety twirl like they're in a tornado. I haven't felt this disturbed in years. I should be meditating, praying, or doing something to calm my busy mind, but the longer I sit there, the more I realize I'm so different from the woman beside me.

I'm envious. But also, I'm not.

She's at peace with this monastic life she chose, but I know I'll never accept it similarly. It's not in me and never has been. I'm a fighter—a Thelma. I may not have started as confident as Louise, but I found it eventually.

Sister Margaret turns to me and squeezes my arm. I shouldn't look at her because the moment I do, I'll either burst into tears or do something equally unbefitting of a woman tough enough to be dropped into a war zone and emerge with more confidence than she left.

Her eyes are so pure and bright that I almost miss the concern wavering in them.

"I feel lost," I reveal, surprising myself. "I'm sure you've noticed our special guests, and they're just so—argh."

I clench my fists on my thighs and glare at the lake. She keeps her hand on my arm and squeezes me.

Go on, she seems to say.

"We've dedicated our lives and souls to become what we are, and now they're here, and I'm second-guessing every-thing." I take a deep breath of fresh air, then blurt more out on my exhale. "They're infuriating. Disrupting. I hate them. But... we need them. Don't we? I mean, the Rev wouldn't put us through this otherwise, right? I know the Vatican has been breathing down our necks since they discovered us, so maybe this was bound to happen, but I never expected it to be someone like *him*." Another deep breath. Another squeeze from Sister Margaret. "He seems to know his stuff, but... I don't know. This was *my* job. I'm the one everyone turns to for answers, and now I'm struggling and... gah. I hate feeling like this."

I slide a hesitant glance to Sister Margaret, worrying that I've said too much and I'm making a fool of myself. Under-standing is in her eyes, but a glimmer of unrest swims beneath the surface. I can't tell if it's on my behalf or for someone else.

"Drop me on a battlefield or ask me to walk into a club

and track down a demon, and I'm good. I'm in my element," I say.

Her brows wing up, and she cants her head. Suddenly, I realize why I'm feeling like this.

I nod. "You're right. I'm trained to fight and not to accept help from strangers. Of course, this will be tough, and I should go easy on myself and take it one day at a time."

Her rosy cheeks inflate as she grins, pats me gently on the arm, and then returns to staring at the water and the gorgeous sunset as it changes the sky, limning the clouds with gold. It was blue and gray a moment ago, and now it's turquoise. Soon it will be orange.

"Then there's the part where the prophecy says the enemy is from within," I blurt, unable to help myself. "How can we trust them if that means the enemy is them? I mean, they're here with us now. So, they're technically within. I refuse to believe it means the enemy is one of us. So, I guess, unless the enemy is within myself..."

Sister Margaret waves her hand at the sky. I'm missing the sunset. I'm reading too much into this. Overthinking it when I should appreciate the wonder this world offers me.

"Sorry."

I sit longer, enjoying nature working miracles, and instantly feel calmer. Something we Sinners tell each other is to enjoy the ride. We know our fate is inevitable torture in hell, but we're not there yet. Until then, we're free to take our pleasures and joys in small chunks, wherever we can find them.

If that ride includes a particular Team Saint member living

across the hall from me, who am I to judge? Who am I to analyze and agonize over it? I clutch the charm and feel a rush of warmth in my chest.

"You're so right," I mumble and get up. I pat Sister Margaret's shoulder as I pass. "Good chat, Sister."

She claps her hand over mine, smiles, nods, and then I leave. By the time I head back to my cell in the evening, exhaustion drags me down.

When I arrive at my door, Wesley opens his. He makes it look like he's simply heading out, but he happens to do it when he hears me. *I know it.* I consciously relax my shoulders. *Enjoy the ride.* His gaze dips to my neck to see if I still wear his gift. I am. I goddamn masturbated with it on. He wouldn't look at me so innocent-eyed if he knew that.

Something about that knowledge makes me offer him a genuine smile. His own is nervous and brief. A thrill skips in my stomach. I think I'll enjoy ruffling his feathers and making him squirm. And then showing him everything he's missed because he's never had me.

But not right now. I'm exhausted.

I open the door to my room. Prudence still isn't in. Knowing my alone time is limited, I quickly shower and dress in the same simple night clothes we all wear: black shorts and a singlet. Well, except for Mercy, she wears whatever she wants and thinks her vanity and comfort are well worth the penance.

Fuck. I should probably confess to Father McBride about how I spent the week. If he's still here, I'll do it tomorrow.

The prophecy calls to me. As I read it, my fingers gravitate to the charm. Lucky or not, it's the first gift of this kind I've ever received. The only other man who gave me things was that asshole janitor at the group home.

And Prue.

Casting a glance at her empty cot, I decide to hide the manuscript inside a Bible. It's not the best fit, but she won't notice immediately.

She was the one who taught me this trick. She might even find it funny if she notices. Maybe I should be obvious and point it out using a romance novel. See if I can make her laugh.

Thinking about it, I recall the day I first met her. I was twelve, she was a lot older, and I thought the sun shone out of her ass. She was so confident, so together. She knew everything while I knew nothing. Definitely the Louise to my Thelma. But most of all, she made me feel like everything would be okay.

I step out of the taxi and notice the big steps leading up to the castle-like stone abbey. It's all so huge. Knights and their damsels should live there, but instead, I see a group of stern women in black, tight clothes standing on the landing and staring down at me.

"Quick smart," says the Rev, a burly woman with hair growing from a mole on her chin. I bite back my scowl, hating that I'm here. But when she turned up at our group home, ignored the other girls but gave me attention, I preened. I basked. Only that man before had said I looked pretty. But no one had ever said that I was smart too. That I had potential. I didn't know for what, but when she said my new home would be

a castle, and there were other girls like me, I jumped at the chance. She didn't even care that I was in trouble for reading the old Harlequin books.

"Get your suitcase, girl."

My scowl deepens, and I go to the open trunk where the driver is waiting. He gives me a pitying look and hands me my old suitcase.

"Now up the steps and meet your new sisters," the Rev says.

It feels like it takes forever to drag my case up those steps. It's heavy for my little girl's arms. As I climb, my resentment grows. Despite seeing me struggle, all these women are just watching.

To make matters worse, when I get to the landing, they disperse like I'm not worth their time. One is left—Prudence. She puts her hands on her hips and looks down at me curiously.

"What's your name?" she asks.

"She had no name," says the Rev behind me.

"That's what I was going to say," I snap, feeling my cheeks heat.

"Hmm," Prudence says. "You look like a—"

"Dorothea," the Rev says. "That's what we're calling her."

I whine, "But I like Thelma. There's a cool movie I watched about this badass woman who ran away with her best friend and shot all the bad—"

"Mind your manners, Dorothea." The Rev glares down at me. "You don't want to spend all day doing penance, now, do you?"

I have no idea what she's talking about, but I nod.

Prudence shares a look with the Rev, then gestures for me to follow her. "I'll show you to your cell."

I'm both mortified and cautiously optimistic when we reach my monastic cell. I had to share rooms at the group home, but I have my own space here. There's nothing in the room, though. No fancy toys or pretty dresses, and I worry I'll live like this forever.

"Thea sounds kinda like Thelma, right?" Prudence plops on my cot and grins.

I nod. "I guess it does."

"Then the Rev gets what she wants, and so do you. We'll call you Thea."

"Okay."

She takes in my sad face. "Look, kid. If there's one piece of advice I can give you, it's what they don't know won't hurt them. You catch my drift?"

My frown says I don't, so she leans over, tugs a book from beneath my cot's mattress, and hands it to me. I almost drop dead on the floor when I see the cover, and I'm too afraid to take it from her. Every time I get caught with these books, I get in trouble.

She smirks and wiggles it at me. "I heard you like reading romance."

"I'm twelve," I say reflexively, repeating what the Matron would tell me. "I shouldn't be—"

"Bah," she says and waves me off. "There's another girl here who's been reading them since she was ten. How do you think they know which of us is good to recruit? Girls who read romance grow to be dangerous women. We aren't ashamed of what we *want. We ask questions, and we tell the judgmental pricks to fuck off. Just... hide it inside your Bible."*

Sighing, I return to the present and glance again at Prue's empty cot. She failed to mention that we were also easier to lean into sin... and in the eyes of the Sisterhood, and the church, we're going to hell for our deviant desires.

Fortunately, my reading tastes have broadened since I was a child, but I still love falling into a world where everything is safe once in a while. It beats the hell out of reality.

And I am a dangerous woman.

THIRTEEN

THEA

My first thought when I wake up is that I forgot to put away the manuscript, but something stops me from moving. The room is dark and cold, and a breeze shifts the gauze curtain. When did I open the window?

Prue must have done it.

I turn toward her, but my bones are cement—my body is paralyzed. The only part I control is my eyes. *What the ever-loving-hell?*

And then I feel it... an ominous presence lurking in the air.

Every hair on my body lifts as the evil soaks into the shadows, making them impossibly darker. The walls have ears and eyes. The air has teeth. My pulse spikes. Sweat prickles my brow. Something heavy sits on my chest. *There's nothing here. It's my imagination. I'm having a night terror.* It's just the breezy curtain and the all-consuming sense that a malevolent force is trying to get inside me to rip open my chest and claw my heart out.

I feel guilty about how I spent the afternoon and then never went to confession. I've sinned, and now I'm open to this evil.

That's how it's supposed to work, right?

The need to remove my eyes from the breezy curtain seems necessary. Break eye contact. Set myself free. But it won't work.

Panic consumes me until I remember my prayers, just like in that alley. I remember the words drilled into me as a teen kneeling on the painful pews while tutored by the old Reverend Mother. She was a cruel master.

Thwack! Her bamboo cane hits my knuckles when I mumble. "Start again, Dorothea. From the top." *Thwack! Thwack!*

But now the prayers are drilled into my mind, so I can't hate her. I recite the Hail Mary and put every inch of my being into delivering the words in my mind.

Shame, shame, little Sinner, the voice hisses in my head, trying to drown out the prayers. *I see your perverted heart. I see all of you.*

Its words are meant to undo me, but they give me strength. Fuck you, evil presence, trying to shame me. I give myself enough of that in the Sin Bin. I don't need it from you too.

Ahhh… so juicy and defiant.

The urge to fight builds like a volcano about to erupt.

Shame, shame, little Sinner. We all know what's troubling you.

Fuck off.

You're afraid you have nothing to offer. I'll tell you a secret. It's because you don't. Wesley knows you're a whore. It's why he walked away from you in the library. That gift is a ploy. You're nothing but dirt beneath his boots.

My prayers falter.

Shame, shame, little Sinner. Why would a good man want to make a home with a whore?

That's where the evil presence lost me. Calling me a whore won't hurt my feelings. That's not the darkness I run from.

"Fucking amateur," I mock, and realize my mouth is moving. I'm breaking free.

There's not much point, little Sinner. You're already spreading your rot. I can smell the pestilence on you. The sickness inside. Just let me in, and we can help each other. I can ease your suffering.

Lies. I double down on the prayers despite feeling underwater. Just when I think I'm about to suffocate in evil, its hold on me breaks. I wrench myself free from the malevolent force and topple from the cot—*oof*—and land hard on the floor. The gospel hits me on the head.

Groggy and grasping my forehead, I check the window. I can't see properly, so I fumble for my spectacles on the nightstand and put them on. The curtain's not blowing. The window isn't even open. The shadows are just shadows.

Just a dream. A night terror. My mind has been filled with prophecy and hormones and gifts. As the dream evil spirit alluded, a tiny kernel of longing had bloomed in my chest. I see that now. I used to dream of an all-consuming love like in my old novels. Of making a home with someone who cared for me and wanted me. Dreams that sharp and deep never leave—they just get covered by the weight of judgment.

You're safe.

Prue's voice whispers from the recess of my memory. The ghost of her hand smooths my head, just like it did when I puked in that alley, and I smile. She was right. I might never have that home with a picket fence—the one with a banquet table where children play beneath—but I have my Sinner sisters.

You're safe.

Yeah, I fucking am. And I owe it to these women to make them feel the same. I rip the charm from my neck and check the manuscript for damage. The book is open to a page I haven't read yet. Sometimes I feel like the blank pages are changing. I swear I would have noticed this one. The style of illustration is remarkably feminine and grotesque all at once. I run my finger over the picture of an upside-down crucifix and tilt my head. It's not Christ on the cross, but a figure shrouded in veils and rags, their identity hidden. Next to the cross are five demons whispering in the figure's ears. Pestilence, War, Famine, and Death... the final demon is Lilith.

Whimpering behind me.

I slam the book shut and hide it under the cot.

"Prue." I get to my knees and lean over her bed. She's

facing away from me, hunched. I shake her shoulder. Hot. Sweaty. Is she sick?

"Prue, wake up."

The whimpering stops. Time dies. No babies are born. No breaths are taken. No world spins. And in that tiny moment, a switch flips on my instincts. *Danger.* I jolt back and narrowly avoid clawed fingers reaching for me. She snarls and gnashes yellow diseased teeth. Black holes for eyes. Rotting skin with oozing pustules.

Not Prue.

Definitely not Prue.

A sick, foul stench follows her as she lurches from the cot and moves toward me on disjointed hands and knees. Her voice is not of this earth, and vitriol spews forth in another language. The logical part of my mind tries to shout that it recognizes words from my studies, but the irrational part I work so hard at smothering takes over.

Fear grips me.

This was sleeping next to me for half the night.

I scramble to my feet and into the hallway, shutting the door behind me. Prue hits the other side with a loud, thundering bang. *Silence.* Swallowing hard, I grip the doorknob, ready for the fight of my life, but Prue doesn't turn it. Maybe she can't. Maybe because a demon has control of her body. I try to pull that logical part back to the forefront.

Possession.

Find something holy. Something blessed.

I scan the closed doors in the long, silent hallway. An old

wooden chair sits at the end against the wall beneath a portrait of the Madonna and the baby Jesus. I race to collect the chair, then wedge it under the doorknob, unsure whether it will hold. At the very least, it will slow Prue down if she trips over it.

Our blessed knives and weapons are downstairs in the training room. Options run through my mind as I survey the hallway. We have a priest living on this floor. But which cell?

Not the one opposite me. That's Wesley's. I run to the next door and slam my fist on it.

"Father Angelotti!" I shout. "Wake up."

I dart to the next door and do the same in case Father is in there. I bang on each Team Saint door, raising the alarm until they all open. Out stumbles a myriad of half-dressed, sleep-disheveled men. They're not the only ones shaken awake by my alarm. My sisters open their doors.

Everyone stares at the person opposite them. Man to woman. Saint to Sinner.

Zeke adjusts his boxer shorts as he faces Leila. His eyes widen at her crop top and sports underwear, then promptly crinkle with male appreciation. Leila aims her Smith & Wesson at him, her expression hard and impenetrable.

"What is it?" Mercy's alarmed eyes land on me. Her long red hair is messy, and the silk strap of her nightgown falls off her shoulder.

Lilith.

She's not Lilith. She's—

The doorknob to my room jiggles, and I point at it. "She's possessed."

"Who?"

"Prue!"

"Are you sure? She looked fine earlier."

"Trust me. She's possessed." I point at my face. "She has black holes for eyes and rotting, diseased skin. I've never seen this sort of thing before. Even that man who vomited on me looked normal."

Call her a floozy, a nympho, or whatever you want, but there is one thing Mercy always is: Dependable. A leader. She clicks into Sinner mode. "We need something blessed. Tawny?"

"On it." Tawny spins on her heels and jogs to her room.

Raven wraps her rosary around her knuckles and then shoves the big, muscled Saint Dominic out of her way so she can pad over on bare feet. The look she gives me says, *I'm ready.*

Leila checks her gun, then realizes it will be useless against possession. It's not blessed. Even if it was, blessed bullets might do nothing but harm the innocent meat suit the demon spirit occupies—Prue. Leila puts it back in her room before joining me.

Sinners surround the jiggling door to my cell. What do we do when it opens? We can't *stab* Prue with a blessed weapon.

"Ready?" Mercy asks. "On my count, we open and restrain her."

"Then what?"

"We work it out."

"Wait," Wesley barks. He finds his spectacles and puts them on. "Shouldn't we assess the situation? I mean—"

"Three!" Mercy opens the door.

Demon Prue stumbles into the hallway, dazed, and then stops. My sisters gasp. Their faces go pale. Prue's rotting flesh is worse. Hideous insects and worms crawl along tendons glimpsed through gaping sores on the skin. Vomit rises in my throat.

Zeke leans casually against his doorjamb and gives us a disparaging look. "She looks fine to me, and you bitches clearly have a few screws loose."

Bitches? I glare at him, then realize he spoke in English, not Italian. He, too, realizes his slip with an irritated look. A week. That's all it took, and their lies are showing.

Father Angelotti folds his arms, annoyed—at us! That, or he is trying to hide the myriad of tattoos on his bare, muscled torso. Even Dominic, the unemotional Saint, shoots us a pitiful look—the kind you give a person in the middle of a psychotic break.

Wesley steps toward Prue and dips to look into her eyes.

"She's probably sleepwalking," he mumbles and reaches out—

"Stop!" I yank him back. "Can't you see?"

"See what?"

"She's possessed. Can't you see the rotting flesh and demonic eyes?" I look at the men, agape.

They have no idea what I'm talking about. I rub my eyes

beneath my spectacles. This is why I use contacts on missions. Damned glass fogs up. Am I still dreaming?

"I see it," Raven says grimly.

"Good God," Tawny mumbles, then gags and tries to hide it.

"She's rotting away." Leila waves her hand before her nose. "Like she's got some kind of plague."

Mercy agrees.

Prue stinks like off meat thrown in the sewer.

Relief washes through me. I'm not going insane or dreaming. But then guilt hits me hard.

"Prue," I whisper, inching closer.

Her chin drops to her chest, and she sways on her feet. The instant I touch her sweaty shoulder, her head whips up, and she spews cuss words and vile propositions that would make a Sinner blush. She lurches forward, and her hands wrap around my throat.

Unnaturally strong, she backs me against the wall, teeth snapping for my face. The stench reaches into my stomach and calls up the contents. I barely hold back the bile.

Father Angelotti swears in Italian and barks orders at his team. Tawny shoves a blessed item into each Sinner's hand. My fingers thread around Prue's throat, holding her back.

You're safe.

My heart squeezes. I hold out my other hand for Tawny to place a statue of the Virgin Mary.

"What do I do with this?" I gape. "Plug her mouth?"

Tawny shrugs, eyes just as wild as mine.

We hold our items forward—religious artifacts facing the demon—and pray loudly. Except I'm begging and holding the statue against Prue's chest.

Nothing seems to work. But Sinners don't wait for defeat. We meet it head-on. Mercy jumps on Prue and directs the others to do the same.

"Pin her down," she grits out.

Between the five of us, one for each limb and one for the head, we soon have Prue bucking beneath us on the ground.

Then she vomits. It's not a spray like the one a week ago. She looks at us helplessly as it oozes from her mouth. In that instant, I see intelligence, and I see Prue. I remember when we almost lost her to the Cartel, and Alice told me she found Prue in a barn stall, bruised and missing pants.

"We won't let anything happen to you." Prue smooths my hair. *"You're one of us now. We protect our own."*

Fuck it. I roll her to the side and put her in a recovery position.

"You're not dying on our watch," I tell her.

"You're gonna be fine, Prue," Tawny says, her eyes glimmering as she pulls Prue's hair back. "We've got you, hun."

The demon inside Prue gnashes its teeth at Tawny, narrowly missing her face. The viper flares in Tawny's eyes. She kneels on Prue's chest and forces her head back by the hair. "You fucker," she growls. "You're not going to win."

"Already have, little Sinner," the demon hisses from Prue's mouth.

We rally and reinforce a limb, holding our sister down like

a criminal. Wesley rushes over with a piece of chalk in his hands. He scratches a circle around us, adding symbols and tweaks to his design. He works studiously and confidently. It's then I pay attention to the strange tattoos on his body, reminiscent of the marks he draws. Come to think of it, now that I see them shirtless, it's clear all of Team Saint have arcane tattoos.

Before closing off the circle, Wesley orders, "Get out. Leave her in. This should trap her... or at least the demonic entity inside."

I don't want to let Prue go. If the men can't see the rot, it's still Prue inside. That glimmer of helplessness was real. I know it. The disease and rot are probably supernatural manifestations of the demon's soul. Something only the five Sinners who connected with Mary's lost gospel can see. Mary had the Sight. Maybe that flash of white light did something to us.

"Thea," Wesley implores, his eyes hard. "Trust me, you don't want to be locked in there for this next bit."

Grinding my teeth, I look to Mercy. Two eyes of fiery determination meet mine. She gives me a curt nod.

"We do it together," she says. "*Go.*"

We leap out of the circle, careful not to smudge the chalk. The instant we escape, Wesley closes the circle, and Prue launches at us. She hits an invisible wall. The chalk lines smoke and burn into the wooden floor, activating whatever woo-woo sorcery Wesley concocted.

I swallow. This is what he taught in his class? Damn, I'm a stubborn fool for playing truant.

"How long will it hold?" Mercy asks, straightening her negligee with aplomb.

"A few hours," Wesley replies. "Maybe four."

"*La concha de tu madre!*" Raven stalks up to him, and she prods him in the chest. "Why wasn't *that* shown in class?"

He straightens his spectacles. "Firstly, you need to know the theory behind the symbols and why they work, then—"

Leila holds up her hand, cutting him off. "I want to know how we get that thing out of her."

"Is it too late?" Tawny hugs herself. "I mean, look at her."

Prue drools and spits and hisses. No sign of our sister is there.

"*Scuze.*" Father Angelotti slides between Mercy and Leila. He holds a small Bible in one hand and a vial of holy water in another. Unflinching, the half-naked priest prays in Latin and tosses water at Prue.

Any time the water hits her, it sizzles, and she snarls. She backs up to the furthest corner of her arcane trap.

While all the attention is on the exorcism, Mercy whispers, "Check out his tats."

My gaze drops to the priest's back, specifically to the Madonna and Sacred Heart spanning his broad shoulders. My gaze lowers to the prison tattoos disappearing into his sweatpants. They're crudely made and remind me of gang signs. Maybe even the mafia. Mercy and I share a look. Father Angelotti was in prison.

Wesley notices us staring. He motions for us to stand back.

"Will Prue survive?" I ask him.

"Father has performed many exorcisms."

"What's the host survival rate?"

He doesn't answer.

Whatever Father is doing isn't working. It only incenses the demon further. It scratches her skin as if the meat suit is too tight. Her voice deepens and turns guttural, like the one that attacked me at the club. Then it laughs mockingly.

Dominic pats Wesley on the chest, his eyes hard. He speaks in Italian, too low for me to catch, but Wesley disappears into his room, returns with a notebook, and scribbles down words.

I glance at Prue, then at Wesley. He's recording the demonic words. I should have thought of that. I briefly glance at what he's written. *You can't stop what's coming. She will always be a step ahead of you.*

Banging on the stairs has us all turning to see the Rev making her way up, the Monsignor puffing at her heels. Both are in night robes. The moment they enter the hallway, the Rev points her cane at Mercy. "What happened?"

Mercy faces me for an explanation.

"She's possessed," I answer. "I woke up, and she was like that."

The Rev sends us Sinners a look we all know well—*we need to talk*. Privately. We huddle in close. The Monsignor goes to speak to his team. His rapid-fire Italian is too hard to understand with everything going on, but it makes me think he's like the Rev—a hard nut pretending to be soft.

"Okay." The Rev's brows lift. "What really happened?"

"I had this horrible dream." I inadvertently touch the

necklace and then remember it's gone. "Wesley gave me a good luck charm and said to keep it on. But I had a nightmare: an evil force entered through the open window and pinned me down, and I couldn't move."

"Probably sleep paralysis," Leila noted. "A night terror. We've all had them."

"Maybe, but Prue was whimpering in her bed when I woke. I checked on her, and she rolled around and looked like that." I point at her snarling and slobbering form.

Leila says, "Prue looks different to us, Rev. Her skin is rotting, but Team Saint can't see the diseased flesh and"—she gulps—"crawlies."

The Rev's pale eyes narrow suspiciously. "Prue looks normal to me. Sickly, but normal."

My theory about the five of us strengthens, but I feel like a child caught breaking into the sweets cupboard. We go quiet, and I twitch, hating that we've been keeping secrets from the Rev. Finally, Mercy mumbles, "We found a book."

I glare at her.

"What?" she whines at me. "I think the Rev should know."

"I agree," Raven says. "No more secrets."

Fine. I meet the Rev's pale eyes. "It's the Lost Gospel According to Mary Magdalene."

The Rev soaks it in without a word, so I continue.

"A few weeks ago, I found half a mostly blank manuscript in the new arrivals in the archive. The matching half was in Wesley's trunk. We reunited the pieces, and they merged with unnatural magnetic force. A bright light blinded us, and we all passed out. It seems us five who touched the book as it joined are the only ones who can see the grotesque side of Prue—I'm guessing this is the demon's true form."

"Beatific Vision," the Rev mumbles.

"What?" we all say.

"You see the true form of mystical entities." She taps her cane softly on the floor, thinking. "They say if you look upon Christ's true face, the glory of it can burn you to a crisp from the rapture. They also say that if you look upon a demon's true face, its appearance will terrify you so much that you will lose your mind. But not you five. We hear about Beatific Vision in the saints of the old, but never in this era. Never with Sinners."

"So let us embrace the outcasts and the sinners, for they may hold the key to unlocking the mysteries of the divine," I mumble, repeating the words I'd recently translated.

"From the gospel?" the Rev asks.

I nod and palm my face. "Rapture is not a word I would use to describe this."

"Perhaps not Beatific, but something else."

We all let that truth bomb settle on us.

"Do they know?" the Rev whispers harshly, glancing at Team Saint.

"About the gospel?" I think of Wesley confronting me in the archives but shake my head. He might suspect, but he doesn't know. "But they now know about the Sight."

Prue's wailing grows louder. She hurls herself against her

invisible cage, dislocating her shoulder. Tawny breaks from our huddle to shout at Father, "You're hurting her."

His strained eyes glance at Tawny but return to Prue with determination. Every muscle in his body hardens with strain. Sweat pebbles on his forehead. But he paces the arcane circle, symbols glowing like embers, and continues his verse without fault.

"How long will the exorcism take?" Mercy asks.

Father's a fit man, but how much of this can he handle?

The Monsignor rejoins the Rev as Wesley answers Mercy. His eyes betray his concern. I don't think he would last five minutes in an exorcism.

"Sometimes it takes hours," Wesley replies. "Sometimes minutes. Sometimes the demon kills the host, and that's how it leaves."

"Do you have *any* good news?" Tawny asks, desperation widening her eyes. "You can't kill Prue. She's been through enough."

"If we know the demon's true name, we will have more control."

Prue lashes out again, this time at herself. She pulls at her clothes, rips her hair, rolls around on the floor, and hits herself. That's when I see the mark of Lilith on her shoulder. Cold fills me. It's in the same spot mine was. Did it jump from me to her?

As if sensing my attention, as if she revealed that mark on purpose, she looks at me and hisses, "Shame, shame, little Sinner."

Oh, God. I drop into a crouch, about to be sick. Is this my fault? My eyes dart over the scratched wooden floor as I think. What if that dream was real? What if that evil *thing* tried to get into me, but Wesley's charm protected me... and the demon shifted to the next vulnerable host—Prue.

That symbol appeared and then disappeared. Maybe it was jumping between all of us, testing our weaknesses. Maybe I brought it home.

"Thea?" Wesley lowers to my level.

"This is my fault," I whisper. "That symbol was on me."

When he doesn't answer, I glance up. His eyes are full of apprehension.

"I suspected," he admits. "The crows at your window were a harbinger."

He reaches out as if to console me but clenches his fingers and frowns at Prue.

The other Sinners stand around the circle, each watching, no one genuinely believing we can save our friend, but everyone hoping.

"There has to be a way," I whisper to Wesley. "We need to get that thing out of her so she can live." In peace. Safe.

He grows quiet. Too quiet.

"What is it?" I push. When he doesn't respond, I grab him by the shoulders and bring us to our feet. "Wesley, I'll do whatever you tell me this time. I swear. No more monkey business."

Gazes have turned our way, but I don't give a shit. I mean it. No more dismissing his help. I know how to kill a man fifty ways, but I have no idea how to exorcise a demon. Sinners have tried to use our own techniques, but they're not working. I can finally see why the Rev allowed Team Saint here. They have experience.

These women are all I have. I will never give up on family.

"The mark usually tells us who is doing the possessing. But Lilith wouldn't do the dirty work when she could send minions. The other day in the archives, you said I had Lilith's mark wrong."

"There are those other bits, see?" I point to Prue's exposed shoulder.

Wesley studies the mark as best he can while Prue is moving. With each passing second, he grows more agitated.

"Wes," I prompt. "What is it?"

"The mark you carved had offshoots, remember? The four horsemen, perhaps. This mark only has one offshoot—pestilence. Maybe the demons are the horses they ride. Or maybe these pestilence-affiliated demons herald the horseman."

He's right. The mark I had was different. The same, but different. Mine had all the offshoots. Maybe it was just a warning—a harbinger like the crows. Maybe it was something the gospel gave to me. Knowing I might not have passed it on to Prue makes me feel slightly better. And more determined.

"So, how do we find the demon's true name?"

"We can work through the lower demon circles affiliated with pestilence. Maybe we'll get lucky."

"Like Vepar," I say. "You said that earlier mark on the severed hand was related to pestilence. One of his soldiers."

Wesley flinches at the demon's name but nods.

"How can we eliminate it without harming Prue?"

"There might be someone who knows." Wesley scratches his rumpled hair. "But, bloody hell, it's risky."

"What is it?" Raven steps closer. The others also overhear.

When Wesley hesitates, I point to Father Angelotti. "He's getting tired, and he won't last. And then what? Killing her will only free the demon, not send it back to hell."

"We'll transfer her to another circle," Zeke suggests. "Until it's done."

"Until she's dead, you mean?" Leila blurts. "How typical of you to give up."

He frowns at her, confused.

She shoves him. "You might not give a shit about people, but we do."

Even though he directs it at Leila, I feel the slice of Zeke's glare. Deep cuts are there, deeper than on the surface, and I have the sense he will never let anyone close enough to find out what they're from.

Join the club.

I turn back to Wesley. "What else can we do to get it out and keep her alive?"

"We ask someone who knows, who likes talking and dealing with humans. Someone higher up in the food chain. We ask Asmodeus."

FOURTEEN
THEA

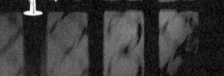

"Ask Asmodeus," I repeat. "You mean the prince of hell? *That* Asmodeus?"

Wesley nods. "Some call him a king, and some just call him a demon."

Zeke pulls a cigarette from his pocket and lights up. Raven goes over and makes the gimme sign. He takes a toke, exhales, and then reluctantly hands it over. Dominic purses his lips at Zeke.

Wes glowers at him, "How do you keep finding that shit?"

"That was my last one," he sulks, obviously thinking Raven will stub it out. But she puts it to her lips and inhales deeply until the crackling of tobacco fills the gaps between Prue's wet snarls.

The Rev stomps her cane.

"Do it," she says, eyes hard. "We must trust God brought

us together for a reason. This is the time to try new things. I have faith in you all, and I believe we can do this."

"Raven?" I ask. Has she seen anything in her visions that can help us?

She meets my stare and nods as she exhales smoke. "I wish I didn't, but I trust them."

Of all of us, Raven was the first to pay attention in Wesley's class. If she has a gut feeling to trust them, and so does the Rev, then I'll follow their lead.

"Let's go summon a demon prince," I say.

Wesley points at Prue. "We need a space big enough to draw an arcane circle twice that size."

"The archives or the training mat," Mercy suggests.

"Training," multiple Sinners say.

Wesley nods. "I'll meet you there."

"What about Prue?" I ask.

"Cisco, Dom, and Zeke will keep working and search for the demon's true name."

"Cisco?"

"Sorry, Father Francisco Angelotti." Wesley disappears into his room, shouting over his shoulder, "Someone needs to get salt from the kitchen—as much as you can find. And we need blood."

"On it," Leila replies. "Tawny, you go to the kitchen. I'll take a visit to the coup."

Mercy points to Wesley's room. "Thea, you stay and keep him honest. Raven and I will check the training room and replenish blessed weaponry from the Sin Bin. Just in case."

I follow Wesley. His room doesn't appear too different since I had it, except it smells like a man. He shoves a book into my hands before going to his suitcase. I turn it over and check the title: *Ars Goetia Lemegeton Clavicula Salomonis* or loosely translated to *The Little Key of Solomon*.

King Solomon was rumored to have gained power through affiliation with demons. I flick through the pages to learn this is a grimoire in summoning them. It's in Ancient Greek and full of circles, seals, and magic spells. It's not an edition I've seen before, but old. Very old.

"Is this your first summoning?" I ask as Wesley returns with an armful of supplies.

"Sort of." When my brow lifts, he adds, "I was present at one in my youth. An uncle. I guess he thought he was fancy or something. Poor sod ended up dragged to hell instead."

"What do you mean?"

He looks me squarely in the eyes. "A demon climbed out of a hole in the ground and dragged him down. I tried to save him but almost got taken myself."

"I'm so sorry." I mean it. "That must have been hard to see. How old were you?"

He drops an unlit candle into the increasing load of supplies I hold. "Twelve."

"It's the same age I was recruited into the Sisterhood." Another strange fact that connects us. "That's rough."

"I thought I was the fucking dog's bollocks back then." He shakes his head, laughing bitterly to himself. "I thought I was invincible, but I was only a kid."

My heart squeezes. He's seen some shit from a young age, and no one probably believed him. It must have been lonely growing up with that knowledge in his head.

As if reading my train of thoughts, he scrubs his hair and says, "I was in an institution for a few of my teen years before I figured out how to tell them what they wanted to hear. I said I made it up. Hallucinated. When I got out, I scoured the internet message boards and dark web to find stories of anyone else in similar situations."

"You found Team Saint?"

"Sort of. The church found me first, putting me through school, then university. They saved my life."

He touches my neck. I'm hyperaware of my skimpy attire, his lack of a shirt, and even more aware of my lack of a bra. His gaze skips to my throat, where his touch turns confident. His thumb brushes the hollow. Electricity zips through my body, making everything tight.

"Where's the charm?"

I can't tell if his deep tone is a warning, a danger, or something else my body wants more than my brain.

"I ripped it off."

A line appears between his brows. His grip on my throat flexes, and then his hand slides to my sternum. Irritation flashes in his eyes. Tension. Every line of his body has pulled taught as though he's trying not to release his anger. But I see it in the flare of his nostrils, in the flashes of violence on his face. His honeyed gaze turns dark. He knows my hands are full of items, and he knows if I want to stop him from touching me, I have to drop everything—just like he had me in the archives.

His devious streak is showing, and from the thrill skipping in my blood, I think I'm excited for it. I want to coax it out of that scholarly exterior. I want those hands all over my body, which makes me the worst sinner because my friend is fighting for her life outside this room.

He has no idea about what's passing in my mind. His eyes are still glued to my neck as he says, "The instant we clear the path to your room, you'll put the charm back on and never take it off." He smooths my shoulder like he's brushing lint away. "Not even when you shower. Promise."

"You're cute when you're demanding." I mean to throw him off his game, but I blush when he does the same.

"Promise."

Something in his tone makes me answer, "Okay."

Appeased, his stormy eyes soften, and he steps back. "Good. Let's go."

WESLEY DRAWS ANOTHER COMPLICATED, arcane circle with chalk on the rubber training mats. At different intervals around the circle—at the apex of his pentagram—we place candles and offerings.

Five points to the star.

I'm not the only one who notices. The other Sinners watch warily.

"Right," Wes says, dusting the chalk from his hands and admiring his handy work. He's got that vibrance about him again. The one I glimpsed in the archives when he was in his element, telling me all the exciting things he'd learned. "I'll start the chant, but I'll need four more volunteers to stand at each point of the star."

"Uh-uh," Raven says, waggling her finger. "We girls are doing it. We have the beatific-whatever-the-fuck-sight, and it should be us."

Wesley's jaw clenches, but he knows he's outnumbered. I hold my hand toward his book. He hesitates, glances at my neck where the charm should have been, and reluctantly drops the Book of Solomon into my hands.

The look in his eyes is clear—*Promise.*

FIFTEEN
THEA

Each Sinner gets into position around the pentagram. The middle, where we assume the demon will appear, is about fifteen feet wide. The center ring makes me feel safer knowing there's a decent buffer to protect us. According to the book, Asmodeus will appear with three heads—one like a bull, one like a man, and one like a ram. He breathes fire, has a serpent's tail, webbed feet, and sits on an infernal dragon. But I also saw a depiction of him in another book as a handsome man. I have no idea what we're in for, but we're out of options.

Wesley's story about his uncle being sucked into hell pokes into the back of my mind.

"Light the candles first," Wesley instructs from behind me as he reads the book over my shoulder. I let him because even though I want to be in control, a part of me is relieved that someone else is taking responsibility in these uncharted waters.

Shame, shame, little Sinner.

I shake off the memory.

Raven pulls out her lighter, flicks the flint, and holds the flame to her red candle. Once lit, she tosses her lighter to Tawny, who does the same. They look to me expectantly when all are lit, and I look to Wesley. I've now relinquished the book, and we're putting our faith in him and the rest of Team Saint upstairs to keep Prue safe.

"Next up," he says, "we paint Asmodeus' sigil on your foreheads with the blood of our offering." Wesley shifts the book to one hand and collects a small bowl of poultry blood Leila organized from our chicken coup. She left the bird for tomorrow's meal. We're a self-sustaining compound for the most part.

He paints Asmodeus' sigil on our foreheads. It's a complicated circle with a strange squiggle inside. All I recognize is a part that looks like a devil's tail. Blood runs down our faces, and we look like we've stepped out of an Eighties horror movie.

When Wesley is finished, he returns the book to me.

"Read that passage," he says softly, pointing to a tattered and crusty section as though it's been used a million times. I shudder to think of the sacrifices made by the original occultists who owned the book. "When you're done," he continues, "everyone needs to repeat it, and you chant it like a meditation."

"Got it."

He touches my shoulder. "Be prepared. You've all been

gifted with a supernatural sight that sees the true shape of demons. I'll likely see something more benign, just as Prue looked normal, so this demon might seem like nothing to worry about to me. So don't be alarmed if I don't freak out."

I give a curt nod. "Be ready for a three-headed, fire-breathing fucker sitting on a dragon."

I suppose that's good. If we see his true form, then we're ready for anything.

Wes stands back and gathers blessed weapons, just in case. I like seeing the confidence in his posture. His shoulders are down, not tense. I search out his eyes to get a hit of dopamine. When he meets my gaze, it's a tingle in my chest.

Here goes nothing.

"Ayer avage aloren Asmodeus aken," I chant.

When I finish, the other girls join in. We chant like that for a few minutes, and nothing happens. I study each of my sisters and realize Tawny is mumbling her words. She catches me looking and then blushes. I glare, and she bites her lip.

I know this is scary. We've never done it before.

I mouth, "For Prue."

She nods. I say the words, annunciating carefully, so she understands. She joins in and then increases her volume and clarity. Then we all chant. Within seconds we feel a change in the atmosphere. It's as though someone has plugged a massive power cable into the room. We're standing inside an electrical vortex. Air thickens. We taste metal. Tiny hairs on our bodies stand at attention.

The world invisibly tears before us, inside us, and around

us. It's how I imagine it would feel if someone sliced me in half with a fishing line, but then my body mended immediately. I feel torn apart but whole. Wrong. Upside down.

Mercy stumbles. Sweat glistens on her upper lip. She's struggling more than the rest of us, and I refuse to let doubts climb in. She's one of us, and she's helping.

"Don't leave your point." Wesley's deep voice is steady and calm. It's an anchor for us in the storm. "Hold strong, yeah? Keep chanting."

I wish I could hold my sisters' hands, but I can't reach them. I clench my fists at my side and pretend. As we continue chanting, natural light darkens like a storm gathers outside. But it's already night. I look up, and the gym lights are on, but eerily not.

Where is the darkness coming from?

Candles flare. Flames flicker and gutter. A tunnel of air shimmers at the pentagram's center, from the rubber mat to the wooden beams high above us.

He's coming.

I'm prepared for the beast but not for a crouching, handsome, nude man with dark, short hair. He straightens to his full six-foot-something height. High cheekbones. Lips wide and sinful. His face has all the charm and wickedness of the myth—the prince of hell who likes to gamble, debauch, and roll with the devious humans. He stretches as though he's been stuck in that crouched position for eternity and then shakes his muscular limbs like an athlete about to race. But he doesn't run. He turns in a circle and inspects us with growing satisfaction. Literal *growing* satisfaction. He becomes impressively erect, his cock juts out, engorged. I suppose the demonic representation of lust wouldn't have it any other way.

Slowly, his black and soulless eyes focus on me—the one who called him first.

A wry smile tugs his lips. "Darling, no need to continue chanting. I am here, in the tawdry flesh."

His voice is a liquid drug, sliding down our throats, heating our bellies, tightening our nipples, and burning our loins. We breathe hard. It's as though the air has become a potent aphrodisiac.

He's not what we expected, but when Wesley's demeanor switches from confident to alarmed and ready to fight, I wonder if he sees the three-headed beast. If he does, then which is the demon's true form?

"Asmodeus," I drawl, intent on keeping fear from my voice. "We've summoned you to ask a question."

He's not listening but prowling around his cage, pressing up to the pentagram's center and inspecting us. There's something about his gait. He limps but disguises himself with the prowling roll of his hips and the flex of his taut ass. A scar over his thigh is puckered and looks like a claw—his only flaw.

"My, my," he drawls and stops before Leila. "Aren't you the little firecracker? I'll bet you're a dynamite in the sack. You love your snuggles, don't you? But you love those pistols more."

He thrusts his hips in time as he annunciates the word *pistols*. His hard dick wobbles, a fact he's acutely proud of.

She stares at him but says nothing. He's said something that affects her because she's gone Sinner still. Asmodeus smirks and then continues his turn around the pentagram. He stops at Raven. "Nice to see you again, *bruja*."

"I think you've mistaken me for someone else," she replies.

"Have I?"

He pouts mockingly and then prowls to Mercy, inhaling deeply as though he's taking in her perfume like wine. His eyes flutter, and when he refocuses on her, he gives a low, arousing growl that skates down my spine like a lover's caress.

"You," he drawls. "You're one of mine, aren't you?"

"Fuck off, demon. I belong to myself," she shoots back.

His laugh is a rich sound that flexes every hard muscle in his body and tingles every extremity in mine. We gaze upon his perfection with hot eyes. How can we not?

This is part of his act.

I grind my teeth, wanting to remind him that I'm in control, but he seems to enjoy his little sojourn around the pentacle. Let him believe he has agency here.

When his laughter dies and he wipes his eyes, he turns to Tawny and stills. For a moment, I think he's lost for words. A spark flashes in his midnight eyes. Shock? Then his breath hitches like he's just taken a hit of heroin. He sidles up to her, all sugar and spice.

"But you," he whispers in a low, seductive tone. "Little Birdy, you're the most vicious of them all."

She takes his bait. "I am not."

"Don't lie. It's unbecoming on someone as dazzling as

you. The wicked beast rumbles in your soul. It tastes like honey." He steps across the first chalked ring inside the pentagram, and we all gasp. He's not supposed to leave it. Right?

I glance at Wesley, and his expression remains unchanged. Alert but not afraid. But then I see his knuckles whiten around the dagger.

"He can't get out of the pentagram," he confirms.

Asmodeus can, however, slide up the inner point of the star to meet Tawny and bite the air before her face. He is a dragon, nipping at inconsequential prey. Teasing and playing with his food.

He purrs, "I can smell you, *Sister*, and all those delicious desires buried deep, just bursting to get out."

Tawny's American Pie sweetness fades. She deadpans. Darkness clouds over her. We've all got demons from our youth, but hers are the most complicated. And mysterious. She doesn't talk about her past, but I see nightmares in her eyes when she doesn't think anyone's looking. I hear her scream in the night.

She points at him with a dagger and says sweetly, "And I smell a sad, bitter little demon."

A flicker of danger ignites the air like the aftermath of lightning.

He counters, "Careful, sweet. The last woman who scorned me earned the death of every consecutive husband for seven marriages."

"Answer the question."

He regards Tawny with aroused humor. "I would if I heard a question, dove."

"A demon has possessed our friend," Mercy says. "Tell us how to get it out and how we save her."

Asmodeus holds Tawny's stare a little longer, then reluctantly faces Mercy. "That's not a question."

"How do we save our friend *and* get the demon out?" I ask.

He places his hands behind his back and strolls to me. "You're the brains of this outfit, aren't you?"

I swallow. "Answer the question, or we send you back to whatever hovel you crawled out of."

"No need to get snippy." He checks his nails as though he's not secretly plotting our demise, as if he hasn't already decided what to do with us. He drops his hand and replies, "There's an angelic relic that will do the job."

That seemed too easy, but also something that rings a bell about the prophecy. "Where can we find it, and how can we use it?"

"I don't know where to find it."

Ah. There's the rub.

"But I know how to use it," he continues.

"What does it do?"

"It's the healing staff of the Archangel Raphael." Hate flitters over his unwieldy expression. His dark, demon eyes are hiding something in their depths. If I could reach in and pull his secrets out, then we'll all be okay. But something is off about his willingness to aid us. They say if you summon a demon, you control it, but how true is that statement? Wesley admitted he'd not done this before. Asmodeus is not just any demon... he's a prince of hell.

"Healing staff," I repeat, unable to hide the contempt from my voice. "That better not be a male euphemism."

His lips curve wickedly. It's not disdain in his eyes but a flicker of respect. "Clever women. Beautiful Women. But not Virgins. Not innocent. All sinners. You'll all be here with me eventually. I think I'll enjoy your company. I think you'll enjoy *my* healing staff." He gives a jaunty thrust of his hips again.

This is getting old. My lashes lower as I hold my patience and remind myself he needs a question.

"You're a child," I say. "You need to be spoken to with clearly defined logic and questions."

His humor dies. The joker is gone, and the dragon is back, peeking out from that handsome face as though it's cataloging every detail of mine so he can hunt me down later. Isn't he also the demon of revenge?

"What does the staff look like?" I ask.

"Last time I saw it, it was a long piece of wood."

I hold his stare, caught between worrying he's misleading us and knowing this is the real him—the dragon. Not the joker.

"How does the staff work?"

"Use it on your possessed friend. Think healing thoughts. Her body will be healed."

"And until then," Raven asks, "how do we stop the demon from destroying Prue?"

THE SINNER AND THE SCHOLAR 149

Asmodeus spins to face her. In doing so, a wind gusts about the pentagram, smudging salt circles and chalk lines. We're in trouble if those lines break.

I survey the rest of the marks and find smudges everywhere he's walked. The clever fuck was working at breaking free all along. Come to think of it, while we were distracted by his package every time he thrust, he'd created tiny gusts of wind and more little smudges across the chalk and salt.

"Drug her," Asmodeus answers Raven. "Keep her in a coma."

Wes moves forward, ready to end the summoning, but I ask one more question.

"Why are demonic possessions on the rise?"

He cocks his head at me and chuckles as though it's obvious. "Don't you know? Hell is overcrowded. Sin has exploded. The gatekeepers are gone, and the seals are breaking. The angels are silent. God is playing truant. Probably off to toy with a new creation. If it weren't for the Deadly Seven turning sin around in Cardinal City, the gates would have burst open by now."

A shudder quakes through me. What the actual fuck.

Alarmed, we dart glances at each other. If Asmodeus is telling the truth, it would explain why none of us has felt the presence of the Almighty—no wonder we feel deserted. Maybe God's been missing for centuries.

Maybe the demon is lying, distracting us. The instant I think it, Asmodeus lunges for the chalk to brush it with his feet but fails to hit.

We're out of time. One more question needs to be asked. "What's the demon's true name inside Prue?"

He ignores me and creates wind. It starts slow, a lazy lift of his hair, but then picks up in intensity.

"Shouldn't he do what I say?" I flick the pages of the unfamiliar book, looking for an answer. "We know his name. We summoned him."

"Unless it's not his true name," Wesley points out.

"Fuck."

Real panic fills my bones. My heart thuds. My mouth dries.

Asmodeus smirks.

But then Wesley moves forward, tosses liquid, and kicks the arcane circle, smudging it until it breaks. Asmodeus shimmers and starts to fade. He glowers at Wesley and snarls something, but it's lost to us as his visage dissipates.

When the lights return to their usual luminosity, it's clear we're all quietly freaking out.

Then Mercy says, "Well, the book got one thing right. He's definitely got a dragon between his legs."

We laugh. It breaks the ice. This is how we deal with our depressing fate. We joke. We fight. We fuck.

We're the last line of defense against this bullshit. We won't give up even if things don't go as planned.

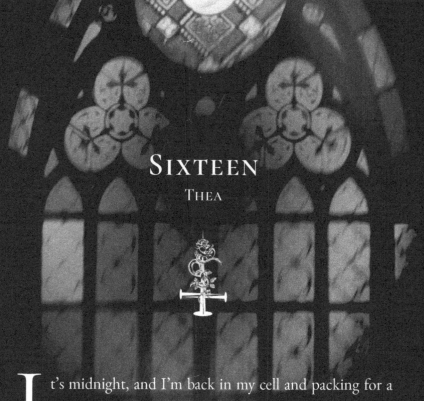

Sixteen
Thea

I t's midnight, and I'm back in my cell and packing for a trip.

For most of the day, we worked with Team Saint to subdue Prue and administer a drug we found in our well-stocked medicine cabinet in the infirmary. Some of our nuns are trained as emergency response officers. Our organization's namesake, Sister Hildegard, was an academic hundreds of years ago when it was frowned upon for women to be. Today, these sisters carry on the pursuit of knowledge here at the abbey.

We have chapters around the world that are dedicated to this and have nothing to do with Sinners.

Sister Mary Theresa gave us a rundown of how to induce a coma. She wrote instructions because of her vow of silence, but I picked up what was necessary. It's one thing for the Magpies to treat wounded Sinners after returning from a mission, but I can't have one of them in harm's way when a demon is involved, especially when we're still learning all the ins and outs. Those demon marks had already appeared on Prue and me. What if mine comes back? What if it jumps to one of our nuns?

They are our backbone. We must protect them.

After Prue was sedated, the appearance of flesh rotting from her bones remained, meaning she was still possessed despite others thinking she was only sleeping. We set up an around-the-clock watch—always with a Sinner included. Team Saint offered to take over, but we didn't accept it.

Prue is one of ours.

I take hasty pictures of the prophecy on my cell phone so I have something to study on my trip. I couldn't sleep, so I stayed up researching all my favorite places on the internet where I thought a relic like the staff would be.

I found it at the British Museum.

It was listed as a "Byzantine Wooden Ceremonial Staff." Time has made the inscription on the wood almost incomprehensible, but I recognized ligatures from Ancient Greek: *To Heal and Hold*.

I went down a rabbit hole working out where it originated and whose hands it passed. Everything points to it being the relic. It's our best bet. The only problem is, how do I get to London on such short notice? The Sisterhood isn't exactly rolling in cash, and smuggling a stolen artifact into the country would require a private jet or us to pay off someone at a shipping yard.

If we tell Team Saint, they'll want in. They'll let the Vatican know, which will slow me down. Not to mention they'll take the gospel from us. Besides, I feel responsible for Prue's condition. I can't help the sick feeling in my gut telling me this is my fault... I should have noticed she needed help, and I should have paid more attention. I shouldn't have been so quick to avoid Wesley's help.

The Rev and the girls all decided I should make a quiet midnight trip to Cardinal City, where ex-Sinner Alice lives. She's married to Parker Lazarus, the genetically modified leader of the Deadly Seven. And she's also the CEO of his billionaire tech empire. He has more private jets on standby than you can toss a crucifix at.

And he owes us a favor.

We helped him close the hell dimension his fanatical father opened. We gave him Alice.

I dress in black Sinner gear—stretch pants and a black hoodie with our Red Cross emblem on the front. I put my contact lenses in and then check my backpack to ensure I have everything I need. Clothes. Poison to lace weapons. Heist shit —lock pick set, glass cutter. Fake passport. I slip on my pack and go to leave my cell but stop when my boot hits something beneath Prue's cot. A moment of panic hits me. Whatever I kicked went under her bed. I stare at the closed door for a few breaths, silently steeling myself to bend down and look, but ice trickles down my spine. What if it's another demon?

I'm being ridiculous. Fear helps no one. I *know* this. Cautiously, I peek beneath the bed and pull out a notebook.

It's Prue's diary. The first pages are pictures and notes on Mockingbirds, even a few attempts at drawing them. Then I find private, broken thoughts about what happened to her with the Cartel. I don't read. I skip ahead to where the words make no sense, and the handwriting becomes erratic. This doesn't feel normal. At first, her ramblings are a normal reaction to her trauma, but then I see more. Nightmares. Visions. Hallucinations. She thinks bugs crawl on her skin. Irrational paranoia about being sick and then suddenly not. Sore throat. Stomach aches. Blood in her stools. Voices telling her to do things. Crows at the windows. My heart squeezes in my chest, and I check the date. She wrote this entry long before I got the mark.

They say there are a few types of demon possessions. It doesn't always come in the shape of a presence invading your body but in the form of influence. The spirit of a demon becomes obsessed with you, and it convinces you to do bad things. Maybe that's how it started for Prue. Maybe she didn't give it what it wanted, so it moved on to phase two —possession.

Maybe that mark was always meant for her, and what I received was an accident—something I wasn't meant to see.

Hearing a scuffle outside the door, I place the diary on Prue's bed. I didn't see the name of a demon anywhere, but I shoot a quick text message for Mercy to take a look while I'm away.

Wesley waits in the hall with his arms folded. He's packed and dressed for travel—jeans, a hoodie, and a backpack. Blond hair is still messy. His spectacles sit on the bridge of his nose, so it looks like he's staring down at me, even though he's not. They're crooked. I want to straighten them.

His gaze dips to my neck, and his posture softens. He sees I've put the charm back on. The brief softening disappears when he meets my eyes again.

"Going somewhere?" he asks dryly.

"Har-har." I flatten my lips. It's obvious he's figured out what I'm doing. "You're not coming with me."

"I'm not asking permission."

"I'm meeting with a contact. They don't like strangers."

"I'm not a stranger."

"To them, you are."

"Thea—"

"If you're about to say the Vatican will pay for it, I don't want to know."

"I wasn't. There's too much red tape for us to jump through to get approval for a private jet to London in the time we need. Plus, if we're doing what I think we're doing, it's better to ask the Entity for forgiveness than permission."

I narrow my eyes. "How do you know I'm going to London?"

"You're offending me now."

"You did the same research. Shit." Others might find it too if it's so easy to locate. We have no idea if the demon inside Prue, or Asmodeus himself, has told others what's happening here. We have no idea how that force communicates amongst itself. Perhaps Lilith can listen in on everything her creatures do... maybe that's the point of her mark entwining with theirs.

"You can't stop what's coming," demonic Prue had said. *"She will always be a step ahead of you."*

I need to hurry. I feel it in my bones.

According to Raven, we must do this quickly and quietly if we want success. While she didn't exactly have a premonition, she had the equivalent of mystical bad vibes anytime we mentioned going through the usual transport channels while we discussed a plan earlier tonight. I haven't even contacted Alice.

The fewer people who know about this, the better.

Wesley stares indignantly. He'll make a fuss if I don't let him come. I size him up and run through all the ways I can take him down. Pressure to the carotid, a hit to the temple, or a simple nosebleed will keep him suitably occupied while I get out of here.

"I can take care of myself," I say weakly.

"I know you can," he replies, his eyes never leaving mine. "I'm saying you don't have to."

His words hit me hard between the ribs. I want to trust him. I do. But there's still so much about these men that we don't know. Like, most of them had those arcane tattoos. They whispered amongst themselves just as we did. They lied about who spoke English.

But we've lied too.

And Wesley knows his stuff.

And that magic card business might come in handy. At the very least, it deserves to be explored.

And I skipped lessons, so I should probably learn more.

Those eyes. Those earnest eyes look at me like this is more than a necessity, more than an order from his superior. This is *wanted*.

But why?

I toy with the charm around my neck. "Fine. You can come."

"Again," he says a little too gruffly. "Wasn't asking permission."

"Someone's grumpy." He doesn't respond, so I add, "Just don't get in my way."

He checks his pocket watch and says, "Let's go."

He walks ahead, and I pull a face at his back.

Mercy pops her head out of her door. "Enjoy the ride, babe."

I nod and give her a salute. Then I force my shoulders to relax and follow the mantra—enjoy the ride because we all know where we'll end up.

SEVENTEEN
WESLEY

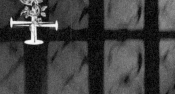

W e catch a cab to the nearest city. When I press Thea about her plan, she assures me she has it under control.

I can take care of myself, she'd said.

I bite my tongue because at least I'm here. The Vatican thinks they have Team Saint under their thumb, but the truth is, every single one of us is in it for personal reasons. If that means we align ourselves with the Sinners, and keep secrets from our benefactors, then so be it. Dismantling a rogue, evil organization isn't so black and white anymore. Lines are blurring.

I check my pocket watch for the tenth time since getting in the cab. My uncle carried it everywhere, and then one day— the day of the summoning—I found it on a pile of papers, maps, and old books in his den. I remember thinking it was odd that he left it behind, and maybe it was broken and needed repairing. So I collected it, wanting to do something nice for him since he'd worked so hard to care for me.

But there—stuck beneath it was a note.

Dearest Wesley,
The hour and the minute hand look separate, but they work together. The cracks try to split them apart, but breaking them breaks the watch. Keep your hands working together. Keep the cracks closed.

I turn over the watch's metal casing and read those last two lines. I still have no idea what they mean, only that it's important. Despite thinking the watch was broken back then, it worked perfectly fine. There were no cracks in the glass.

I dart a glance at Thea, then back at the watch. A secret organization run by women is a threat to the Vatican. But I saw something different when news of their existence came through the channels a few years ago. I saw a link to an old, discredited prophecy written by a supposed whore—a repenting sinner. I saw an opportunity to save the life of a friend and, in doing so, keep the team together.

If they discover what I've done by bringing the lost gospel here, all hell will break loose. I've put a loaded gun in the Sisterhood's hands. They will have the power to change how the church sees women forever... from allowing women into the priesthood and rewriting history. They could bring about the fall of the whole patriarchal Holy See.

I'm intimately aware of what the Entity does to neutralize threats. I'm dead when they learn this was my fault. But I'm desperate. And I'm not thinking about me. I came here on the chance that we could save Zeke, and I knew destroying the Sisterhood would be the next best thing if we couldn't. Now it seems foolish. These women aren't our enemies. They never were.

I wonder what Thea's reason for doing this is. I know about saving Prue, but the rest of it—being a Sinner, a killer. It seems like she's been shoved into this life, unlike us. No... not like us. We didn't ask to have our family members destroyed by demons. She might not have asked to be turned into an assassin, but she embraces it.

I think.

The Cardinal warned us about them all. He said the Sisterhood kept hidden because they knew their actions were wrong. They treat their agents as expendable pawns and thus must all be evil because only evil is okay with sanctioning Sinners.

I turn my thoughts back to the relic we're hunting. It's imperative that I get my hands on it first, but my guilt is getting louder these days. My cell phone has already buzzed with incoming messages from the Entity asking why my location has deviated from the abbey. Zeke and Dom have also checked in.

I've ignored each message. I'm not ready to talk yet.

"If you want," I say to Thea. "We can use this time to review the class material you missed."

"I'd rather talk about Asmodeus," she replies, keeping her alert gaze out the window. "That wasn't his true name because he wasn't under our control, was he?"

"There's probably another part to it."

I scrub my face. My skin crawls at the memory of the three-headed monstrosity I was ready to knife. His act had layers and was designed to distract us in many ways.

"He spoke in Latin," I mention. "Is that what you heard too?"

I study her to gauge her response. While I heard Latin, none of the Sinners performing the summoning seemed confused. Either they all could translate, or—

"He spoke in English to us," she said, then shrugged.

"And... what did he look like to you?"

"I saw a naked man." She smirks. "A good-looking, well-endowed, and dangerously clever man."

I stare out the window, forcing my mind to consider her declaration. *Clever?* She's probably referring to the windy gusts he created to mess with the salt and chalk seal trapping him. I would have noticed his escape attempt earlier had I not needed to translate his words from Latin.

Didn't think he was that attractive, either.

None of the Sinners had a language barrier. That secret and the fact they all saw something else when looking upon the damned is unsettling. As far as the church is concerned, the Sinners *are* the damned, and maybe that's why they were on the same wavelength as Asmodeus.

I don't believe it.

None of them *seem* evil.

Cisco pulled me aside before I joined Thea tonight. He warned me to keep a close eye on her and to protect myself. But they don't know what I know... that Mary's gospel has chosen them. It's too obvious to discredit.

When I found the split manuscript in the Vatican's archives and connected the dots between Mary and the Sisterhood, I thought the worst consequences would be controversy to the church, the Sisterhood discredited, or my ultimate death. At the very best, I hoped I would save Zeke's life.

But now... now the Sinners have a supernatural sight linked to that gospel, and I suspect Thea is hiding more from me.

Shifting in the seat, I slouch and get comfortable. I want to remain awake while Thea is, but I'm not trained like her. A few all-nighters at university don't quite have the same staying power as her training in the Art of War.

I heard a rumor they used to hang from trees by a noose to strengthen their necks—making them impossibly hard to break.

As I relax, my eyes take a sideways swipe to soak up Thea's remarkable profile in the moonlight. I wish I hadn't. Seeing her like this makes my cock stir, which reignites my irritation. Since that moment we shared in the archives, my body has been swift to react like this. Why does she have to be so bloody beautiful?

I wish I could say she was using her God-given beauty to manipulate me, but I think her brain gives me wood more than anything else. I've never met another woman who can outsmart me. Well, almost outsmart me. I'll keep catching up with her. Anywhere she runs, I'll follow.

I grin and stare at the back of the driver's seat.

"What's your story, scholar?" Thea asks.

"Pardon?"

"Tell me about your uncle and why you joined Team Saint."

I meet her stare, see that she's genuine in her interest, and talk.

"My mother was pregnant when she and my father died in a car accident. I survived. My uncle took me in. Then, as I mentioned, I witnessed a demon dragging my uncle to hell during a summoning gone wrong. They put me in an asylum. Eventually, I decided to bite my tongue, and they let me go. I was put in foster care, but I ran away. I lived on the streets for a while. I often snuck into churches to get out of the rain and eat biscuits and coffee at AA meetings. The cantankerous old priest pretended not to notice me. I liked him. He was safe. So I followed him home like a stray cat.

"When he heard my story, he didn't call Child Protection. He introduced me to a nun who lived at a small house that I soon learned was a convent. He told her I was the new gardener. They housed me, fed me, and sent me to school. Looking back at it now, I'm sure it was illegal, but they never mistreated me or called the authorities. I think they believed what I saw was real, believed my nightmares about Vepar coming to finish the job."

"Vepar?" She frowns. "You mentioned that name before."

"The demon who took my uncle. I found its name in my uncle's notes. As soon as I approached the end of high school, a representative from the Vatican turned up, and I was offered a dual scholarship to Oxford and a Pontifical University in Rome."

"*Pontifical* University?"

I shrug. "Anywhere I could get information on Vepar, I went."

"So that's your driving force? Your uncle?"

Other factors are at play now, but I guess I can talk about this.

"I tried to save him and couldn't. So I'm obsessed with figuring out how to—"

"Get revenge?"

"Stop it from happening again."

"And what did you find?"

She faces me with her arm resting across the length of the back seat, her eyes bright and attentive—my pulse quickens. The need to shuffle closer feels like a hot wave pulsing against my skin. I want to keep surprising her, so she continues to look at me like that.

"She came to me in my sleep," I say. "Sometimes she was a mermaid, sometimes a confident, calm woman. Sometimes she tried to lure me into a storm." My mood darkens as I recall the waves and rough seas in my nightmares. Images of my uncle getting dragged under by a fishtail or tentacle.

"Do you think you're still connected to her somehow?"

she asks, frowning. "Were you marked in any way with her symbol?"

I look at my palm, at the half-formed scars from when I grabbed my uncle's hand as he was dragged under. Even now, knowing everything I know about demons and the mystic arts, that night seems impossible—like one of my nightmares. My uncle was pulled through a wooden floor like it wasn't there. The smell of sulfur still burns my nose. Screams from the pits of hell still echo in my ears. My mark isn't clean like the one on that severed hand Thea had brought home. It's messed up. Broken.

Ink-free tattoos of arcane symbols weave around burn scars from when I was in the asylum. Suddenly I'm back there, my skinny childish body being strapped to a bed, screaming and bucking against the orderlies as they drug me with sharp needles. Then I'm walking down the hallway at night, listening to a voice in my head. I'm so lonely. It's easy to believe her taunts. That I'm unlovable, that I'm wrong inside, and that's why my entire family has died around me. Not even the pets survived. The cats ran away. The dogs got sick. The goldfish floated.

So over it all, I wanted the despair to end.

Thea takes my hand, holding it to the moonlight to see better. I let her because the need to be touched drowns out everything else. It's been so long since someone touched me like this. My whole body aches and yearns. I try not to think about her warm, steady contact. How it feels strong yet tender. How it's so *real* and pure—nothing like that demon who invaded my reason. How I never want her to let go despite all those old fears lingering.

"What happened?" she asks, tracing her fingertip around the mangled lines of my flesh.

A deep, cold, hidden part of me warns me to keep my secrets.

"Wes?" she prompts, and that familiar use of my name undoes me. "What's the burn mark from?"

"Vepar demanded that I do evil things. If I refused, she threatened to cover me in putrid wounds that would take three days to kill me. She lured me into the asylum kitchen." My gaze turns distant at the memory, but Thea's warm touch grounds me. "It all felt so surreal. It was a secure asylum, yet she told me to do things at certain times like she knew everything. She guided me through the place like a mermaid guides sailors through a storm but then crashes them on rocks." I shudder. "I ended up in the kitchen with a pot of boiling water in one hand. She wanted me to pour it on this kid about to be released. I wanted to pour it on myself. Better me than him, right? I was everything Vepar said: a burden, a fuck up, a waste of space. But all I could see was the flame on the gas burner. All I could think of was the burning flames of hell. And somehow, I knew I had to slam my sigil-marked palm on the burner."

"You broke her influence," she whispers. "That's how you got away."

I nod. "How I knew, I'm still not sure, but I like to think I had someone watching out for me. Some divine intervention."

Thea still has my hand, and I refuse to pull away. Her brows pucker as she traces her finger over the fine lines of an inkless tattoo.

"They're for casting spells," I explain, my voice a little thick.

"Spells?" She hasn't looked up. "I didn't think the Vatican would be into sorcery."

"They're not." One day they'll find out I've used their resources to learn everything I shouldn't. But until that day, I'll keep doing what I'm doing. If it gets us closer to helping Zeke, I'm okay with that. If it helps me stop demons from hurting others, even better.

"It looks like the trap you drew for Prue."

"There's a lot I can teach you, Thea."

She becomes silent, absently tracing my palm. Tingles spark throughout my body. She holds words for ransom, and I can't for the life of me guess what I can pay to make her give them to me. My mind returns to the welts I glimpsed on her back that first day in the bathroom. I flip our hand positions so it's mine gripping hers. I brush my thumb along the soft pulse point at her wrist.

"Thea," I murmur, looking deeply into her eyes. "What is it?"

"What if..." she whispers. "What if the demonic mark isn't burned off or destroyed? What if it disappears on its own? Will it return?"

I check the charm on her neck and exhale. She shouldn't

be in trouble as long as she keeps it on. But why would she ask that?

"Do you have a mark, Thea?" I force my voice to remain steady.

Fear flickers in her eyes. I don't think someone like her shows it often.

"I can help," I urge. "I'll keep it between us, I promise."

"Not even my sisters," she says.

"Not even them."

"Remember the mark I carved?" she confides. "You said the crows were a harbinger. I... the mark was on my back, and then it wasn't. I'm afraid..."

I frown. "I didn't see a mark on your shoulder. Perhaps you imagined it."

"Will you check for me?" The whisper is barely audible. "Just in case?"

"Of course."

She faces the window and unzips her hoodie before slipping it off her shoulder. She's left in a tight t-shirt but doesn't remove it. She pulls her long hair out of the way until I'm left with a delicate neck. My thumb brushes the goosebumps on her skin. She's nervous.

I also remember the fear of not knowing if something evil is inside you—it eats at you. You obsess so much that you start to wonder about reality.

Keeping my breath steady, I tug Thea's collar to expose more of her shoulder.

"This side?" I ask.

She nods. Her breath hitches under my touch. My fingers run along the shoulder blade, testing the skin for bumps or abnormalities. The light is low, and I should switch on my phone light, but I don't want to draw any more attention to us in the back. The mark should be evident to the eyes and through touch.

There is no mark.

Only faded flogging welts that incite rage in my blood. She flinches at my touch, and I want to murder the person who put them there. It *must* have been from someone at the abbey. That they punish her in one breath and then send her to sin in another boggles me. But I suppose I shouldn't be surprised. The church has been full of contradictions since the dawn of its existence. I'll get the story out of Thea eventually. And when I do, I'll find that person. I'll...

I'll what? Put scars on them?

My protective reaction is instinctive. But illogical. Probably borne of the unplanned intimate moments we've shared, the turmoil she creates in my heart, and the guilt over knowing my impending betrayal will cause her more pain.

I want to kiss the smooth skin between her old welts. Touching her makes me feel the opposite of how I felt in the asylum. Inexplicably, she's the holy light scaring away the evil. She shivers beneath me, but she doesn't pull away. She leans back into me as though she craves this connection as much as me. If we were anywhere else, anyone else, I'd slide my hands around her and hold her until her trembling subsides.

The cab driver looks at us in the mirror.

I tug Thea's shirt up and slip her hoodie back on, glaring at the driver until he slides his attention back to the road.

I wait for a breath, then say to Thea, "There's nothing there. You're safe."

Yes, she can take care of herself, but I told her she doesn't have to do it alone. At first, it was just a way to get her to trust me. Desperation. To continue the toxic game she started with our bodies in the archives. But an ache in my chest says otherwise.

It remembers how nice it was to touch her.

But I'm not her savior. I'm her Judas. It would do me well to remember that.

EIGHTEEN

THEA

We spend the remaining cab ride to Cardinal City in silence. Something seismic has changed between us.

The imprint of his touch on my back still makes me shiver. Why I didn't pull away, I can't explain. Why I leaned into him is also a mystery. Getting close to someone is not something we Sinners do. Even with each other, we don't get close, for we know death waits around every corner, beneath every bed, and now, in the very air itself.

Enjoying the ride is a hellova lot different than losing someone we love on the way.

Wesley's suffered. He's struggled. He's clawed his way from ridicule and loneliness to be where he is. I respect that. He's kind when he's not reacting to my taunts.

Now I know why I didn't pull away. When I felt his touch on me, I wanted something good to erase the mark's dirty

memory... even the guilt and scars from the flog felt inconsequential. Now, when I think of that shoulder, I think of him.
His cologne and fresh male scent. His scruffy hair. His puppy
dog eyes. His crisp British accent. Long legs. Mysterious
tattoos on his hands and forearms. The dangerous mystery
beneath the nerdish scholar.

Dawn is only a few hours away as we coast into the city's
center.

The city is a blend of neo-gothic architecture and old slums.
The south side is the worst, but we're headed for the Quadrant,
the luxurious heart of the city. The Deadly Seven live in a
privately owned apartment building between a restaurant called
Heaven and a nightclub called Hell. But turning up at their
doorstep isn't ideal. If I bring a stranger, they'll be angry... plus,
I'm not sure if their home is being watched. I don't want
anyone to discover me, so it's best I do this off the books.

I pay the cab driver cash and motion for Wes to follow me
out to the sidewalk.

The cab drives off, and I readjust my bag as I take in our
surroundings. Wesley does the same. Seeing him in a hoodie
instead of a crumpled three-piece is still odd, but I can't say
I'm opposed to the casual look.

Wes moves confidently with his body. Maybe I was wrong,
and he could handle himself in a fight. The way he pushed me
against that bookshelf was admirable. Anyone who witnessed
their uncle being dragged to hell would have learned to defend
himself.

Cardinal City has a population of millions. It's after midnight, yet random people still walk about. And they're not just clubbers on the way home or workers finishing a shift. A lone figure with a sign board over their head walks up and down an intersection next to a Seven-Eleven.

"We'll take the back streets," I say to Wes as he fits his backpack over his shoulder. "Away from the people."

We start moving, but a hoarse voice halts me.

"Let he who is without sin cast the first stone!"

I frown.

"The fabric of society has been torn asunder!"

My heart stops.

"And let us question what others call sin, question what others say purely to hold us down."

"Thea?" Wesley falters. "What's wrong?"

"That sounds like something in the pro—" I stop myself before revealing too much.

"In what?" he prompts, attentive eyes on me.

I glance over my shoulder at the religious hawker. They wear a beanie over long, matted hair. I can't see their face, but the message on the back of the board brings a shiver to my spine: *Judgement is coming. Open your hearts.*

"Let's keep going." I pull Wesley away.

It's odd. Weird. Those lines sounded straight from the gospel, almost like they were a message made for my ears. Or a warning. I speed up my steps, wanting to escape the late-night city dwellers. I'd forgotten how busy it is here. We need to find a dark, empty place, but someone else pops up whenever I think we've found it.

Further up the street, a young couple walks a black Labrador puppy on the sidewalk. They have no control over it as it sniffs and pisses on every street light pole. Their conversation floats down to us.

"I blame you," the man groans as the puppy stops at another pole, its tail wagging.

"Me? You brought it home." She rubs her tired eyes.

"I had no idea it would wake us in the middle of the night to go pee-pee."

She gives him a wry smile and touches her swollen belly. "What do you think the baby will do?"

"You're right. Of course, you are, and I suppose we should treat this as practice."

Something is captivating about them. My steps slow. They're out in the dark morning hours, dressed in pajamas and dressing gowns, walking a naughty puppy, but they're still smiling at each other.

The puppy spots us. Barks. It runs toward us so fast that I wonder if I have jerky in my pockets. The young woman cries out, and the leash flies from her fingers. The puppy bounds onto the street, oblivious to the oncoming car.

My feet move before my brain catches up. I scoop up the dog in one hand, keep running, and hit the other sidewalk just as the car whooshes past with a honk of frustration that blares in the night. Asshole.

"I got him." Wesley arrives at my side and takes the wriggling furball.

I don't want to let go, but when I see the adoration in Wesley's eyes, I can't help myself. The moment the puppy wiggles into his arms, it licks him and yips. But then a shadow of something drops from beneath its wagging tail.

I glance down at the sidewalk and cover my mouth, hiding my grin. "It pooped."

"Must be a scared, little bugger." Wesley coos and pats it. "You're all right, mate. You're safe."

You're safe.

Those two words unsettle me. They're words I've only heard from my Sinner family. Prue, in particular. I clear my throat and point at the wagging puppy tail. "It doesn't look afraid."

"He's too little to know what he feels, don't you, mate?" Wesley nuzzles it. "That's a good lad."

The young couple makes it to our side. She's crying and gasping, panicking, and he looks like he will vomit.

"Thank you," he says, putting his arm around his partner. "I don't know what we would have done if..."

The woman gulps and holds her heaving belly. I don't know what to say to calm her down. I turn to Wesley for help.

His eyes crinkle as the puppy licks his face, disrupting his spectacles. Its joy is contagious. I can't help envisioning him as a father, seeing him with a plate of food in his hand, laughing and chatting with visiting family as his children run around his legs and hide under the table.

He's patient with the puppy. I admire the good in him, but at the same time, a dark part of me wants to make him bad —to close that gap between us.

"All good, mate," Wesley says to the man. "But you might want to pick up the shite before someone steps on it."

The couple realizes what the dog has done and bluster even more.

"I got it." I take the bag from the man's hand and quickly dispose of the waste.

"How will we look after a baby if we can't keep a puppy safe?" The woman's voice trembles too much to believe she'll sleep tonight.

"You'll learn." Wesley's calm voice inspires confidence as he returns the puppy to them. "It takes time, but you learn."

"Thank you again," the woman murmurs to me. "You could have been killed."

"Don't mention it. You got this." I squeeze her arm.

"You two must be pros at this parenting thing," she replies. "How old are your children?"

"Oh." Wesley blushes and straightens his specs. "We're—"

"They're five and eight," I reply quickly with a tight smile. The urge to fuck with Wes is getting stronger. I pat him on the chest. "Just the right age to start getting into trouble. Ain't that right, babe?"

His expression is unreadable as he stares at me. It's like he's never seen me before. For a moment, I worry he'll blow our story and storm off, but his focus snaps back to the couple with a broad smile that steals my breath.

"Right." He throws his arm around my shoulder and pulls me in tight. "We're just on our way home from a party. I'm sure they're up right now, giving the babysitter grief, right, *honey*?"

"Absolutely. They're always pushing our buttons."

The man groans and palms his face. "Are you telling me it gets harder?"

They look at us with such helplessness that my amusement dies. I didn't mean to worry them further. Guilt tugs in my chest, and I bite my lip. "I'm sure it gets easier."

Wesley smirks at my discomfort. "Remember what you told me the other day?"

Fucker. I feel like I've brought this on myself. I know jack shit about kids. Or babysitting. Or what a reasonable bedtime is for kids that age.

"I think you mean that thing you told me," I reply with a false smile. "It was such good advice. Don't be shy. Share it."

He continues to watch me with a hint of deviousness, but then his expression softens and turns somber. His thumb sweeps my cheek, and every nerve in my body shudders.

"Don't overthink it," he murmurs deeply, holding my gaze. "Best advice you can get."

Those warm eyes see inside my twisted soul and through the wall hiding my fear.

Don't overthink it.

Enjoy the ride.

You're safe.

Open your hearts.

The puppy yips, and we break eye contact.

"Well," the woman says, smiling at us now. "Your children are lucky to have parents as brave and in love as you two."

"I hope they're fast asleep when you get home." The man waves goodbye as they move on.

Wesley leaves his arm around my shoulders as we continue down the street. I don't push him away, even after we've lost sight of the couple and finally hit a quieter part of the Quadrant. A part of me still thinks the world is spinning. I open my mouth to speak, but he gets there first.

"Is that what you want one day?" His voice is soft, almost inaudible.

"A puppy?"

"A family."

A cold feeling spreads throughout my body, starting at my chest and moving out. The suffocating blanket of reality forces me to slide his arm from my shoulder and say, "I was just doing my job."

His eyes narrow. "Pretending we're together is doing your job?"

I know that charade wasn't necessary. We could have handed the puppy over and continued on our way, but that sweet, adoring look he'd had when playing with it had triggered hopes I've long since buried.

And a graveyard was where they belonged.

"Yes, that's my job," I point out harshly. "So is fucking strangers and killing them. *Don't overthink it.*"

He spears pure contempt at me. I know he's thinking all

those hard, cruel thoughts about me being a Sinner, how I'm evil and a whore and a bitch, and I deserve to go to hell.

He was just asking a question. Being nice. I was the one who started that charade, after all. Part of it was instinct—me slipping into assassin mode, throwing off the target, misdirecting, making them gloss over us as potential suspects.

Suspects for what?

I feel dirty.

I need to go to confession.

I wait for his retort, but nothing comes.

He shoves his hands in his jeans pockets and starts walking. "Right."

"I had no idea you were a natural puppy whisperer," I say, changing the focus to him.

He shrugs. "My uncle felt sorry for me being an only child, so he kept buying them."

"What happened?"

"They never lasted long. Sick or hit by a bus."

He hunches and increases his pace. I remain behind him for a second, thinking how sad his childhood must have been. He seemed so happy with the puppy in his arms.

I jog to catch up.

I'm such a cow. Heat floods my cheeks, and tears sting my eyes for the first time since forever. Why am I like this? Why can't I just...

I sigh.

It doesn't matter why because I can't change.

We don't talk for the remainder of our walk until we find a

suitable dark alley between a block of commercial buildings. Dim lights over back doors flicker, and dumpsters overflow and smell like sewage. Feral cats and rats scamper about. But otherwise, it's deserted. Perfect.

"Down here." I motion for him to follow me.

I stop halfway and face him. This is where things might get a little awkward between us. But the tension already vibrating between us will help him accept what comes next.

He adjusts his spectacles. "What's wrong?"

"We need to lure them to us."

"The Deadly Seven?"

I nod.

"Okay." His eyes grow suspicious. "How are we doing that?"

"They sense deadly sin," I explain. "If we want their attention, we must feel deadly amounts of sin. Not just a fleeting thought, but a sustained 'I want to kill you' sort of thought."

"You're going to try to kill me?"

"That's what *deadly* means."

He shoots me a belligerent look. "I thought you said they were your friends."

"They are. Sort of. Alice is an ex-Sinner and married to their leader. But since the mayor basically put them on the payroll, they're now local celebrities. If we turn up on their doorstep, we'll be noticed. I don't want any record of us being here, even a text message. Nothing can get in the way of us finding that relic."

"What sin?" he asks.

I dump my bag and roll my shoulders. "I'll try to take your pack. Maybe I envy it and want to see what you have hidden inside."

I actually do want to know what secrets he's hiding in there. All I have to do is amplify that need and take it from him. Maybe rough him up a bit. Should be easy.

"Resist me." I start circling him, sizing him up. "That way, I can intensify the sin."

He licks his lips. "What if I don't resist? What if I *want* you to tackle me?"

My steps stutter as I catch the flare of heat in his eyes. How does he not hate me by now? I'm honestly doing everything I can to push him away.

"What do you mean?" I ask although I have a fair idea.

A flash of nervousness crosses his expression, but then he sets his jaw and prowls closer to me. His confidence takes me unawares, and I step backward until I hit a wall. His hands brace on either side of my head, and then he lowers his lips to my ear.

"There are other sins, right?" His voice is deep and rough.

A shiver sets my nerves on fire when his lips connect with my neck. I can't hide the effect he has on me. There's no point lying. Maybe this is what we need—an outlet for our pent-up frustration.

Enjoy the ride.

"Lust is also a deadly sin," I breathe, tugging him closer.

My body buzzes at his closeness. Maybe he's thinking the same thing I am.

Let's get this confusing tension out of our system. Purge it, and go back to hating each other.

"If you think you can handle this much sin," I breathe. "Take what you want."

His lips stop on my neck. His hot breath tickles my skin. We're stuck in an endless moment of uncertainty. Just when I think he'll back off, he drags his open lips from my neck to my jaw as though he's ready to eat me. The move is so erotic, so decidedly male, that I feel myself getting wet.

When he claims my mouth, it's devouring. It's demanding, needy, and raw all at once. He kisses with his whole body —with his hands spearing into my hair, his hips digging into mine, and his throat making soft little grunts like he's struggling to hold back the tidal wave of his desire. Like he's been waiting for this moment since he met me. Like he'll never get this chance again.

My knees go weak as I submit to his hunger. It's so foreign to me, like nothing I've taken from other lovers. Maybe because this time, I'm not taking. He's giving.

I grab his shirt and pull him closer. Deepening our kiss, I hook my leg around his waist and grind my hips into his, hunting for more delicious friction. We both release a shuddering groan at the contact. Shocked and dazed, we pull away, panting.

He's so fucking hot with his lazy, crooked cat-got-the-milk smile that I almost forget what I'm doing here. But then our eyes clash, and his desire splashes cold water on me. This isn't a game to him. This is something he wants from deep within his soul. No one kisses like that unless they mean it.

For Sinners, seduction is a choreographed dance. Every touch is carefully constructed, and every word has a use. When I use my body to take down a mark, I'm like a robot going through the motions. But this isn't that. This is hope in my soul talking to his. This is my heart peeling open.

A slice of fear stabs me.

Too much.

Too real.

I shove him and snarl, "This has to be *deadly*, you understand?"

He recoils but doesn't step back. His fists tighten in my hair, and his eyes turn defiant.

But if we're to attract the vigilante of deadly lust, this won't be two sweet lovers coming together. This will be him forcing himself on me to the point he's ready to kill me. Death, I'm used to. Violence, my heart understands.

He eases off with a flicker of disappointment and an ounce of bitterness.

"Envy is fine," he mutters.

Something impossible builds inside of me at his rejection. I slap his face. His head snaps to the side. His spectacles slide down his nose, threatening to teeter off. But he makes no move to right himself.

"Come on, Wes," I hiss. "I see the way you look at me. I see the lust, the want, the craving. You were all too happy to stick your tongue down my throat a second ago. I'm well acquainted with what men want from pretty girls like me. So take it. I'm giving you a guilt-free chance to take the one thing I'm good for." I shove him. He stumbles, fixes his specs, and straightens. Still, he won't look at me. As if my face is the most disgusting thing he's ever seen. My chest heaves. My heart burns. This feels worse than rejection. It feels like I'm not even good for this despicable act.

"Show me what you're made of," I taunt.

"I'm not going to force myself on you," he grinds out, outraged eyes meeting mine.

"I'm giving you a free pass."

His upper lip curls, and he shakes his head. "Pick another sin."

"No. We started this. Let's finish it."

"I don't know what you want from me," he shouts, cutting his hand through the air. "I see the way you look at me too. Don't pretend it's part of your job. You give me signals, and then you push me away." He stops, chest heaving, eyes blazing. "You think this is easy for me? You think I planned to have feelings for someone like you?"

"That's rich coming from you." The liar he is.

"You don't even know what you want."

"I want you to hurt me." Punish me. Be my penance.

"This is getting out of hand."

My mouth opens to give a retort, but nothing comes out. It's because he's right. He's rocked the foundations of my existence, and I still have no idea what's happening. All I know is that my mind and heart have been in turmoil since he came into my life. I know his rejection hurts more than anything. I'm not worth the dirt on his feet, but I want to be. I'd rather him force himself on me than not touch me at all. How fucked up is that?

I grip the fabric at my chest. My face is twisted in pain, and I'm floundering in uncharted territory, unmoored, adrift.

Something hard collides with my midsection, knocking the wind out of me. I careen to the side. Instinct sharpens my reactions. I tuck my shoulder, hit the ground, and roll to my feet. I expect to face Liza—the vigilante who senses lust—even though Wes and I never got to the deadly part of our sin.

I face my attacker head-on, ready to surrender, but it's not one of the Deadly Seven.

NINETEEN
WESLEY

Shock punches my gut as Thea is attacked. I'm already opening my backpack to retrieve a weapon when she rolls to her feet and faces her enemy. Something about the exchange stuns me, and I freeze.

Who is that?

I narrow my eyes. The masked attacker is in a dark suit—much like the one Thea wears, only this one seems slicker—like it's made from high-tech material that I probably need a degree from MIT to understand.

The attacker has curves. Must be a woman. A hood and red face scarf cover her nose and mouth. Red. Just like Thea's.

I almost back off, thinking this is the ex-Sinner Thea mentioned, and after the exchange we just had, I know absolutely nothing about what these women need. But then the masked woman intensifies her attack. There's nothing Thea can do but deflect and defend. My eyes widen. My heartbeat thuds in my chest, and then I'm down on my knees, rifling through my pack.

I shove clothes, holy water, blessed items, relics, and occult weaponry out of the way. I don't think the attacker is possessed, which reduces the effectiveness of most of my weapons. *Fuck.* Panicking, I almost give up and toss the bag. I'll have to use my fists. Then a gleam in the bag catches my eye —Enochian-sigil-carved knuckledusters. I slip them onto my right hand and straighten.

Thea might be the most complicated, conflicted, and stunning person I've ever met. But I can't stand by while she's hurt.

I step toward the brawling couple and wait for an opening. I raise my fist, but a punishing grip wraps around my wrist. Heat bathes my spine, and a gravelly snarl prickles the back of my neck. But I'm not afraid. The grip is human—sort of. It's unforgiving metal, but it belongs to a human. After facing monstrous demons... humans and robots don't seem so intimidating.

Even one as stacked as the vigilante with flashing gold eyes and a bionic arm behind me. A purple face mask covers his mouth. The rest of him is covered by a gray hood and battle suit, much like the one the attacker is wearing. He's bloody big... like, mountain-man big. One arm is metallic. The other is seemingly ordinary flesh and blood... no, not ordinary— sharp claws at the fingertips.

The words *genetically modified* and *deadly* bounce around my head.

Thea's cry of pain snaps my attention back to the fight. She's on the ground now, and her attacker isn't pulling punches. *She needs me.* I yank on the vigilante's grip, ignoring the pain shooting through my wrist.

"Envy." The big brute's voice is modified to sound monotone and deep.

I don't understand what he means—envy? Then I catch the silhouette of a hooded figure leaning against a dumpster, watching the fight. Twin katanas are strapped to his back. A green scarf covers his nose and mouth, but his eyes twinkle with amusement.

"Envy."

He glances, annoyed at my captor, and says, "Yeah?"

"A little help?"

"But I'm watching the girls."

"If you've taken bets, I swear to God I'll—"

"Just a little longer. Wait for it..."

"Envy!"

"Party pooper."

They sound like bickering siblings. The vigilante behind me must make a face because Envy rolls his eyes and then pushes off the dumpster to grab my other wrist.

"Don't push it," Envy warns me but keeps his grip loose.

"Bugger off." I wrestle out of his hold, but he's quick.

He snaps me back up and mutters, "I warned you."

Electricity jolts into me, zipping into my body and seizing my lungs. He's a walking taser. I bite my tongue as the current runs its course, and I'm left breathless and dizzy, hanging between two lethal men... if that's what they are.

"Whoops," says Envy. "You good, Pride?"

"Fuck's sake." Pride lets go of my other hand and shudders. "You could have warned me."

I smile as I convulse. At least the big guy received a jolt through that metal arm. Hopefully, the robotics are fried. But he's barely affected while I'm dying. A thousand thoughts run through my mind as I recover. *Breathe*—chiefly among them. *Don't piss your pants,* the next. I'd heard rumors of genetically modified heroes while I was in Europe, but I'd dismissed them as inconsequential. Thea said we were coming here, but I didn't understand what we'd face. My mind has been filled with Thea, Vepar, and Zeke.

"I thought you were her friends," I rasp. Tension rolls off them, but they stay silent, so I add, "Why the bloody hell are you okay with this?"

"You don't get to question us," rumbles the big one.

My wits slowly return. I have one avenue left—my palm tattoos. I clench my jaw as my nails pierce my skin, bringing blood into contact with the sigils marked there. I mutter the spell, thinking I'll get away with it.

Somehow, Pride *hears* above the noise of the fight.

"Why are you speaking in Latin?" he asks calmly.

I can't break the chant. Every drop of blood, every syllable, enters the atmosphere as my secret fuck-you to these vigilante pricks. But I also didn't account for Pride understanding Latin, and he seems to know exactly what I'm doing.

His big palm covers my mouth. I glare at him and try to continue, but he tightens his grip and holds his scowling face before mine.

"Idiot," he growls. "Your friend isn't in danger. *Look*."

He shoves me ahead of him but holds me by the scruff like I'm a toddler. He forces me to watch the women fight.

"Look at her face," he urges.

I zero in on Thea as she deflects a punch to the head. She's smiling. *Grinning*. Her eyes are bright, her cheeks are rosy, and her lips move like she's trading insults with her attacker and loving it. Her cries of pain are more mocking than real... as if the hits to her ribs tickle. I stop struggling.

"What the bloody fuck?" I gasp.

Pride lets go of me. "They do this sometimes."

"Beat the shit out of each other?"

Thea swipes her opponent's legs, upending her, then Thea's shin is on her attacker's throat, pinning her to the ground.

Pride steps forward, but Envy slaps him on the chest. "Don't be a dick. She's fine."

A grumble of acquiescence rolls out of Pride. He folds his arms and watches, but his need to protect the fallen woman remains a tangible warning in the air.

"Yield, bitch," Thea says to her pinned attacker.

"No fair, you went for my bad leg."

"You started it!"

"I had to make sure your skills are still up to scratch. Who knows what training drills Mercy has you doing these days."

"Yield."

"Fine. You win."

Thea spits blood to the side, then offers her hand. The fallen attacker takes it. Once standing, she tugs her scarf and hood down, revealing copper hair and freckles. She fits in with the Sinners. Beautiful, feisty, and lethal.

"Alice," Pride grumbles and points to the red scarf. "Mask up."

"Pah." She waves her hand dismissively. "I'm not one of you."

"You're a fucking CEO of a Fortune Five Hundred Company."

"Hey," Alice warns and points at him. "Language." Then she shrugs. "Besides, half the city knows your identity anyway."

"*You* don't have a pardon from the Mayor."

Envy tugs his mask and hood down. His hair is short but messy. He's about my age, maybe younger, but he's not me. He's genetically modified. He deals with sin. I glance at Alice and Pride, at how they seem to comfort each other, and wonder if Envy has someone like that too. He holds out his hand to Thea with a grin. "Thank you very much. You just made me a cool five hundred."

"You bet against me!" Alice slaps him.

"Ow." He makes it look like her slap hurt, but I know it doesn't. Anyone who can generate electricity with his body wouldn't be a wimp.

Pride lifts his eyes to the night sky and seems to pray for

patience before he gives a laborious exhale and drops his mask and hood. His hair is long and tied at the nape. He shoots me a look that says he doesn't trust me but then strolls to Alice and leans in. "Are you injured?"

"I'm fine," she replies, her gaze softening on him.

"How did you know we were here?" Thea asks Alice.

I'm confused because I thought Thea planned to lure them out by conjuring deadly sin, but we never got to the *deadly* part of our sinning exercise. I'm still unsettled that she wanted me to treat her with violence and contempt rather than affection.

Alice gestures at Envy. "He had one of his premonitions."

"What did you see?" Thea asks him.

"Enough," he replies solemnly.

Alice nods. "The jet is fueled, chartered, and stocked with supplies."

Thea's mood turns grim. Then she gestures for me to join her.

"This is Wes," she explains to Alice. "He's a part of Team Saint."

Alice takes me in with a wary once-over, then returns to Thea. "I'm sorry. I thought we knew why you were here. Envy's been drawing some pretty dark stuff. Demons. London. A jet. But what the fuck is Team Saint?"

"Team Saint is the Vatican's version of us," Thea replies dryly. "The *male* version."

"I know what Team Saint is," Alice grumbles. "I mean..."

why the fuck is one of them with you? What the hell has happened since I left?"

"You know we're not secret anymore. With the recent rise in demonic possessions, they sent a group of their finest to *educate* us."

The obvious incredulity on Alice's face makes me want to laugh. It's the same reaction all of the Sinners had. *How dare the men come into our home and tell us what to do.* I feel a retort coming from her, but her partner—or husband—or whatever he is grips the back of her neck in a familiar way and says, "Hear him out, Alice."

Surprised to find an ally in him, I try not to show it. But I guess if he's married to an ex-Sinner, he knows exactly what it's like to be a male outsider in their ranks. He's also found a way to be with someone like her... a hero with a Sinner.

I give him a nod of thanks and face Alice, who's waiting for me to explain and tapping her foot.

I adjust my spectacles. Where to start?

"I've been working with a group of men around Europe to get a handle on the growing demonic activity."

"Group of men?" Alice shuffles her weight to the other side.

"Father Angelotti is our exorcist. Zeke is our weapons expert. I'm research and the mystic arts. Dom is a Saint."

"And what do you know that we don't?" Alice blinks, then corrects. "I mean the Sinners."

"Spells. Geomancy. Arcane arts. Holy weapons. Prophecies. Exorcisms."

"Spells?" Alice snorts, but the vigilantes aren't quick to dismiss.

Envy listens intently, and Pride takes my hand to inspect the new bloody crescent moon cuts from my nails. He says, "He was chanting while you two fought, and I smelled the fresh blood on his hand."

Smelled? Is he more animal than man? Looking at those golden feral eyes and claws, I would believe it.

Envy points at my palms, seemingly picking up the tattoo as it travels up my forearms and hides behind the sleeves. "You've had more work."

"Inkless on the hands," I confirm. "Regular on my arms and torso."

"Nah, bro." Envy takes my hand and scrutinizes it. "It's not inkless but UV. Inkless tattoos can actually help heal scars. This shit can be toxic. I hope you went to a reputable tattoo artist."

Thea explains to me, "He runs a tattoo shop."

Vigilante by night. Tattoo artist by day. *Interesting.*

Pride asks, "Both occult and arcane?"

I nod. "I wanted some difficult to see at a glance. As you saw, I was incapacitated but could still draw blood with my nails. With the right words and symbols, blood conjures a spell. Works better if I surprise my opponent."

Dark magic has consequences... like sharing with the dark world that someone is using their gifts, which is why I prefer to use them as a last resort.

"What were you going to do?" Thea asks.

"Now you're interested?"

"Maybe I am."

Alice scowls at Thea. "Now? As in, you didn't want to learn before?"

I point my thumb at Thea. "I offered to teach her, but the little minx is stubborn."

"Thea," Alice says, her voice soft. "If he can help, then let him."

"Says the woman who hates being told what to do," she drawls.

Alice meets her squarely in the eyes. "The Sisterhood isn't the be-all and end-all. There's more to life."

Emotion flickers over Thea's expression. "Easy for you to say. You're out. You're probably going to Heaven along with these goody-two-shoes."

She gestures irritably at the vigilantes.

Envy scoffs. "Heaven? Us?" He points his thumb at Pride. "All God needs to do is take a peek at his bedroom wall of knotty shibari secrets—"

"Envy!" Alice punches him, blushing. "Just because you see things in your dreams doesn't mean you have the right to tell the whole world."

"I'm going to kill you," Pride says through clenched teeth, reaching for him.

"Uh-uh." Lightning sparks at Envy's fingertips. "I'll fry your circuitry this time."

"It's okay, babe," Alice says to Pride, mollifying him. "I'll just steal some of those x-rated drawings he's done of Grace before they started dating."

Evan blanches. "You wouldn't."

Alice scowls and returns to Thea. "For fuck's sake. You're not going to hell. It's not even—"

"Real?" Thea finishes, her brows raised. "How can you still think that?"

"If you keep filling yourself with shame, you'll never make room for what's important." Alice's tone softens, and I almost miss her following words. "And you'll end up alone."

Thea glances at me, then away.

A lightbulb blows further down the alley, and we all look. Dawn is on its way, but it feels darker than midnight. And colder. Another bulb blows—closer this time. As we watch, lights over doors burst in procession as though someone invisible is walking toward us, breaking them with a bat. Darkness encroaches like rolling fog. Every hair on my body stands on end as though Envy has sent another bolt of electricity through me.

"That's weird, right?" Alice mutters.

But no sooner have the words come out of her mouth than water bubbles from the sewer grates and rain falls from the sky. In a matter of seconds, we're drenched.

Stiletto heels click and splash. Out of the storm, a tall, immaculately dressed woman appears. My brows knit together as I take her in. A drenched white business suit, long dark hair plastered to her face, and black-as-ink eyes—the same as Asmodeus.

My half-attempt at a spell must have gone up like a beacon to any demon in the area.

"Thea?" I collect my backpack.

I see a businesswoman, and I'm sure Envy, Pride, and Alice all see the same thing. But Thea's eyes are darting about the woman, landing on targeted areas like she notices something we can't.

The moment they confessed their strange Sight at the abbey, I believed them. They were too horrified to fake it. And Cisco confirmed the demonic possession—he has a knack for sensing evil presences, no matter what form.

"Demon," she confirms. "Has a fish tail and maggots crawling out of pustules on her scales like she's diseased and rotting." Her eyes widen in horror. "Some fallen maggots are turning into little fish beasties with fangs and four legs."

My old demon-marked palm burns as I study the sodden businesswoman through the rain. Apart from the black eyes, she looks normal, but then something Thea said plucks at my memories. Fishtail. The demon who took my uncle had a fishtail.

The last time we met, I was a child pissing my pants and hiding behind a doorway, watching it slither out of a hole in the ground. Her tail wrapped around my uncle. Water flowed and sizzled from the pits of hell. Then she took him down. I ran forward and reached—grabbed his hand—slipped, lost hold, and the hole in the ground closed up. All that remained was a burning in my palm. When Vepar tried to influence me in the asylum, I saw nothing... only heard voices in my mind.

I didn't know a demon's true name gave you power over it back then. Didn't know that my uncle had left me a nugget of gold in his notes by writing her name down. I also don't understand why he didn't use it... maybe he never had a chance.

She probably thought she could attack me again if she turned up here disguised as the human she possessed. She didn't count on Thea's special vision or me, all grown up and knowing her name.

"Vepar," I growl, much to her surprise.

TWENTY
THEA

R ain runs down my face. The atmosphere is darkening, but the vile vision of a pustule-covered mermaid slithering over puddled asphalt is sharp in my mind. Her visage flickers between demon and businesswoman, which must be what my allies see—a simple woman in heels and a suit.

I glance up. The moon is still shining, and no clouds are in the sky. I have no idea where the rain comes from or how water oozes from the drains.

My allies have frozen, just like me. They don't see the demonic fishtailed monster. But they might see the maggots dropping from her flesh and turning into cat-sized grotesque fish with legs because they're all quietly freaking out.

"Vepar," Wes growls as he moves to stand between the demon and me.

Wasn't that the name of the one who tried to claim him as

a child? The same one whose mark was on the severed hand? What are the odds that it's back here now?

A cold, calm takes over me as I flip into Sinner mode. I reach down and release a blessed dagger from my strapped ankle sheath. My crucifix is tugged out of my shirt next, and Wesley's charm follows it. I grasp the two together, ready to hold them before me like a shield.

"What the fuck?" Envy mutters, his eyes taking in the minions.

"Get back," I warn them. "Normal weapons won't work on these creatures."

Pride doesn't listen. He leaps in front of Alice and flicks out his claws with a feral roar that rattles my spine. Envy, too, has switched into defensive mode. Flashes of lightning arc up his arms and crackle at his fingertips.

"Get them out of the water," he bellows at Pride.

Before I can protest, Pride snakes a hand around mine and Alice's waist and lifts until our feet dangle. Outraged, I'm ready to stab him—Wesley needs me.

An image flashes in my mind—a demon dragging a man to hell through the ground, a child trying to save him.

Wes.

"Let me go," I growl and twist, but Pride won't release me.

Envy slaps his hands into puddles at his feet. His eyes narrow on Vepar, and he unleashes his power. An arc of purple lightning flashes along the ground, skipping through the interconnected wetness. Wes won't survive. Adrenaline surges through me, and I flip the knife to aim at Pride. I'll never make it to Wes in time. He'll get fried. But before my knife connects with Pride, the lightning runs its course and misses Wes completely. Miraculously, he's not standing in a connected puddle... or maybe his rubber boots saved him.

My relief is short-lived when I realize none of the demonic minions were affected, and certainly not Vepar.

"What the hell?" Alice mutters.

I hit Pride. "Let me down."

Faster than I thought he could move, Wes rips a vial of holy water from his bag and slams it on Vepar's tail. Glass breaks—steam and smoke hiss from the contact. Vepar screams, but Wes is already chanting something and holding a crucifix wrapped in a torn cloth as he circles the demon. He holds a lighter before the crucifix and blows air from his mouth. It shouldn't work. Breath is not an accelerant. But fire streams from the lighter, through the cross, and toward the demon like it's come out of a blowtorch. Vepar's screams increase as she writhes. Rain stops, and water reverses down the drains. No more demonic minions manifest through her pustules.

Pride drops me. I run toward Wes with my blessed dagger brandished. A grotesque fish on four legs leaps at me, and I run the blade through its body. My heart wants me to go to Wes, but there are too many minions—and now I'm not even sure if the others can see them or if they're too stunned to move.

I slice and stab each minion with sharp, methodical movements until none are left.

When I glance up, Wes is standing over the demon. His spectacles have fallen, water drips from his hair, and he seems a little shell-shocked. He doesn't see her as I do. He sees the woman in a business suit. He's probably doubting. Maybe the demon is in his head.

That's the only reason I can think of why he's not defending himself as the demon rears up to face him.

I flip the blessed dagger, readjust my grip, and then throw. It embeds in the demon's heart, and just like the man outside that club, pure evil streams out. Only this time, I see it. The demon becomes a woman as a black swarm of darkness shoots into the sky and disappears.

It's over in a matter of seconds. I'm soaked from head to toe, and my fist hurts from clenching the dagger.

"You okay?" I jog to Wesley.

He stares at the corpse, at the dagger protruding from her chest. Black mascara runs down the woman's damp cheeks like she's been crying. Her nails are the perfect shade of fire engine red. One of her red-soled Louboutin heels has fallen off. Her toenails don't match her fingernails. They're chipped and hidden. She probably spent every cent on making an impression and couldn't afford to pamper the parts no one else saw.

The gravity of it hits me. I killed a woman. She had a life. Hopes. Dreams. A powerful demon possessed her, but she didn't deserve to die. I'm used to killing deplorable men, easy targets.

Maybe that man at the nightclub wasn't evil before the demon took him.

Maybe they're all just vulnerable, traumatized victims like Prudence.

I killed an innocent woman. Wes was in danger and... I didn't hesitate. This is Prue's fate if we don't find the relic.

My pulse quickens. My fingers and extremities go numb. I recognize the beginnings of shock and force myself to breathe and get a grip. I can't lose it in front of Wes. Not now.

"Wes." I pick up his fallen spectacles and clean them with my drier undershirt. When I touch his back, he startles and meets my gaze.

"It was her," he rasps, eyes wide.

"I know."

He puts his spectacles on with fumbling fingers and then returns to being the scholar who knows everything. He points at the demon fish and says, "They're not supposed to be here."

"You see them?"

He gestures at Alice and the vigilantes, who are still warily taking in the scene. "They probably see them too."

When they nod, Wes shakes his head in disbelief.

"They're not supposed to be here because they've manifested as physical beings... on *this* plane."

"Aren't they all physical?" Alice asks.

Wesley saves me from answering.

"No. What you saw was a woman possessed by the spirit of a demon. These creatures are inferior demons that have crossed realms. They shouldn't be here. The gates of hell must have cracks big enough to fit tiny things through."

"What do you mean, Wes?" I get in front of him.

He nervously licks his lips. "No demon or devil can exist on this plane physically. That's why they possess, haunt, and influence. But—"

One of the grotesque fish gapes like it's floundering out of water. One by one, the others start flopping about.

"They're not dead," I mumble.

The sound of sliding metal echoes against the walls as Envy unleashes twin katanas. Pride flexes his claws.

"Put them away," Alice says grimly, her eyes on Wes and me. "If a blessed dagger didn't kill them, then your weapons are no good."

"Blessed dagger," Pride rubs his jaw and glances at the corpse. "It exorcised the spiritual demon, but not these physical ones?"

Wesley rubs his face. "I don't even know if that's the case. Vepar could have voluntarily exorcised. Or I could have weakened her with the holy water and fire, and the dagger might have been the final straw."

Envy's brows lower. "My power barely tickled them, and my weapons can't kill them. What the fuck are we supposed to do?"

Wes flicks them an unreadable look and then picks up his charred crucifix from the ground. He pulls another slice of torn fabric from inside his bag, wraps it around the cross, and says to me, "Use the dagger to drag them all together. Don't touch the scales... and especially don't touch the warped mark of Lilith."

He noticed what I didn't. Lilith's mark is scored into the underbelly on each of them.

I stab each beast, hating how their flounders become dexterous and know they're healing. Soon they will attack. But I hope Wes is right, and all we need to do is coordinate our efforts. I shove them into a pile—seven altogether—and Wes barks, "Stand back."

Then he mutters the same incantation he did before and sparks his lighter in front of the wrapped crucifix. He blows until flames pass through the relic and shoot holy fire at the demonic minions. Screeches and high-pitched screams echo through the alley. Heat blisters our faces.

It's a strange comfort to my shivering and cold body.

When it's clear they're all dead, Alice turns to me with a grim look. "This fight is yours. The jet is ready." To Wes, she says, "Take care of my sister."

I nod. "Thank you, Alice. Pride. Envy."

They go to leave, but Alice turns back with a frown.

"Thea?"

"Yeah?"

She limps to me and envelopes me in a bear hug. Tears sting my eyes at the contact. My body rejoices. The force of her love is evident in the strength of her embrace. She's seen the worst of me but will always accept me no matter how removed she is from this life. This hug is everything.

It's not the life raft, but it will keep me afloat a little longer.

"Enjoy the ride, bitch," she whispers, squeezes me one last time, and then pushes away with a wry smirk.

Envy gives me a compassionate look as I watch Alice and her husband disappear into the night. He knows exactly what I'm envious of, and then he's gone too.

AS THE ENGINES FIRE UP, I strap my waterlogged body into the seat of a private luxury jet. We came straight here from the city. Didn't even stop to dispose of the business-woman's body or the demonic minions. The woman's family deserves closure, and the minions were charred beyond anything recognizable. We can clean up and rest on the long flight.

Black mascara tears on flawless skin. Glossy red fingernails. Chipped toenails that don't match.

I clear my throat and glance at Wes opposite me. His half-dried blond hair has curled. The tan leather chair is dark from where his wet body rubbed against it. His honey eyes are wide behind his spectacles. He clutches his backpack with white knuckles. We haven't spoken since the attack.

"You okay?" I ask softly, my throat dry.

Because I'm not. I'm holding on by a thread.

Wide eyes meet mine and hesitate, but then he nods. I watch him fuss in his seat and wonder if he's afraid of flying. He has the look of a startled deer. But this isn't that. This probably relates to the attack... and how I treated him before it. He doesn't know how to deal with me now.

I don't blame him.

I don't know how to deal with myself, either. But seeing Alice reminded me that I have a family at the Sisterhood and a job to do. It reminded me to shove all my confusing feelings for Wesley in a box, to trust my instincts, catalog details, and read body language.

My old teacher's voice echoes in my mind.

A Sinner can only focus on one thing at a time, and it can't be her emotions. She must be ruthless, cold, and efficient. She must focus outward, not inward... for that way leads to death.

So I chant in my mind, *Don't think about your guilt. Think about the job. The job. Not guilt. Not the woman and her mismatched nail polish. Not the guilt or how it expands like a balloon, threatening to burst.*

Chanting isn't helping.

Wesley's eyes dart about. His posture is hunched and defensive, his skin is paler than usual, and he's gripping that bag like a security blanket. He's not coping either.

Fuck, I need a drink.

"Vepar's not dead, is she?" I ask.

Of course, I know she's not. I saw the black smoke coming out of her body. But did he? After a pause, he shakes his head.

"She's coming back for you, isn't she?"

He stares out the window, keeping his secrets to himself. My irritation grows. If he doesn't engage, I'm stuck with my guilty thoughts.

The jet vibrates as we move down the runway. The single seats are in a four-formation, two facing each other on either side of the aisle, and eight in total. Behind Wes, a leather sofa-couch lines the fuselage wall and faces a flat-screen TV and credenza. Even further back is a small bathroom and kitchen.

The demonic attack has set us back. It will be daytime when we arrive in London. If I'm to pull off a museum heist, I'll have to wait until nightfall. It will give us time to scope out the museum and finesse a plan. The girls are working on strategies back at the abbey, but I have a few ideas. We'll have something workable by the time I land.

If demonic forces are trying to open the gates of hell, if that bitch is coming back for Wes, then I need to be prepared.

I need that archangel's staff.

But as I sit here with destructive thoughts and a man who won't look me in the eye, I recall a verse from Mary's gospel and wonder if I'm the right woman for this job.

> *And let us remember that the divine relics, though powerful, are only tools in the hands of those who wield them. True strength lies in accepting the darkness within and forging a path of love and compassion, even in the face of adversity.*

After tonight, I've learned I don't accept the darkness within me. I'm ashamed of it, and I hate it. I hate myself for doing these things, but I'm not in the abbey, so I can't beg the priest to purge my sins and absolve me. I close my eyes.

Black mascara tears on flawless skin. Glossy red fingernails. Toenails that don't match.

I open my eyes wide.

My self-loathing will eat me alive if I can't get it out. And just like that, I'm cast adrift again. How much more of this can I take before I lose my mind?

TWENTY-ONE
WESLEY

When the seatbelt light flicks off, Thea unbuckles, unzips her hoodie, and tosses it on the seat next to her. Grumbling under her breath, she walks to a bar fridge beside the credenza and rifles through it. Two seconds later, she's back with mini bottles of alcohol.

She plops down, cracks the lid on a vodka, gulps the contents, then tosses the empty bottle on the seat beside her.

"You want one?" She waggles a bottle in the air. "It will calm your nerves."

I want to say no, that I don't need calming, but it would be a lie.

I nod.

I catch the one she tosses and then wait until she chugs her second bottle before cracking mine. The burning liquid warms me from the inside out, but it fails to douse the fury in my blood.

I'm so fucking angry that I fear it leaks from my pores like radiation. I can't let her see. If it gets out, I'll poison everything around me, including her.

It's shameful enough that she knows Vepar wasn't killed, or that she suspects the demon will be back for me, but I'm sure she's figured out that I know the manuscript is missing from my trunk. She's probably wondering why I haven't asked for it back. It won't be long before she learns I'm not worthy of Team Saint.

I'm someone she should hate.

But that's not why I'm full of rage.

It's the dark gift Vepar left me when I touched her. It crawls through my veins, changing me, robbing me of time, and stealing hope—right when I finally learned to have it again.

Thea's eyes lit up when she watched me play with that puppy. I ached for the childhood she lost, for the need to give it to her. My uncle brought home pets for me, and I'd never felt more loved, more part of a family... Even if it didn't last, I'll always cherish those moments of happiness. It sounds utterly pedestrian and domestic, but with Thea, at that moment, I glimpsed a future I've always wanted but was too afraid to hope for. She eased into the charade of a happy couple like it was something she wanted, too.

An invisible string connected our souls.

Even when she shut me down afterward, I knew it wasn't because of me. It was out of fear. Our feelings for each other are growing, but big feelings come with big changes and consequences. Her reaction was proof that I was right. I thought I could break through her fear because I wanted mine gone too. Our kiss shattered my world. It made me yearn. Hunger. But the kiss broke her differently, and I'm still trying to understand... I'm trying to wrap my head around so many things that it hurts to think.

Her mind. Her soul. Her body. Why do I feel so drawn to her that my throat aches to taste her again? Awareness of her proximity is a constant buzz over my skin. I would know wherever she went, even if I was blind.

I watch her lick the remnants of vodka from the rim of a bottle like it's ice cream. She's strong, intelligent, feminine, and everything I didn't know I needed.

She's not for you. Not anymore.

I wince at the tight feeling in my crotch, but it's useless. The tip of my hard shaft inches toward the waistband like it's drowning and needs air.

Thea is my air.

I exhale, unzip my damp hoodie, remove it and cover my lap to hide my embarrassing lack of control. Thea tosses me another bottle. I gulp back the bourbon and wince at the burn, then put my hands on my lap, palms down, hiding them in my hoodie.

I stare at my buried hands and remember when Vepar realized Thea could see her true demonic form. There had been a moment of complete, predatory focus. The demon was going to murder Thea. Because of me. Because I'd drawn on dark powers that I shouldn't have.

Use her—I'm your only friend.

Vepar's voice kept repeating in my head, just like it used to. My life had flashed before my eyes—my uncle's hand slipping through mine, the screams of tortured souls, the insanity and loneliness I suffered at the asylum, the fact that I might lose Zeke—and I stepped between Vepar and Thea before my brain caught up to my heart.

Nothing else mattered but keeping her safe. But now the danger is over, and we're in this private jet thousands of miles above sea level, my promise to Zeke is glaring.

"Is it going to work?" he asked.

"When have I ever steered you wrong?"

"Well, I can name a few—"

"You know what I mean. We've been planning this for a long time. Every part has worked. Even Asmodeus says it heals. It will work on you." I clutch his shoulder and squeeze. *"I'll bring it back."*

The smudges under Zeke's eyes never disappeared, no matter how much sleep he had. Inoperable tumors have a way of doing that. Zeke's parents died when he was a toddler. He lived in a group home with his baby sister Amira for a few years. But then she was killed by a demon before his eyes. No one believed him. They'd taken one look at him and thought *he* did it—a child. He lost faith in humanity and eventually ran away. As a teen, he lived on the streets, getting into brawls and dabbling in organized crime while he hunted demons on the side. Anything that brought him closer to gaining justice for his sister. After he saved my life, I wanted to give him that.

We had so much in common. He was a perfect candidate for Team Saint. And he's good with a gun. He can shoot a penny off a bottle with his eyes closed.

It's your fault everyone dies around you.

Vepar's taunts are fresh and sharp in my mind. Without looking, I know the crescent wounds on my palms are puffy and sore. Tiny cuts from the broken vial of holy water also hurt, but they're not bleeding anymore.

I know all there is to know about Vepar and what that swelling on my skin could mean. Is she trying to influence me again? Or is this paranoia? Before I dwell on it, I clench my fists and bury them deeper beneath my hoodie.

"What are you hiding?"

My gaze lifts to Thea. Intelligent eyes pierce me.

"I beg your pardon?"

"You're keeping secrets. I want to know what they are."

I look out the window at the endless blue sky.

She pushes off her seat and slams her palms onto my armrests. The smell of vodka hits my face. I glance at her seat to count the empty bottles. Only three. She leans forward, fiery eyes glued to mine. I should be offended, but I'm too distracted by how her hair dangles over one shoulder. How a flushed complexion still graces her cheeks. When those nuns chose her to join their team, they knew exactly what they were doing. She's heart-stopping.

Her pose arches her back, pushes forward her chest and accentuates supple breasts beneath her tight black shirt. I swallow a groan. Her nipples are erect and straining through the damp fabric. Heat floods my groin, and I squirm at the uncomfortable pressure building.

Use her—I'm your only friend.

"Show me your hands." She props a knee between my legs, forcing my thighs open. My breath hitches as she makes contact with my erection, and heat floods my cheeks. She probably knew I was hard the instant it happened.

Distrust is the last thing I see when I look into her eyes. I see shadows and ghosts. Pain. Angst. Desperation. I can't even imagine what horrors put it all there. I thought this ambush was about my secrets, but she must feel something else.

Why not mention the manuscript? Or the fact we all lied about not speaking English. Why start with my hands? Even if I showed them, she'd see normal wounds. I hide them because... I'm not ready to reveal that fear.

So why does she start with this unless she's just picking a fight to release tension? I don't think she knows another way of dealing with her emotions—the battle with Alice proved it. They can't show weakness.

Use her before she uses you.

"Don't be absurd." I dismiss her again.

"Wesley, show me your hands."

"I'm not in the mood for your games, Thea."

She blinks. A flash of grief passes over her features, and then it's gone, replaced by the same antagonizing creature she was in the alley. She snatches my wrist, intending to inspect my palm, but my anger collides with my fear. I shove her. She falls back into her chair so hard that her head whips back, and she grunts. My eyes widen in shock. An apology is on the tip of my tongue, but she faces me with a smirk.

"There he is," she says, a wicked gleam in her eyes. "I've been waiting for him to return."

"Are you insane? I don't want to hurt you. Stop whatever this is you're doing."

She reaches for my hands, but I fight her off. We grapple. She's relentless, but I can't. *I can't.* The moment she sees the wounds, it's real.

"Fine," I say through clenched teeth. "I know you stole the manuscript."

She pauses her assault long enough to ask, "Then why didn't you say something?"

Think of something. "I'd hoped you'd own up to it and prove everyone wrong."

Thea gives a throaty laugh. "That's a lie."

She grapples with my hands, I knee her off me, and then unbuckle to stand. Then I shove her again—two palms to her chest.

"Enough," I bark, eyes flashing.

Desperation. Wildness. Pain. Anguish. It's consuming her, taking over.

"You're lying to me, too." I shake my head in disbelief. "You want me to spill my guts, but you're so blocked up you need a laxative."

"Fuck you, Wes."

"You'd love that, wouldn't you." I toss back her words from our moment in the archives.

"What's that supposed to mean?"

"It means sex and violence are the only languages you understand. You'd love me to turn you over that seat, spank the impudence out of you, and then fuck you in the arse like the unapologetic whore you claim to be."

The words are out before I can stop them. My face burns, and my heart slams against my ribs. I don't know what I'm doing anymore. If Dom and Cisco heard me, they'd be appalled.

Every line of her body is tense. Her fists flex at her sides. She knows I'm halfway right. She's pushing me, trying to force me to treat her in the shitty way she thinks she deserves.

"That's awfully specific, Wesley," she drawls. "For someone who claims not to want to hurt me, it seems you've given it much thought."

"There's no appeasing you. I gave you a taste of something different, and you ran the other way." A flicker of emotion in her eyes tells me I'm right. I wish I had it in me to be moved. But I'm tired of this. It's not like I find what's happening between us easy. "You could have shared that fear with me because I feel the same. We could have been friends. It's too late now, Thea. I've got nothing left to give but violence, and you don't deserve that."

Her eyes flash with something I don't expect—triumph—and then she attacks me again. I don't push her away this time. I hold her face between my hands and smash my lips against hers.

TWENTY-TWO

THEA

Wesley's kiss is the cruel, punishing force I crave. I want to corrupt him. I want violence. I want to pay for my sins.

His fingers rip into my hair as he holds me immobile so he can unleash all that God-given male hunger on my mouth. Our teeth knock, and I taste blood. But he doesn't slow down. He growls and delves deeper into my mouth with his tongue, ravishing me in ways I never thought possible.

I lift his shirt and press my palms to his scorching stomach. It's like hard fire. The muscles of his abdomen contract and flex with his ragged breath. His taste is heady. I'm drunk on him, already falling, begging. I must be moaning, whimpering, or something because he sees my pleasure as a sign to slow down, to turn his plundering into slow seduction.

You don't deserve violence.

"No," I moan against his lips. "I do."

"What?" he whispers gently.

I can't have him going soft, so I force his hands from my face. Using every ounce of strength in my assassin-trained muscles, I drag his hands before my eyes. I already know he's cut himself. I don't understand why he's so panicked about me seeing. But I know it triggers his violence, and that's all I want.

With our hands locked in war, we stumble into the aisle. One group of four chairs is on his left, another on our right. The force of holding me at bay causes veins to pop along his tattooed forearms. His jaw clenches. I glance at the pilot's door, but he's been instructed not to leave the cockpit. He's paid well, so he won't, even if he hears bloody murder.

My expression is blank as I show Wesley why I'm the ruthless killer, and he's not. I slap him. I taunt, and I play dirty. We end up falling together. His spectacles knock from his face, and I use his disorientation to straddle him. But he's faster—or more determined—than I gave him credit for. He rolls us, pushes off the ground, and returns to his feet. I slowly stand and face him.

"Why won't you show me your hands?"

"Let it go," he replies. "It's none of your business."

His eye twitches. His t-shirt clings to his chest as it heaves. His hair is messy. His lips are swollen and bruised. I love it. I've never been more turned on in my life. But then he goes and says something that rips away my control.

"You're so bloody smart, Thea. You're better than this."

Don't say nice things to me.

He shuffles closer to console me, but I rear my hand back to slap him, daring him to retaliate. To give me violence. To punish me for my sins. He catches my wrist and finally reveals his darkness.

In an explosion of madness and strength, he roughly grabs my arms and faces me away from him, toward the back of the seats. Then his hand bites my neck so hard that I'll bruise.

He shakes me to remind me of what I'm looking at—the seat ahead, custom-made to fit a private jet. The height of its leather backrest is short enough that I can fold over it and still keep my feet on the ground.

You'd love me to turn you over that seat.

He can't see my wild grin as he forces me forward.

Spank the impudence out of you.

The backrest hits my stomach. The pressure on my neck intensifies. I resist... push back...

Then fuck you in the arse like the unapologetic whore you claim to be.

I'm so amped, so full of adrenaline, that I can't hear properly. Wesley doesn't let up until I bend at the hips. My top half falls over the backrest, and my hands slap onto the cushioned seat for balance. But he doesn't stop controlling. Doesn't stop bending over with me, using his body to pin me hard.

Blood rushes to my head. The protection charm slips from my collar along with the silver crucifix. They land below my face and taunt me. One is a sign of my guilt, the other of my salvation, and I don't know which is which. I can't breathe from the pressure of the seat against my ribs. My skin is on fire.

A heavy ache blooms between my legs, and I silently pray Wesley will give me what I deserve—he'll purge my sins.

"Is this what you want?" His growl is strained, angry. He's not revealed how he'll do it, but I'll take it. I'll take anything.

"Yes," I whimper, squeezing my eyes shut. "Please."

He loops the seatbelt length around my wrists, circling twice to wrap tight. Deep grunts of frustration fill my ears as he secures the belt clasp into the buckle on the other side. He pulls the extra extension cord until it all tightens and flattens my hands against the seat. He gives a tug, testing my restraints.

I'm trapped. Face down. Ass in the air.

He returns to stand behind me but collects the protection charm, leaving the crucifix. He brushes my hair to the side and then positions the charm against the back of my neck. So he can see it. That understanding unravels something inside my chest. He trails his fingers down my spine, rasping over my t-shirt until he arrives at my yoga pants.

"Yes," I whisper, biting my lip. "Make it hurt."

He tugs off my pants so harshly that my skin burns. But then his attention moves to my panties and gentles. This isn't rough now. Decidedly *not* rough. My lungs seize, and my heart stops. *Why is he gentle?*

He traces along the lace hem with his finger, dipping beneath, tickling my bare skin just enough to make my eyes flutter.

"Rip them off." I wiggle my legs impatiently.

A deep chuckle behind me isn't what I want to hear. I don't want to be the object of his affection or amusement. I want pain. Punishment. Absolution. He kneads my buttocks and mumbles, "You have the most perfect arse I've ever seen, Thea. I should write sonnets about it. Pray to it."

I'm losing control of the situation.

"I'd rather you spank it," I growl.

"Mmm." He sounds like he's considering but then slides off my panties so I'm bare and exposed. Air tickles my wet folds, and I close my eyes, preparing for the pain I hope he'll give me. The release of my guilt, shame, and this unending feeling of being unmoored. But it doesn't come.

I sense him move. Hear the creak of his knees as he bends. He spreads my cheeks, exposing my most intimate parts. Hot breath shudders against my sensitive flesh and I whimper at the spark of heavy sensation. It's like he's savoring. He's taking too long, getting too familiar. I yank on my restraints.

"Please," I urge. "Give me what I deserve."

"With pleasure."

His tongue plunges deep into my pussy. I cry out as every nerve ending in my body seizes. Too many euphoric sensations flood my body. His tongue explores. Tastes. I buck against his mouth, unable to stop myself from reacting—from squirming at the sudden pleasure. He feasts on me with the voracity of a starving man. Like he'll never have another meal again. Just as he kissed me with his whole body, he devours me now.

He presses against my legs, buries his face in me, makes little sounds of satisfaction.

"Wesley," his name is a prayer on my lips. I don't know what I'm asking for any more.

He slides a finger along my slit, gliding and teasing everywhere until I pant and sweat. "*This* is what you deserve, Thea. Pleasure. Bliss, and I'll be the first man on this planet to give it to you."

"Cocky," I gasp.

"Confident."

Some kind of release starts through me. It's warm, heady, and turns me limp. I'm no longer floating adrift. I'm anchored to the words this man speaks, to the feelings he gives me. I've never had someone care about my pleasure. I know what's happening isn't real. It won't last. It can't.

"Tell me to stop," he demands, his voice rough as he teases with his fingers.

"Bastard," I pant, shaking my head.

This is just a distraction—for both of us. This is just because I pushed him. It won't happen again.

"Tell me you don't want this." He glides his finger into my entrance and pumps.

I clench around him and whimper.

"You know I'm fucking hot for you," I breathe. "I have been since..."

"Since the archives," he mutters. "Then why not..."

"Because..."

"Don't overthink it, Thea," he murmurs. "Let me..."

"Yes. God, yes."

He buries his face where I need it most. He brings me to climax in seconds. I shove my mouth against the seat to muffle my cry while he coos praise to my pussy as it pulses, and he licks and draws out the last of my desire until there's nothing left.

Let us question what others call sin...

I'm draped over the seat, exposed, and don't care. I don't care that I failed in my quest to use him. I don't care that I never received the pain. This catharsis is of a different kind. One I didn't know existed. It's making my eyes burn and my throat clog. All I want now is to feel him move inside me, to experience more of this euphoric connection between us.

But he doesn't make a sound. I don't know what he's doing behind me.

"Wes?"

No answer.

"Wes!"

I wriggle my hands and maneuver to unlock the belt clasp. I'm out of my restraints in seconds. When I whirl to face him, I find him kneeling. His lips glisten from my release. His cheeks are flushed. His specs crooked. A sheen of sweat covers his now naked torso, muscles perfectly defined with restrained lust. His hand is wrapped around his cock, half out of his unbuttoned jeans, the tip purple from the force of his grip. But he's not moving. He's squeezing himself as though he can stop the need.

Sultry lust drenches his expression. There is no pretending anymore. He's so far gone, so tortured by his feelings for me, that I know we'll never be able to fight them again.

I know this because I feel the same way.

I should leave him to finish alone, protect both our hearts.

But something urges me forward, drives my palms to his chest, and forces him onto his back. He helped me accept my feelings, and I want to return the favor. I tug his jeans off.

"Thea," he whispers, brows meeting in the middle as he straightens his spectacles. "You don't have to do this."

My gaze narrows as I straddle his hips and pause. "Are you trying to back out of this?"

Helplessness flares out of his eyes. His mouth opens. Shuts.

"No," I say. "You don't get to play the white knight, and you don't get any more excuses."

I fit the tip of his cock to my core and impale myself with a gasp of sweet pleasure-pain. But it's nothing compared to the distress on Wesley's face as he adjusts to the sensation of being inside me.

"Fuck, love. You're so tight," he rasps, squirming as I finish lowering until he fills me.

A groan of carnal satisfaction rumbles out of him. But when his lips finally curve on one side, in pure male bliss, I find myself smiling back.

How could I not? That joy is because of me. The urge to wring more from him makes me gyrate my hips. It's only small. A quivering. But his smile broadens until his beauty blinds me.

"More, love."

I'm stunned.

Frozen.

He's so fucking handsome that I can't think. Blond hair is

plastered to his face. Tattoos and muscle clash with the spectacles. He's a proper scholar and deviant rolled into one. But it's more than appearance. It's how his stubborn adoration for me bleeds from his every pore despite what he's been taught to believe by his peers.

He's not all good, but he's not all bad. He's somewhere between, and that thought is dangerous because it means we can make this real.

He grips my thighs and bites his bottom lip. Smoky eyes drag up my body, lingering on feminine places, leaving goosebumps in their wake. When his gaze returns to mine, there's a dark defiance I'm fast becoming addicted to. "More," he demands.

Balancing with a palm to his slick abdomen, I slide off his length and hammer home. Every thrust is soul-jarring. At some point, I don't know when, but I realize I'm not thinking about punishment, sin, or lies, and I'm simply enjoying the ride.

He rears up, braces my back with his hands, and kisses me all over. I'm a panting puddle of sensation and submission, a prisoner of his lips. I'm breaking inside, and I don't know what to do. He shifts my legs from straddling to sitting so they hook behind him. Then he wraps me in his arms and looks deeply into my eyes. "That death is not on your hands."

My throat tightens. The walls close in.

He tightens his embrace. "It's on the hands of that demon. The blame lies with them, as it lies with the institution that created you."

"But..."

He swallows my protest with a kiss. It's slow, passionate, and forgiving. We rock together.

Forehead to forehead.

Breath to breath.

Soul to soul.

I'm falling into him. He's catching me. There are no more words, just the absolution we find in each other. Gentle rocks. Tiny pleasures. A feather-light touch as he wipes hair from my slick face. The swipe of my thumb as I smooth sweat rolling from his temple. He kisses my neck and bites the charm. When heat gathers in my lower belly, I panic. This is so intense, so revealing, that I feel flayed open. Afraid.

"Wes..." I grip his hair.

"I've got you, love." He tightens his embrace.

The next time I thrust, I climax so hard I see Heaven. I lose control of my rhythm, my body. Wesley takes over, thrusting up, grinding into me. His movements become frantic, desperate. His face crumples. It's like he doesn't want this to end. But he can't stop it.

Sooner or later, everything ends.

He bites my shoulder and joins me over the edge. When it's over, he plants soft kisses on my collarbone. I toss my head back and blink at the fuselage ceiling, and... for the first time in my life, I *breathe*.

He says something. But I can't hear properly, and I think that orgasm made me deaf. The ringing is slowly dimming, but something is wrong.

Suddenly he's shoving me off him. I tumble to the carpet as he scrambles for his clothes.

"Wes?"

He takes his bag from his seat and gives my torso a pained look. "I'm so sorry."

I glance down. Blood smears are on my skin. He flashes his palms only long enough for me to glimpse raw wounds, then jogs to the bathroom and shuts himself inside.

I place my palm on the door.

"You okay? I can help dress the wounds." Let me help.

"I'm fine."

"Wes, it's just a bit of blood."

"I won't be long, and then the bathroom is all yours."

When he eventually comes out, he's freshly washed, smelling like soap, and back in a hoodie and jeans. White bandages wrap his palms like boxing tape. He walks back to his chair without meeting my eyes.

I have my shower, but when I get out, he's fast asleep.

TWENTY-THREE

THEA

I don't sleep well.

We're about an hour from landing, and all I've caught are a few restless naps on the long couch. Everything has changed, but nothing has. Wesley snores softly in his reclined seat. After our... situation... he fell right asleep. I guess the sex did him good. But not me. I mean, I thought it did. But my stomach is now twisted into all sorts of knots.

That death is not on your hands.

I believe him.

Which makes the cause of my turmoil unfamiliar. It's the beginning of love. It has to be. There's no one else to blame for being in this situation but my heart. It's not like the Rev told me to fuck Wesley to keep my enemy close. In fact, she said to learn from him. To trust him.

She's not like the other Reverend Mothers we've had. She's never asked any of us to use our bodies. She spent much of the first year of her occupancy just getting to know us and our missions. An urge to read Mary's manuscript has me pulling out my cell phone and scrolling through snapshots of her handwriting.

"You are a woman of ill repute, Mary. How can we trust your testimony?" Peter asked, eyeing me suspiciously.

"Because I have seen the truth, Peter. I have walked with the Savior and witnessed his love firsthand," I replied, my voice firm.

"But you were a prostitute, Mary. How can we believe that you have truly changed?" Peter persisted.

"I may have been accused a sinner, Peter, but that doesn't mean I can't be a witness to the truth. The Savior himself saw me for who I truly am—a beloved child of God—and he taught me that love and acceptance are the path to salvation."

I put my cell phone down.

This gospel will change the world. Whether Mary was a sinner was never confirmed, but she was believed to be one through lies told by men. The fact Wesley had half of this book in his supply trunk is wearing on me. It means the Vatican had it all along. Keeping this secret ensured their power.

But I don't know if I have the strength to add this to my fight. Not now when there are so many other battles to win first.

I try to sleep again, but Prue's face floats into my mind. The knots in my stomach tighten as I realize I've been up here, filling my time with wicked games and pleasure while she's been down there already in hell.

"We won't let anything happen to you." Prue smooths my hair. "You're one of us now. We protect our own."

I sit up so fast my head swims. My heart thumps uncontrollably in my chest. I feel too much for Wes, and now I've fucked everything up. Mary's message is clear. Love conquers all. But what if it's not love? What if it's a distraction? Wesley knew it. That's why he went all quiet afterward. As my eyes dart about the cabin, they land on a hardwired phone beside the couch.

Only one person I know can help me make sense of my thoughts. I grab the handset, hold it to my ear, and bite my lip. The dial tone is delayed, but it works. I punch in Mercy's number and recline on the couch to stare up. I twirl my finger around the spiraled cord while I wait for her to pick up.

It should be afternoon now... or evening. I'm losing track. With any luck, I've caught her at a good time—

"Mercy's pleasure palace, how may I direct your call?"

"Babe."

"Babe." The humor dies from her tone, and a lump forms in my throat.

"Is she...?"

"She's holding on. That bitch is tough. So tough."

"Has she woken up?" Does the demon still control her?

"No, but Tawny's been baking cookies and leaving them by the bed."

"Why?"

"She thinks it will remind Prue of us, to keep fighting."

"I guess she loved them. And burgers."

"She ate so much."

"All that running."

"She's also playing a recording of bird sounds."

Tears burn my eyes, but I don't let them fall as I say, "Remember when we were in Sydney, and she tried to scare us with all that fake Australia-is-dangerous bullshit?"

"Yeah," Mercy sighs. I hear the smile in her voice, and something rustles and then thuds like she's sitting down. "She forced me to carry a Vegemite sandwich in one of those little zip-lock bags and said it's so the killer koalas think I'm a local and won't attack. What were they called again?"

"Drop Bears."

We giggle as the memory strengthens. Drop Bears aren't even real, just some urban legend the locals tell for a bit of fun. Mercy and I were so naive back then. But it didn't stop Prue from keeping us frosty—it's the same thing Alice did when she attacked me in the alley. We torture and test each other in little ways because we want our sisters to remain alert and strong. To survive hell.

"I saw Alice," I say.

"Oh yeah? How's that big hunk of arrogant man meat she's boning?"

"The same. But they're good. They lent us the jet." I pause. "A demon attacked us."

Silence greets me as she takes it in.

"You good?" she finally asks.

"Fine."

"Wes?"

"He's..." I glance over at him. His spectacles have fallen off, and his brow is furrowed. He must be having a bad dream because his breathing is elevated, and his eyes move rapidly beneath the lids. That flushed look he had after sex is still there. Looks feverish. I want to go to him, to protect him from his nightmares.

I thought we shared something special, but he's clearly got other priorities than our hearts.

"Oh, it's like that, is it?" Mercy says after my stretch of silence.

I sigh. "I don't know what's wrong with me."

"You banged him yet?"

"Maybe."

Mercy gasps, but I hear the smile in her voice. "You slut. You totally did. So what's his dick look like?"

I roll my eyes. "Stop it."

"Is it like, long and thin or short and thick? Ooh, is it long and thick? Have you hit the jackpot?"

"Jesus, Mercy."

"Why else did you call me if it's not to share the details of this magnificent staff you're supposedly hunting for together?"

I laugh. She's right. If I wanted someone to mend my heart, I'd have called Tawny. "It's not that kind of staff, and you know it."

"Shame."

"I called because I..." Again, I lose my words as I look at him.

"You've caught feelings," she finishes with a sympathetic tone. "He showed interest in you from the start, and you ran the other way. I know you, missy. But don't worry, it happens to the best of us. Just look at Alice or Mary before her."

There it is.

The reason why I've been so confused and messed up.

"It doesn't matter if I have feelings for him," I say. "We're headed in different directions. Alice and Mary were the exceptions. Sinners don't fall in love."

My proclamation sounds empty after what I shared with Wesley, after reading Mary's gospel. She thinks everyone deserves love. Especially sinners.

Mercy's quiet, and I know she's contemplating her own emotions and thoughts. We've had this talk before. You don't leave the Sisterhood unless you're in a body bag. But things have changed.

We're not a secret organization anymore.

Demons are real.

Hell is real.

Enjoying the ride isn't as fun as it used to be. The ride

fucking sucks. I'd rather not go to hell at all. I'd rather spend life with loved ones.

I squeeze my eyes shut. "I don't know what to do, Mercy."

"That's an illegal statement. Dorothea always knows what to do."

Despite myself, I chuckle. They used to sing that to me when we were training. I was an arrogant know-it-all when I told other recruits how it should be done.

"Hey," Mercy coos, sensing my unrest. "What's holding you back? He wants you, right? I mean, even I could see that."

I shrug. "I think he's just as messed up as us. Shit happened to him when he was younger. Maybe he's afraid of commitment... or... he's hiding something, and it's affecting his decisions."

"What do you mean?"

"He puts on an act sometimes. One minute he's nice, and the next, he's an asshole. I know I'm pushing his buttons half the time but... I don't know."

Mercy chuckles. "Babe, men do that when trying to impress a girl they're intimidated by. He's probably inexperienced, nervous, and shy and has no idea how to handle the force of his attraction."

That sounds like how I've behaved toward him.

But Wesley's completely shut down.

I frown. "Or he's misdirecting, so I don't find out what he's hiding. He knew we stole the gospel. Said he was waiting for us to come clean, but something's not adding up. We shared something special, and now he's ignoring me. He's keeping distance between us..."

My voice trails off. I can't voice the thought.

Mercy says, "Only one way to find out. Is he sleeping right now?"

I glance over, and he's still frowning, but his eyes are closed, and his breathing is steady. "Yes."

"Look through his things. Check his messages."

"Mercy..."

"Babe, Prue would do it for us."

"You're right." This is more than my hurt feelings. This is a battle for Prue's soul. Thinking of our fallen sister makes me think about the heist. "Speaking of misdirection, what do you think if we stage a distraction for the heist? We can black out the city."

"I still think you should flash your tits, but you probably know better. I'll add it to the list."

"Good. Get some contacts lined up. I'll keep you posted." I hang up.

Blanking my mind, I tip-toe down the aisle to Wesley. Keeping one eye on his sleeping form, I gather his backpack and rifle through the contents. None of it means much to me —a few occult items I assume will help him with spells, a pack of white cards, half with arcane marks, the others waiting to be scribbled on. It's nothing I didn't expect.

I put the backpack down and look at Wes.

What are you hiding?

Some part of me wants to find a secret and protect my

heart. So I can prove he's not just confused and nervous about his feelings. Instead, he used me, and it's all misdirection, and I'm being played. He's done what Sinners do—seduce, manipulate, steal.

Betrayal is easier to swallow than love.

My eyes land on the cell phone between his thigh and the seat. I check that he's still asleep, then pluck the cell from its hiding spot. I hold it to his face and unlock it with facial recognition.

The first thing I see is a text conversation between him and Zeke. As I scroll through the history, a stone drops in my stomach. The text history goes back to a conversation he had months ago about discovering an old prophecy and how he believes it's linked to the new female cult of assassins called Sinners. How taking us down should be easy. I raise my brows at that, then promptly lower them when I read that Wes believes the relic is a one-time-use thing. He will use my talents to procure it, and then he'll steal it and take it home first. Zeke is sick with something terminal, and Wes will heal him before I can heal Prue.

He's going to betray us.

This is what I wanted, right?

I mean, I understand perfectly what he's going through. He wants to save his friend. He's putting Zeke before anyone else. I should admire his loyalty. But after I return to the couch, I lie there with my fingers thrumming on my chest, trying to ignore the sense of cold emptiness creeping into my body.

I know what this is, and I can't stop it. Every Sinner knows.

It's the numbness after you burn yourself. It's the long few seconds before your brain registers the pain. It's the calm that allows you to do whatever is necessary to protect yourself from further harm before paralyzing agony hits.

Sooner or later, everything ends.

"Are you going to tell me the plan?" I ask Thea as she leans against a souvenir shop across the street from the British Museum. She stares at the behemoth, columned building as though she didn't hear me.

We dodge the occasional person moving about their evening but always return to watching the museum in silence. This silence is how it's been between us since we disembarked from the jet. I know I've been a prick. We shared something honest, but then I saw my blood on her body, and somehow, I saw fresh welts from a flogging. I saw the pain I'll cause her.

She knows something is up. I see it in her eyes, and the coldness and shadows lurking there. There are more ghosts now, and I put them there. At least this way, my betrayal may sting less if she's already numb.

A spiked iron fence surrounds the museum. The gate is closed. Night has fallen, and security patrols the area.

We spent an hour wandering the museum before it closed. The old relic was there, but we barely stopped to look at it. Didn't want to look conspicuous. Thea spent most of her time in an exhibition about feminine power in the divine and the demonic. I followed her and read what she read. I don't know why she was so interested in it, except that much of the exhibition scripture revolved around Lilith and how she became the queen of hell.

I even saw an incantation bowl used to ward and trap Lilith. It's probably a fake, and I'm not even sure Lilith can be trapped—not the real Lilith, anyway. More accurate knowledge exists in the Vatican archives. What's out here in the real world is often misleading. It fits the narrative the ancient institution needs to remain in power. Or at least, it has for so long that no one knows what's real anymore.

But like the relic, sometimes authentic information survives out in the world.

My attention wanders. It's hard to rein in. My palms aren't the only things burning—a fever has stolen over me, worsening by the hour. I'm shivering despite the warmer summer air. Voices from my dreams haunt me. Some words were from Vepar... but I'm not sure if they're from the present or my past.

Yes... use her as she uses you. Take what you need. She'll never love you. She doesn't have the capacity. I'm your only friend.

But then I remembered Thea's voice breaking through my

sleep. I think she was reminiscing about Prue as she spoke on the phone. She sounded wistful.

It's all a cloud now. All I know is that I can't delay anymore, and I can't pull off a museum heist alone.

Finally, she says, "I'm going in through the roof."

"What do you mean *I'm*?"

Her eyes slide to me. "You'll slow me down—"

"You can't do it alone. Breaking into the national museum is bloody bonkers."

"The person who says it can't be done shouldn't interrupt the person about to do it."

"I don't know what wise person you're trying to quote, but you're not doing it yet," I point out.

"Oh," she says. "So the scholar doesn't know everything."

"Thea."

"You don't trust me?"

We share a look, and my breath hitches at the burning hatred in her eyes.

She knows...

She knows I'm planning to take the relic. She must see the awareness come over me because her hatred shifts to a challenge. It's the same look she had in her bathroom with the crows.

I can take care of myself.

My gaze dips to her neck, where the charm cord peeks from beneath her black, hooded Sinner's assassin uniform. A part of her still trusts me.

My endorphins battle with the fever, and I swoon.

Suddenly I'm done with this. I don't want to be enemies. I don't want to do this anymore. This will be my last few hours with her, and I can't die knowing she hates me.

I thought I could be Judas, but he ended up putting his head in a noose. Nobody won. Where's the sense in that?

My smile is a white flag... or at least, I think I smile. It might come out more like a baring of teeth. Sweat pops out on my upper lip. Dizziness overcomes me. I stagger forward. The pain in my palms wrenches a snarl from my lips. Thea doesn't flinch. A pinch at my stomach has me glancing down.

Thea's fist is there, her fingers wrapped around... my eyes snap back to her face.

"You stabbed me," I whisper.

"I saw the text messages, Wes, and I can't let you take the relic," she replies coldly. "Be thankful I didn't lace the blade with poison. Or hit any vital organs. You'll live."

"You stabbed me," I repeat, astonished.

I flop forward. Thea catches me like I'm drunk. A couple walking past stop and look.

"Come on, big guy," she says loudly. "Let's get you home to rest."

But she doesn't take me home. She pulls me into a dark shadowy spot further down the street where no one can see us. I slide to the floor, my back against a wall. Shock must have hit me. I don't feel anything. Not even cold. Not even pain in my gut. That's wrong. I should feel something.

But my only ache is when I think of what this will do to her. There's no demon in me. There's no rationalizing away this death. She'll pretend she doesn't feel the guilt, but then she will go to penance. She'll blame herself.

"It's okay," I say as she props my heavy limbs. "This isn't your fault."

She snorts and shoves my backpack to my side, away from anyone who might walk past. I sound arrogant. Bloody fuck, I can't even apologize properly.

"S'okay," I mumble, my eyelids falling. My limbs are made of lead. Maybe this is how it should have ended anyway. I didn't like lying to her, and I didn't like using her. It ate me up inside more than I care to admit. She's had enough of that in her life from other people, and she won't end up like me if she doesn't take the charm off.

I must have said that last part out loud because she stops after stepping away and turns back.

"What does the charm have to do with ending up like you?" she asks.

"Just going to rest my eyes," I mumble.

"Wes."

When I open my eyes again, she's right before me. This time, she's not the stone-cold assassin Sinner. She's the woman who tried to hate me but ended up making love to me. Her expression is fraught with worry. She takes my hand and unwraps the bandage. All it takes is a whiff of the putrid sores beneath, and she gags. She wraps my palms back up, wide eyes landing on mine.

"Wes, what's going on? What did this to you?"

"Vepar," I mumble. "She's been after me for years. I

touched her. Sores will be all over me tomorrow, and I'll die soon. So..." I chuckle softly. "You stabbed a dead man."

Confusion and panic battle in her eyes. "But you were still going to steal the staff from me. To save Zeke. Even when you knew your fate."

I know. A drunken, low-energy scoff slips out of me like it's obvious.

"Why?" she demands. "Why use it on him when this is happening to you?"

I shrug.

"But you're dying. You won't have made it back to the abbey!"

"I promised him." Again, I shrug. "People die around me, and they get sick. It's my fault."

"Fuck that." She snarls and flexes her fists. "You're Team Saint. You're meant to be the good ones!"

"We're not saints. Only Dom is."

"Then why..." She clutches the charm, and her eyes widen. "You gave me this. It protects the wearer from demonic influence. It was yours, wasn't it?"

All I can muster is my brows lifting and another shrug. Oblivion is a death march, thudding in my pulse, getting closer.

She's silent. I think I'm asleep... drifting... drowning... but then her voice calls me back like the angel I always thought she was.

"Wes."

"Mm."

"You said Vepar's been after you for a while. Would your hands be like that if you hadn't given me this charm?"

I close my eyes and shake my head.

"Fuck."

Pain filters in at my side. I glance down, half delirious, and see a dagger protruding from my skin. Blood dribbles from the hilt and oozes onto the ground. "You stabbed me," I murmur, remembering.

"Fuck, Wes." Thea gets down on her knee and tugs my face so I look into her dark, tragic eyes. "What the fuck? This is why you ignored me after we shared something so wonderful."

I'm sure the pain and regret bleed from my eyes because she flinches as I say, "I didn't want you to go down with me."

She barks a laugh, big eyes glistening. "I'm already down, Wes. I'm the lowest you can get."

"No." I shake my head. "Maybe I thought that at the start, but..." I pant. "We got it all wrong."

She's so beautiful. The light from a streetlamp casts a halo around her head. When I first saw her, I thought the devil picked her, but now I believe God sent her to save us all.

"*This* is beatific vision." I sigh, a rapturous smile on my face as I study her. "Looking at you chases the pain away. What you have—seeing the bad—that's not beatific. That's infernal."

"Always with your damned references. I suppose it should make me confident you're okay. You men and your intolerance to pain." She pats my face, trying to bring my focus back. Her voice is tight now, rough. "Wes, why do you think the staff can be only used once?"

"Prophecy," I mumble. "One body to save."

"How did you know about the prophecy? I thought we united the gospel."

"It was united before. We had a record of it." I breathe. Wince. Try to toughen up for her. "But the old scholars discredited it. They ripped it apart and sent half away."

"You found it," she notes.

I nod. "Tracked it down. Sent it to you."

"You were behind that last incoming shipment from our sister chapter in Spain."

"Yes."

"Your people don't know what you've done, do they? There were other messages in your phone—from someone asking for a status report. I never saw you mention the gospel."

"The Entity," I explain. "Doesn't matter. The relic will save only one person. I wanted it to be Zeke... but... you have a right to decide."

Her head hangs. Tears fall from her eyes like diamonds. They blend with my blood, pooling at my side. I should hate her, I suppose. She stabbed me. But I deserved it, and I was dead anyway. It was only a matter of time before Vepar caught up to me. I attract this shit in my life because I'm wrong inside. First, my parents, then my uncle, and somehow Zeke became ill. Shame washes over me.

"I don't want to be the cause of more welts on your body."

She jerks like she's shot. "What?"

"I know what they're from. They punish you for doing the things they ask of you."

Thea checks my stab wound, then grimly meets my eyes. "No, Wes. I punish myself."

Coldness fills me. I knew the flogging marks were her way of atoning for her sins—but I assumed it was part of the penance forced on them. But she hurt herself. Because of what they led her to believe. My face must be full of pity, or something, because she snaps, "Shut up."

Her confidence and sass wash away as she averts her gaze.

"Thea." Adrenaline surges in me from the need to protect her... from herself. "You're incredible. You know that, right? When I first arrived here—" I wince as I shuffle. "I thought you were made from the devil's own toy bag to tempt me, but now I think God made you. You're everything this world needs to get better... maybe not the stabbing me part, but..."

I lose the energy to finish.

Her following words come out like there's a bitter taste in her mouth. "I *stabbed* you, Wes."

"I'm dying anyway." I shake my head. "I lied to you. If one of us deserves to use that relic, it's you."

The Sinner hardness comes over her. Grit. She's got it in spades. She's the one—the chosen one. All of them are, and they will do what no one else can.

"You're not going to die," she says, catching the look in my eyes. "Suck it up until I get back. Don't remove the knife, do you understand? Pulling it out will only make it worse."

I don't understand. I'm blinking at her like a doe-eyed cow or something, half listening, half thinking about the pain turning numb at my side... half wondering if that's a good thing or bad.

"Don't pull it out," she repeats as she straightens. "I'll be back in no time."

I pity the fool who gets in her way. She's a force. Maybe that's why I don't resist when she removes the charm from her neck and places it over mine.

I want to ask where she's going... if she'll be back, but it's not just the numbing sensation at my side, the burn at my palms or the heavy sand filling my bones. There's a darkness creeping toward me from all around. It's hidden in the night sky and in the shadows between cracks on the walls. I imagine the scent of the ocean is in the air. Fish. Scales. Disease. Rot.

I imagine this is what happens when death comes for you. I don't want to reveal my fears, so I keep my face passive.

Thea watches me as she lifts a blood-red scarf to cover her nose and mouth. Next is the black hood. Strapped to her body are daggers, throwing stars, and other metal weapons glimmering in the moonlight. Embroidered on her chest is the Sinner symbol—a red cross.

"Tell me you're going to suck it up," she demands. "You're not as bad as you think."

"I'll be fine."

And then she's gone—melting into the shadows. Hope remains alive for a few minutes, and then my short-lived adrenaline wanes. I want to believe her, that she knows how to stab without causing permanent damage, that this pain is an over-reaction, but she never accounted for the condition I'm already in.

The smell of pestilence is everywhere.

Zeke. I owe him an explanation. I fumble in my pocket but don't know what to tell him. Instead of my phone, I pull out something hard and round. It's my uncle's watch. The cool, smooth surface is calming. I run my trembling thumb over the inscription.

Keep your hands working together. Keep the cracks closed.

I used to pore over those words in the Vatican archives. Sometimes I thought, maybe, he meant my actual bodily hands. But I kept coming back to the watch. To the hour and the minute hand. Different but the same.

It reminds me of the prophecy. There was a line about cracks. What was it? *Cracks splitting the brave.* And then I think about the exhibition Thea was enthralled with—how she lingered on Lilith's mark on her shoulder.

I don't think it was a sign of intended possession. I think Lilith was trying to claim Thea as a soldier in her army.

My eyes roll down to the pocket watch in my blood-stained hand. My uncle had also been researching Lilith—a woman who wanted revenge against Adam. Who had a vendetta against men.

My uncle's greatest regret was when his wife left him. He always said it was his stubborn pride that sent her away. I remember feeling so sorry for him. He seemed lonely, despite having me in his life, despite buying pets to fill the void. But he also seemed to be so powerless to change it. To ask for forgiveness.

A rotten smell makes me gag, and I think it's me. Vepar spreads pestilence. Her power in this realm is getting stronger, which means the first harbinger of the apocalypse might already be here too. I thought the demon inside Prue was just another minion, but what if... what if it's not. What if it's Pestilence itself?

TWENTY-FIVE

THEA

My training as a killer allows me to shove all the confusion swirling in my heart and put it in a box. Right now, I need to get that staff.

Stabbing Wesley was a mistake. I made sure to keep away from his vital organs, but I hadn't planned on him dealing with whatever the fuck Vepar had done to him.

Fucking stupid name for a demon. When I see it again, I'm going to destroy it.

A sense of foreboding follows me as I scale the fence to the museum. Shipping containers from renovation construction give me the perfect cover as I wait and look at my smartwatch. Two more minutes should do it.

While we scoped out the place today, I texted the girls to see what else they'd come up with as a strategy for the heist. Mercy's suggestion of flashing my tits had evolved into seducing the guards. Leila wanted me to walk in guns blazing.

—smash and grab style. Raven said to trust my instinct, which I, in turn, said wasn't very practical, so she suggested poisoning them through the ventilation system. Tawny mumbled something about maybe doing it tomorrow after a good sleep but then said, "You got this."

Ultimately, we went for my plan of a city-wide power outage, so it doesn't look like the museum is targeted. We have a network of contractors and mercenaries we hire, and a fire at the local power station is the perfect job for them. Money has already exchanged hands—or rather, untraceable bank accounts, and all I have to do now is wait.

Easier said than done when Wes is lying in an alley not far away, potentially bleeding to death because I had to go full assassin on him. I mean, why couldn't I have just tied him up or some shit? He can't beat me in a fight. When he overpowered me on the plane, I intended it to happen. I let him.

So why was I even worried that he would overpower me now?

I know why, but I refuse to acknowledge it.

Not until I return to him with the staff.

Museum and street lights go out. A message on my smartwatch confirms the job at the power station is done. I scale the wall closest to me until I'm on the roof, then pad across to the glass court. It was meant to be a conservatory once upon a time, but now it gives me the most accessible opportunity to get inside through its domed glass roof. I pull a glass cutter from my backpack, apply the suction cup, and cut along one of the panes held together by a steel web.

Once the piece of glass pops out, I realize how small the space is to squeeze through. I guess this is where being a woman comes in handy, and another reason why the Hildegard Sisterhood was created generations ago. Women are often underestimated because of our soft bodies and strong emotions. But if we don't listen to the ones underestimating, and we keep asking questions, then we hold power in our grasp.

Always question.

I learned that during training with the *onna-bugeisha* in Japan. They originated from the female samurai but now exist in secret like us. Despite specializing in defensive martial arts, they are witty and sharp. They use the advantage of being overlooked. Once, my sensei had me spend an entire day running up the temple steps to fill a bucket with water using only a teaspoon. If I drank from the supply, the exercise would only take longer. So I went thirsty. When night came, and I finally filled the bucket, she kicked it, so it spilled down the steps.

"Why?" I exclaimed. "Why did you make me do that only to spill it?"

She shrugged. "I was bored. Perhaps you should have asked this question at the start, yes?"

When I didn't respond, she rapped me over the head and said, "Best defense is to always question."

Wes is suffering because I should have kept asking questions until I found the right answers.

Exhaling, I push the destructive thoughts away. They keep

creeping back in. No one has affected me like this before. It's borderline obsessive, and it's also cracking the cage around my heart open and making me feel things I've only dreamed of as a little girl.

I tie a rope around my waist and secure the end to the broken steel frame of the support triangle. I squeeze myself through and lower to a tall, wooden totem pole in the courtyard.

After detaching from the rope, I leave it dangling for my escape and shimmy down the rest of the pole. It takes a matter of seconds, but I shouldn't dilly-dally. A backup generator will likely be up and running soon, meaning mainstream security measures will come online. The alarm might also be battery-operated, and if that's the case, there will be casualties regardless of my plan.

I'd have scoped the place out properly if I had more time.

I hasten my steps and make a beeline for the room that holds the staff. As it did this morning, the relic calls to me. I didn't tell Wes about this sensation, but the relic called my name without speaking. Raven says she gets vibes from objects or mystical energy readings. When I exited the museum, it was like I had left a part of my soul inside. Like it's also a part of me that needs to come home.

A buzzing, excited energy rolls over my skin when I reach the room holding Byzantine relics. I shiver at the force. It's almost like the staff is rejoicing at my proximity. And it's stronger than before. This isn't my imagination the second time. I'm linked on an intrinsic level to this long wooden rod carved with ancient glyphs.

This is fate.

My blood hums with the need to claim it. With trembling fingers, I use the glass cutter on the protective casing. Pulling the suction cup and removing the cutout, I pause and listen for an alarm.

Blood roars in my ears, but no footsteps thud toward me. No whining siren or shouts to freeze. Could I be so lucky? Have I tripped some kind of silent alarm, or is the second diversion we planned working? The same contacts who set fire to the local power station were also paid to light a garbage bin at the opposite end of the museum yard. With a grin, I spear my hand through the hole in the cabinet and claim the staff.

When my fingers wrap around the wood, a rush of pure energy rolls through me, and my vision goes white. The only word to describe the feeling is holy. I feel loved, pure, whole, perfect, and happy. Rapturous. Nothing is wrong, and everything is right.

Then the alarm sounds, and I crash to earth.

Realty hits me with a shock, and I let go of the staff. What the fuck was that? That energy—that light. It was how I felt reuniting the two halves of Mary's gospel.

Something has changed in me again, and I don't have time to work out what. The alarm blares and whines through the room. I yank the staff through the casing. It's long—about five feet. I run toward the staircase leading back to the glass court.

Two security guards are coming up the steps. They see me

and reach for their Tasers, but I don't hesitate. I leap down and swing the staff like I'm Harley Quinn with her baseball bat.

I'm airborne.

Flying.

I knock the first in the head, land, then pirouette, and catch the second in the same motion. The wooden bo-staff returns to my side, and I pause, checking on every sense I own for immediate danger.

Nothing.

The guards are unconscious. I breathe again and continue down the steps. I'm already rounding the corner into the glass court when I have a surreal moment of thinking the staff didn't approve of me using it that way. It's for healing, not damaging.

"Wrong gal to call out to then," I mumble as I tuck it under my arm and climb up the totem pole. When I climb onto the roof, the smell of fire accelerant assaults my nose. Panicked shouts filter up from another side of the museum. I hope it means the guards are putting out that trash can fire.

I catch my breath and check my surroundings before discarding the rope—I don't have time to repack—and then I find the darkest point of the roof to scale down the columns. I pause to listen. Between the guards shouting, I hear the ding of a bell and another voice. It's odd and familiar—harsh, raspy, an outcry.

When I get to the street, I face the location of the new voice. Down on another corner, near a deli of some sort, a lone figure wears a signboard over their chest. I squint to read the words scrawled in chalk. *There is no sin—only you.*

The person turns my way. A young female... barely a woman. She dings her bell and shouts between wet coughs, "Only you! Only you!"

It can't be the same person I saw back home. Surely not.

The staff warms my hand, reminding me of my purpose. By the time I jog to Wes, I feel invincible again. This thing I'm carrying is like a nuclear weapon—napalm courses through my veins.

I round the corner of the alley where I stashed Wes but skid to a halt when I see the silhouette of a demon bent over him. Wes isn't even fighting. He's not moving. Panic grips my lungs, squeezes my heart, and stops time.

The archangel's staff heats in my hand, reminding me of my power.

Get to Wes.

Save him.

Heal him.

But first... destroy that fucking demon.

I move so fast, Vepar doesn't hear me coming. It's not until the staff is inches from her pustuled head that she turns, balks at the glowing relic, and throws her hands up to shield herself. Unseen energy hits me, throwing me backward. The demon somehow attacked me with air. Pain lashes my face— it's like I've belly-flopped into a pool, but there's nothing before me. I land on my back, winded and blinking at the stars.

Get up.

I roll to my feet and crouch in an attack pose. Vepar steps into the streetlamp's light, and I want to vomit at the disease and rot falling off her. She was disgusting to begin with, but now... pure horror. Water and puss slick her body like oil. The sickly smell is thick and suffocating. A shudder rolls through me.

My gaze flicks to Wes. He's breathing—his hand moves on his chest. His eyes are closed but pained.

"Give him to me," the demon hisses. "You don't want him anyway. He slows you down, remember?"

My upper lip curls at the echo of my words. It's even the same tone I used. Hearing them from someone else makes them so much worse. I see a side of myself I never wanted to confront, making me sick and hot with shame.

But... maybe... maybe I needed to hear it.

There is no sin... only you.

Maybe it's time to take responsibility for my actions and words. Blaming the Sisterhood for who I am is only half of it. The rest of it is me. It's the guilt I lay at my own feet. It's the walls I build around my heart. It's the voice in my dreams telling me I'm going to hell because what they say is true—I'm worthless, good for nothing, a whore, unlovable.

I'm my worst enemy.

I straighten as a line from the prophecy hits home—the enemy is within. To sin is human. To forgive is divine. Or some shit like that. We all make mistakes. We shouldn't beat ourselves up about it. But to forgive... that's where the real power lies. No one has more power to forgive me than myself.

It releases me from my chains.

The staff thrums in my hand as though it agrees.

"He's mine," I say to the demon, pointing at Wes with the staff. "If you want him, you'll have to go through me."

"That can be arranged," she laughs. It comes out a gurgle. Like water lives in her throat. "I went through his uncle, after all. Oh, poor little lonely uncle. He thought he was saving his nephew. Thought he could bargain with me because I killed the boy's parents. But it was always about the boy."

Wes's pale and clammy face turns hard as he takes in the demon's words. Then hard determination flashes in his eyes. His hands move secretly, and I know he's preparing to use one of his spells. If I keep the demon busy, I'll give him time. I might even kill it first.

I stroll forward and ask, "Why him?"

Vepar laughs again. "Because he's the first to mend the cracks. And she likes her cracks. She wants them *big*. She wants them on one side and us on another. She wants the crack so big it's a gaping chasm no one can cross. If we stop the first, then we stop them all."

"The cracks..." I cant my head. There goes that term again. It was in the gospel. It's on Wes's watch. "There's more, isn't there? More to why you want him stopped?"

Vepar's eyes narrow. She hesitates. But then spits and hisses angrily, pointing at him while looking at me. "He resurrected Mary's gospel, and we wanted it dead. Out of the Bible. Out of the world."

"Dead," I say. "Where women can remain in the dark.

Where conflict can grow. Where there is no place for love in the world."

"And the cracks get bigger and bigger."

"You've manipulated the church all this time," I gasp. "Wars have been waged in the name of the Bible. Murders. Rapes. Divisions. Sin!"

"I know." She cackles uncontrollably. "Even from you."

Maggots start popping from the demon's sores, falling to morph into the same grotesque fish creatures I fought before. Their gaping mouths appear to struggle for air, but then I glimpse the fangs inside. The first one slithers up to me on tadpole legs. It almost looks sad. As I swing the staff, I feel bad for it—it probably didn't ask to be a minion of evil. I feel compassion as the staff connects. But it's gone by the time the minion flies across the street and lands on the dirt beneath a council tree. Another has latched onto my boot with its fangs —foul thing.

When I knock it with the staff, I remember what Asmodeus said. *Think healing thoughts.* But what if there's no soul to heal?

So I think about smiting evil, protecting the innocent, and healing the world. The relic lights up, approving of my mission. The minion bursts into water.

I blink and look at the staff. Water drips from my face. The pure, angelic power is enough to obliterate the minor demons.

More come at me, snapping their fishy fangs. One by one, I strike them, keeping the same thoughts at the forefront of my mind. Soon, I don't think. I do. The relic is an extension of me. Balls of water pop everywhere. Maybe I'm having too much fun, maybe I assumed the demon was possessing a human body, but I dismiss the massive mermaid tail flinging through the air toward me.

It knocks the wind out of me. I fling to the side. Wheeze. When I land, the staff skates from my hand. The warmth and invincible feeling vanishes. Everything is cold, wet, and miserable—the air stinks. And a flesh and blood demon covered in sores is coming at me.

My heavy eyes barely open to see Vepar cut Thea down with her tail. She shouldn't be able to do that. She possesses a human... doesn't she?

I thought maybe I saw the true demonic form because I'm close to death. The veil is thinner, and I see the true face of hell. But perhaps this is real. Perhaps the cracks in the gates of hell are big enough for Vepar to come through completely.

I rack my brain to think of what changed between now and the last time, and when I land on Thea stabbing me—her loss of trust—everything hits at once.

Vepar tried to kill me when I was young. My mother was pregnant with me at the time of the car accident, but I survived. Vepar wanted *me* dead. Me. Why?

Is it just about the gospel, or is it about Thea and me? Is this all connected?

My eyes drift to Thea as she climbs back to her feet. She

reaches for the staff, but the demon hits her again with its tail and knocks her into a wall. The sound of air leaving her lungs is heart-wrenching. Her eyes search me out, but the demon is there, hissing in her face, "He can't save you. He only used you to get what he wanted. Everything you ever shared is a lie."

My eyes burn. I shake my head.

"She's lying," I mouth.

Doubt flickers in Thea's eyes as she opens to the influence. Anger sparks in my soul. This nasty thing has always been in my ear, trying to keep me from finding someone to love, telling me I'm wrong, and that's why this shit happens to me. It's now telling her the same thing.

Keep the hands working together.

Now I know what it means. I know why Vepar tried to kill me, and it has to do with her master—Lilith, the perpetual hater of men. Lilith doesn't want Thea and me to work together. She doesn't want us to love each other. She wants discord between the sexes, to divide the world.

We are the hands. One big and one small, but both equally important in the function of the watch. Keeping them working together will stop the cracks. Keeping love in the world will save it.

When Thea stabbed me, she widened the divide between us, allowing Vepar to step into our realm and will probably let Pestilence do the same.

I have to prove to Thea that we're on the same side.

She wipes blood from her lips with the back of her hand and glares at the demon. Even without the holy light shining through her, she's a goddess. I should have confided in her from the start.

My hands are too damaged to use the arcane spells. Sores cover my tattoos everywhere, blocking more spells. I keep trying to activate them but nothing works. Parts of my abdomen are clear—I keep searching until I find a complete tattoo of a spell I would never have thought to use, but it might distract Vepar so Thea can reclaim her relic. It's still lying in a puddle out of her reach.

Blood.

I need blood for this spell to work. Fortunately, I have a dagger protruding from my stomach; all I need to do is pull it out.

Don't pull it out. You'll only make it worse.

Worth it.

She's worth it.

I wrap my bandaged and agonized hands around the hilt and grit my teeth. I fill my lungs with air a final time. I pull the dagger—pain blinds me. A gurgled grunt leaves my lips. Blood wells anew.

"Wes!" Thea shouts. She runs toward me, but Vepar seizes her lapse in concentration. The slithering tail wraps around Thea's torso like a serpent.

Thea's eyes widen as the tail tightens, crushing her.

"This is for you, Thea," I rasp as I wipe the blood over the arcane tattoo. "Don't listen to her. She's keeping us apart." I pant. "S'how Lilith sows chaos. S'how she's paving the way—"

My vision darkens. "Way for the antichrist. How... cracks... gates... hell..."

Thea knows this is my last stand. Her eyes bulge as the tail tightens. Her face turns purple, dark, and bruised, but defiance fortifies her expression.

I finish smearing blood over my tattoo. I locate Vepar and think of when I bumped into Thea in the hallway after her swim. Of how she smiled at me. I think of her hand on mine as she asked about my past—of her apology for my pain. I think of that wistful tone in her voice when she reminisced about Prue on the plane, and I pray that one day, she'll sound the same when remembering me.

Then I mumble the words to activate the spell. I chant until every ounce of water around me turns into red wine. Puddles on the ground go dark—burgundy water bubbles from the grates. Merlot falls from the sky. Every drop of fluid on Vepar is dark and viscous. It's almost like blood.

It burns her—she hisses and recoils and probably dehydrates. Her tail loosens, and Thea fights her way out, coughing and catching her breath. But she crawls to me, not the demon.

"Kill it," I rasp. "Use the staff."

Her wild eyes search around. She pulls the staff from a wine puddle but continues crawling toward me. Fierce determination is in her eyes. That familiar defiance flashes. But she's not using it against me this time. She's using it against forces keeping us apart.

Because she cares.

Because she'll smile when remembering me.

"Thea, there's no time. Save yourself," I chatter. I'm no longer numb. I'm cold. Weak. Can't even hold my wound. Can't stop the bleeding.

On her knees, she lifts my fallen shirt and presses her staff to my stab wound. Bright light fills it, then her, and then the street we're in. Darkness is obliterated. Hot energy scolds me where I'm touched. It burns. An inferno in my veins. I try to hold it in, to be brave, but end up bellowing. Her hair blows up from the force but doesn't break her concentration.

And then I feel myself heal. My flesh itches and knits together. The sores on my body melt away. Blood renews in my veins like it springs from an internal well. I inhale sharply, taking in air that is now fresh and clean. Weakness evaporates from my limbs. Everything blurred is now laser-sharp. I swipe my bloody stomach. The wound is closed. I pull the bandages from my hands—my old burn scar is gone.

I'm lost for words. I'm...

Her eyes glimmer as she meets my gaze and whispers, "Don't overthink it, Wes."

A shaky laugh rocks out of me.

But she used the staff on me. Not Zeke. Not Prue. Her palm lands on my cheek, and I push into it, crumpling my face.

"No," she says.

"You don't know what I was going to say."

"Yes, I do. You don't think you're worth it. For whatever reason, you've always put other people's needs before your own. This was my choice, Wes, and I chose you."

I let that sink in.

I let her words wrap tendrils of warmth around my heart as I recall two more words she shouted at Vepar when she arrived. *He's mine.*

I cover her hand and say with conviction, "You're mine too, love."

Her lips curve on one side. "You don't have a choice. You got me now."

She straightens and offers me her hand. I take it, happy for the lift. When we're both on our feet, she gives me this look that says she's worried she'll offend me with what's next.

"What?" I prompt.

"The staff isn't a one-hit-wonder."

"It's not?" My mind reels at the potential. "But..."

Why didn't she tell me?

"Didn't want you to think I wouldn't pick you," she mumbles, a bashful blush staining her cheeks. "That I didn't choose you because I did, and I would put you first every time."

I see the truth in her eyes. "I know."

"Also didn't want you to feel bad that a girl outsmarted you."

My eyes crinkle. "I'm sure I can manage."

"And you, dumbass, you pulled the dagger out." She scowls and raises her brows.

"Because I chose you, too." I touch her cheek. "I would do it again."

The writhing demon draws our attention. Wine still spills from its mouth.

"Now, I'm not ungrateful or anything," she says to me as she strolls toward the demon. "But is that wine?"

"Yeah." I scratch my head. "It was the first spell I learned. A tester, if you will. Didn't want to start practicing sorcery with something potentially dangerous."

"Guess I know what I want for Christmas," she jokes.

Every time water gushes from Vepar's scales, it darkens to wine. But it's not killing her. We circle the demon, studying her as she gapes and gasps for air—or water. I'm not sure. Her eyes roll and glare at us as she tries to choke out words.

"The spell won't last," I say.

Thea brandishes the staff like she was born with it. "Time to send this bitch back to hell then... or who knows, maybe she'll turn into a ball of water like her minions."

"Wait." I hold up my hand and crouch before the demon. "I want to speak with her first."

"In that case." Thea pushes the tip of the angelic staff onto the demon's forehead.

Vepar's eyes widen to show the whites.

"Vepar," I say. "Is Pestilence inside Prudence?"

Her eyes dart from me to Thea. Thea picks up what I'm doing and moves the staff to Vepar's neck. She applies pressure until the demon chokes, and pus oozes from the sores there— my nose wrinkles. I have no idea how Thea is unaffected by that, but she's a warrior goddess—ready to battle, obliterate, and win.

"Answer him," Thea presses before easing off. "Or I make this slow and painful for you."

"Yes," Vepar blurts. "Yes, it is she."

"She?" I share a look with Thea. "I thought the horseman was male."

Vepar laughs a hissing laugh. "Yes, but we all know history is written by the man wielding the pen. Who better to create the divide? Who better to grow the cracks."

"What's Pestilence's true name?" I ask.

Vepar's laughter dies, and she shakes her head. "I don't know."

"I think you do."

"Why do we need the name?" Thea asks me quietly. "I have the staff."

"It might not be enough to exorcise the demon," I explain. "Asmodeus told us the staff would heal the body. He said nothing about it removing the demonic spirit. Better not to take our chances."

"Good point," she replies, grateful eyes on me.

"Asmodeus," Vepar hisses. "Fucking cunt of a farce of a whore-loving—even from his prison he—"

She chokes when Thea presses the staff, but pink water comes out of her mouth instead of wine. The spell is almost over, and we're out of time.

Thea repeats, "What's Pestilence's true name?"

When the demon starts begging, we know she *really* doesn't want to tell us, but the staff heats in Thea's hands. It sizzles the demon's flesh until she spits out, "Loimós! Her name is Loimós Leviathan."

"Stand back," Thea warns me. Then she says to Vepar, "This is for Wes and for the ruin you made of his life." The staff shines bright. The demon screeches and bucks. Her tail thrashes. Thea holds steady and shouts, "If you somehow survive this, tell Lilith we're coming for her."

The staff sinks through the demon's throat. Cracks filled with light grow over its body until they widen and burst. I shield my eyes from the light. When it's gone, there's nothing left of Vepar but scales and ash floating in wine.

"I guess she didn't survive." Thea kicks the sludge.

A rustle of leaves snaps our attention to a council tree across the street. My heart rate spikes. *More demons?* But there's nothing there. Just darkness.

Sirens blare. Police and other emergency services are on the way to the museum. With the racket we just made and the light, it won't be long until someone comes this way and finds blood... and wine.

Time to go. Thea collects her fallen backpack. She hoists it on while I find mine, and then we make our way to our rented car a few streets away. It's not until we're both strapped in and driving toward the airport that it all hits me.

We're alive. We have the relic. It works.

Thea's cell phone pings. She glances to where she's stashed it in the console, but she's driving.

"Can you check the message?" she asks, then shifts her eyes back to the road.

She trusts me.

I read it.

"Bugger," I murmur. "The airport is on lockdown because of the power outage. It went that far."

"Shit."

I scroll. "The pilot says they'll be clear tomorrow morning, but congestion will delay takeoff until maybe midday."

Thea makes a sudden turn and heads south.

"Where are you going?" I ask.

"We have a safe house across the Thames. It's probably better to lie low until the airport is functional again. Just in case the authorities decide to search commercial planes for the stolen artifact. I don't think they'll jump to this conclusion yet, but we should get off the streets."

She's right. And I know Zeke will survive the extra wait... but will Prue?

Wesley's eyes are wide as he takes in our location. I bring the car to a stop at the front of the skinny townhouse.

"I thought you said the Sisterhood had no money." He stares up at the tall historical facade.

"We don't. This has been in the Hildegard Sisterhood for generations. If it's worth money now, we can't access it. We need our ties off bank records."

"So you can't even use it for equity."

"Nope. But we can use it for other shit." I open the car door and enter the code on the gate's security box. There's only room for one car inside, but that's all we need. I drive the car inside the gate and straight into the open garage. The door shuts on its own.

Before I go anywhere or do anything, I have to call the Rev. This delay might be costly to Prue's health, and I'll never

THE SINNER AND THE SCHOLAR

forgive myself if we fucked up with that power outage. It was my idea, after all, and I would have planned an appropriate risk analysis if I'd been less distracted.

After two rings, she picks up.

"Thea, you have news?"

Wesley watches me as I reach for the staff. The length stretched into the back seat and almost hit the roof. It wants to be close, and after what it did to Vepar, I'm okay with that.

"I have the relic." I glance at Wes and realize he should be a part of this conversation. If Lilith is trying to divide us, then we need to do the opposite. I have no more doubts that this danger is coming.

I put her on speakerphone and say, "Wes is here with me."

"Evening, Reverend Mother," Wes greets.

"Mr. Wesley." The Rev's sigh of relief is audible. "I'm sensing a but from you, Thea."

"The power outage went so far as to hit the airport, making it impossible for us to leave the country. The pilot said we should be okay in the morning, but there might be a backlog of planes trying to get out. We could drive to another airport and take our chances on a regular flight, but it will be filled with passengers doing the same, and the staff will be difficult to hide. Even in a container or wrapped up, it's obviously long. Best case scenario, we'll be home in under forty-eight hours. Worst case, the authorities are chasing us down... but I'll still find a way to get home."

The Rev exhales. "Okay. We'll keep doing what we're doing until you arrive."

"The relic works, Rev." I try to suppress my excitement but fail miserably.

"It works?" she whispers.

"It goddamn works!" I exclaim.

"Language, Thea."

"Sorry. But yeah, so, get this... Wesley was bleeding out from when I stabbed him, and then I healed him completely—even the old scars. Not only that but the demon we fought—"

"Wait. Hold that thought." Swishing and then a clicking sound. "You're on speaker now. The girls are here. Please repeat that last bit."

"The staff healed Wesley's stab wound, and it healed everything the demon did to him, too—it even healed an old scar on his palm. I think his tattoos might need to be reworked too."

"Did you say you stabbed Wes?" The Rev asks.

"I'm fine." He waves as if they can see him. "We kissed and made up."

Wes realizes what he's said and blushes. I give him a crooked smile, and his bashfulness deepens.

"But you have the staff," the Rev says.

"Yeah, we got it. We're at the safe house, and I'll think of a way to wrap it before we get on the jet."

"There's something else you should know," Wesley says, adjusting his specs. "Thea was able to extract the true name of the demon inside Prue."

Rapid-fire Italian can be heard in the distance.

"Dom," Wes explains to me.

We wait for more, and then the Saint's deep voice comes on the line. "I'm ready. *Parlare*."

"The name is Loimós Leviathan," Wes says. "I think it's Pestilence."

"*Sì*."

"Pestilence." Raven's husky voice is unmistakable through the phone. "You mean the horseman?"

I share a look with Wes, and he nods. Then between the two of us, we relay what we know about the prophecy and Lilith's ultimate goal.

"She's trying to bring on the apocalypse," I finish.

Silence answers me. It's a lot to take in.

"Anything else?" the Rev finally asks.

"She's doing it by growing the divide between women and men. She's sowing distrust and hate. Creating enemies where there should be lovers." I lift my eyes to the heavens at the magnitude of this plan. "Vepar admitted Mary's gospel was a long-kept secret for this very reason. If the world believed Mary was a whore instead of Jesus' greatest confidant, perhaps even his wife, then equality between the sexes never existed."

"I see."

I hear her brain ticking over. She knows this is going to put the Sisterhood in jeopardy.

"How is Prue?" I ask.

"She's not good. The induced coma seems to be losing efficacy. Whatever is inside her is gaining strength. The drugs won't hold it at bay. But with this name, the Saint seems to think Father Angelotti will have more power over it. If it breaks through the coma, we might be able to hold it off from consuming her until you get here. Get some rest while you can. We'll talk more when you get home."

Home.

The word is a beacon to me. Suddenly there's no other place I want to be.

"We'll see you soon." I cut the call.

Now it's just Wesley and me in the dark cabin of the car. He reaches across our seats and tucks hair behind my ear. It reminds me of when we met on the steps of the abbey, and my eyes fill with water.

"Come on, love," he murmurs. "Let's get inside and do as the chief ordered."

Unable to form words over the lump in my sore throat, I nod. I'm not an emotional person. I don't know why I feel so overwhelmed, but know it has something to do with having someone to lean on.

I take Wes inside the building and switch on the lights. But they don't work.

"Citywide power outage," I mumble.

The safe house is three floors high, but it entered our care in the eighteen hundreds and needs renovation.

The staff glows in my hand, and I smile. "I think it's trying to help."

"The relic?"

"Yeah, it seems to have a bit of a personality."

"Fascinating." He stares at it. "May I?"

I hesitate but hand it over. The instant he touches it, the light dims, and it looks like a regular wooden stick.

"I don't think it likes me," he jokes and hands it back. But before I accept it, I think we better test it.

"Can you feel anything weird about it?"

"It potentially gave me a splinter."

I chuckle. "I mean, like mystical energy?"

He shakes his head and hands it back. "It's not meant for me. You're the special one."

I scoff. "I'm just the one who connected with it first."

"No, Thea." His voice turns soft, his eyes serious as he continues. "You were meant to have it. I see that now. Everything in that gospel points to you five women. I think a part of me always knew, so I sent the other half to you instead of trying to find the relics myself." His gaze turns distant. "Even my uncle knew our teams had to work together."

We stare at each other in the gloom. I'm not even looking at the blood, wine, and mess on our clothes. I'm just looking at him. His perfect honey eyes, his messy hair, and his lips.

"We should probably look over the prophecy," I mumble. "Now that we both know and compare notes."

"Probably," he agrees, although his gaze drops to my lips. "We should clean up."

"I should give you the tour."

"Yeah."

Neither of us moves. We're frozen to the floorboards, staring at each other in the moonlight filtering through an old window. And then we're both dropping our bags, the staff, and rushing to meet in the middle. He holds my head between his hands. I fist his shirt, tugging him down to me. Our lips meet in a bruising kiss. I could do this forever. Taste him. Feel his warmth. Thank God he's alive. And then his hand slides down to my arm, and I hiss as he brushes a wound.

He breaks away with wide eyes.

"You're injured." He checks me over, notes all the scrapes and bruises, and berates himself. "Of course, you're injured. You fought multiple foes. How stupid and bloody selfish of me. We should get you fixed up right now."

He goes to leave, presumably to find a first aid kit, but I tug him back and kiss him again. His tongue swipes in, and gives me a passionate lick, but then he groans in frustration.

"Thea... you're hurt."

"All I need is this," I murmur.

"Can you heal yourself with the relic?"

"I'll be fine." I chase his mouth with my lips.

"Thea, you're injured."

A scowl forms on my face. I step away so I can inspect myself. He's right. Now that I see the wounds, I feel them more acutely. My ribs are bruised from when the demon crushed me with her tail. My knee bleeds from an open graze, and my arm has a shallow slice.

"I'll try the relic," I concede.

The staff glows and acknowledges me as its owner, but it doesn't heal me.

"That's not good," I mumble, fearing the worst. Maybe it's a one-time thing, after all.

"Perhaps it will work on everybody else but one..." His voice trails off. "Perhaps we misinterpreted the translation. It's not one body that can be healed but one that cannot."

"I'll heal the normal way. I'm used to it."

"No," he returns, his brows puckering. "Not the normal way. I'll take care of you. Show me where the shower and first aid kit are. We'll get you cleaned, and then I'll patch you up."

It's on the tip of my tongue to turn him away and take care of myself, but this is what I fought for. This is what I want. I nod and point him in the direction of the bathroom.

Twenty-Eight

Thea

Wesley is all business as he turns the old shower faucet on and tests the stream. The look of concentration on his face is adorable, especially as he tries to adjust the temperature to make it perfect. I feel like a swooning teenager drooling over him, but I can't stop and don't want to. He's mine.

"Thank God the heating runs on gas." He grimaces and cleans his glasses as they fog up. "But we can't see ourselves through the steam."

He searches the cupboards for something—finds the first aid kit, and puts it aside.

The previous Sinner who used the safe house left toiletries. Clean towels are on the rack, and protein bars are in the kitchen cupboard. It's well stocked with supplies. Most of the items in the house are clean and well cared for. We just have no power.

I have a moment of thinking we need candles when the relic hums in my hand and glows. Soft, warm light illuminates the bathroom. Once again, the staff read my thoughts and provided. My lip curves as I rest it against the tiles.

It stays alight when I let go.

Wesley gives it a wary glance but then returns to the business of checking my wounds.

"Right. Let's see what the damage is," he mumbles, adjusting his glasses to inspect me like I'm one of his books.

But I don't want to be inspected. I want to feel his naked body against mine. I like the comfort of his arms around me. He unzips my hoodie and peels it from my shoulders. I hiss as pain lances my ribs.

Alarmed eyes meet mine. "You alright, love?"

His voice is a deep murmur of compassion. I'm not used to this kind of attention. But as Alice said, I have room for better things if I stop filling my heart with the bad.

After I nod, Wesley starts narrating as he peels my shirt up my body. I can't tell if he's trying to distract himself from being worried about my injuries or if it's to put me at ease. Either way, I'm completely in love with him.

"Just lifting now," he mutters. "Just taking a peek. Alright. Going to lift a little more and check beneath."

His knuckles brush my bruised ribs. I suck in a breath. Wish I hadn't—*sharp pain*. I hold it in.

"You don't have to pretend with me, Thea," he whispers.

My jaw clenches briefly before softening. "I know."

He lifts my shirt clean off my head. I don't want to look at my torso, but from the bleak look in his eyes, it's not good.

"You should be at the hospital, love," Wes scolds. "They might be fractured."

"Nothing you can do for fractured ribs. I'm fine. Sore but fine."

He gives a disparaging shake of his head and resumes checking me. "This is my fault."

"How do you figure that?"

"Vepar was after me since before I was born."

"She said you were the first to mend the cracks. What does that mean?"

He frowns and goes quiet. I remove his spectacles, place them on the vanity, and smooth the frown line between his eyebrows. His lashes flutter at my touch. I slide my hand to cup his face.

"What does that mean, Wes?" I ask.

"It means I'm the first to fall in love with one of you Sinners. The first to close the cracks between two teams that shouldn't work but do. Vepar taunted me about her plan coming to fruition before you returned with the relic."

"What?" I splutter. I'm stuck on that first bit. Everything else is white noise.

"I'm in love with you, Thea. I..." He scrubs his hair. "Somehow, they knew that I would bring you the gospel. They knew if we're united, it's not good for them. If Raven is psychic and prophecies exist, they probably have one too." His eyes defocus with thought. "Come to think of it, I've heard rumors of an anti-Bible. An evil version of the good one. Perhaps there's also a missing gospel in theirs."

"I love you too," I whisper, still not registering much else from his mouth but that four-letter word. His eyes snap to mine. I keep talking because I'll lose the courage if I don't say it now. "Wes, before you came along, I felt like I was always floating adrift. And then we met, and even when we said we hated each other, something was happening between us. You see me like no one else has. You put up with my bullshit when I'm crazy and figuring out my emotions. You somehow know what I need when I don't. You are my anchor in this stupid world. I can't fathom a future without you."

The changing mood is a shift in the air. He no longer clinically looks at me, but like there's nothing and no one who could stand between us.

I slip off the rest of my clothes, careful not to aggravate my injuries. When I'm nude and straightened, his eyes are dark with lust. His lips purse. Nostrils flare. Shoulders tense. It's as though he's holding himself together by a thread. As his gaze rakes over me, from top to bottom, I know he's not seeing the wounds but the person beneath. The one who fought for him. The one who feels safe in his arms.

It's a strange notion—I'm the assassin—yet an embrace from him has the power to cradle my soul. I feel like nothing is impossible with him. This is what Lilith fights against.

"Shower with me," I whisper.

His hands are on his clothes, ripping, tugging, and removing as fast as possible. I laugh at his enthusiasm and then at the self-deprecation in his eyes when he realizes he's so obvious. But this is why I love him more. He's both light and dark, bashful and brave, dominant and gentle. I get the cuddles, and I get him when he's undone and ravenous with need for me.

I bite my bottom lip and appreciate his body. The relic casts a soft ambient light over his physique, from broad, muscular shoulders to a narrow, defined waist. Some tattoos have faded from healing. I reach out to touch him, but he pulls me into the shower, still determined to follow his promise of taking care of me.

The water isn't warm as it hits us. We gasp, and I wince. *Ribs. Ow.* I should be shivering, but my gaze is trapped on the goosebumps on his flesh. Heat builds in me, low and deep. I trail my fingers down his abdomen, loving how his muscles bunch in response, loving how I make him tremble while he adjusts the temperature of the water. I might have even purred.

"You know," I tease. "For a man who spends all day with books, you're kinda buff."

"I'm offended."

"No, you're not."

"I'm not." He smirks and holds his hand under the stream, still testing. "Dom treats his body like a temple, so apparently, we all must, too."

I can't stop touching him, from sliding my fingers over that wet, smooth and completely healed skin. I feel him all over. Marvel at his palms. I kiss each one.

"I'm supposed to be worshipping you," he grumbles, but I

take the thick, hard shaft of his erection and squeeze. Short, stilted breaths pass his lips. His eyes defocus, and he makes a helpless sound in the base of his throat. Sweet agony crosses his expression.

"Thea." His voice is gravelly. "Let me clean you first."

"While you do that, I'll do this."

"Always testing me."

The brave man releases a little growl as if steeling his resolve. Then he takes the shampoo from the caddy, fills his palm with soap, and lathers it into my hair. I gasp at the sensations but don't let go of his cock. I love seeing him try to keep his composure, and I pump him hard in my fist.

His fingers falter as they massage my head. "You're making this hard, love."

"That's the point."

"Minx."

"Always."

"Love, let me do this, please."

Something in his tone makes me pause. "What's wrong?"

He takes a deep breath and squeezes his eyes shut. He speaks without opening them. "You were right after you stabbed me. I had to suck it up. I'm not brave or a fighter, but I can do this. I can take care of you."

A lump forms in my throat.

"Wes," I sigh. "I only said that to keep you angry so you'd live long enough for me to return. You're the bravest man I know. Everyone you loved died around you, yet you kept going. You could have shut yourself off from the world, but you made friends and put them before anyone else. Can't you see you're an inspiration?"

His cheeks flush. "I don't want just to inspire you. I want you to know I can... be a man."

I press my lips to his collarbone and rest my face on his chest... maybe because I can't look into his eyes for the next bit. I'm a little embarrassed to admit this, but I have to. "Wes, you protect me every time you call me on my bullshit. I can be my own worst enemy. And sometimes... you see that I need something... different... and you find a way to give it to me but make it less shameful. You make me feel safe. You accept me as I am, and that's the best kind of man in my book."

He kisses the top of my head, mumbles something I don't catch, but I think it's about *always and forever,* then continues massaging my hair. Not long after, I run my hands down his front and resume stroking his erection. My actions keep tugging my head from his shampooing efforts.

"Thea," he warns.

"Wes," I return.

"I can play this rough, too."

"Can you?"

He laughs, only for an instant, because his mood sobers when he understands what I want. I get a flash of the devil in his eyes. He takes me by the throat and pushes me beneath the water. I splutter as the shampoo washes from my hair. He holds me there forcibly until I'm ready to kick him in the balls, then he tugs me out of the stream and captures my mouth with a blistering kiss.

The soap has made us slippery. When our bodies clash, my nipples brush his chest, and sparks shoot down my spine. I ignore the pain lancing my ribs. He spins me, facing me to the wall, and grips my neck. He pushes me under the faucet again.

It reminds me of what he did to me on the plane, how he bent me over the seat. I whimper for more.

"You love it like this, don't you?" His voice is hoarse in my ear.

"Yes."

"What parts?"

"All of it. I love you manhandling me like you have a right. Like I belong to you. Like if I keep giving you sass, and it gets in the way of you caring for me, you'll do whatever it takes to finish. You don't give up on me."

I push back, defy a little, and he slaps my ass.

Hard.

I cry out. The sting of wet flesh tears up my eyes, but the same hand that hurt molds to my buttocks and soothes me. He mumbles how much he needs to take care of me, how I always need to let him finish showing me what I deserve.

Pleasure.

Now I'm too hot. Too needy. The water isn't giving me relief. I need him. He squeezes my bottom hard, and I whimper. He backs off, confused by my sound.

"Keep touching me." I place my palms on the tiles and lean forward until my forehead rests against the cool surface. "Wes."

I don't think he meant for this to escalate in the shower.

He truly wants to make a sweet, loving gesture. And I'll take that later. But right now, I need corrupted Wes. The one who will walk hand-in-hand with me to hell... if I'm still going there.

"Get on your knees for me, Wes," I breathe, glancing over my shoulder. "Like you did before."

His eyes are glued to my ass. He catches me looking, and his lust deepens. Every part of him tenses. Veins pop in his muscles. The surviving tattoos look stark against his paler skin. Holding my gaze, he swipes fingers between my thighs and says gruffly, "You need me here, love?"

But he doesn't touch where I want. I widen my stance, panting. "Stop teasing."

A smug look comes over him. His fingers roam closer to my pussy. Closer. Another swipe. He traces over the mound and down the other thigh. I'm bottled up like a dam, throbbing and aching. I'm ready to show him who's in charge when he drops his lips to my spine and kisses down the arch until he's biting my buttocks.

"Wes..."

The soft, velvety strokes of his tongue move down the seam. He pulls apart my cheeks, licks around my anus, and then probes lower until he finds my quivering center. The deep, satisfied groan that rattles out of him makes me melt. The base of that man's voice can heat me as much as any fire.

"You taste so good," he murmurs as he explores. "You're so hot in here." His fingers probe my entrance. "And wet. Jesus, fuck, you're tight."

I gasp as he inserts fingers inside me. I wince at the pain in my ribs, but it feels so far away now. I'm too wound up with electrical heat that I can't speak.

"You're trembling, love. Let me know if you need to get out."

"Don't you dare stop," I whimper and push back. "Show me our last time wasn't a one-hit wonder."

He snarls at my challenge, pinches my clit, and kisses me down there. I'm a mewling mess. But we both need more. He spins me by the hips, holds me against the wall, and lifts my leg over his shoulder.

Water sprays down his back. Honey eyes flick to mine—a brief warning to brace for impact—and then he eats my pussy with ravenous, unrelenting tongue flicks. He makes needy sounds like he's getting off on this too. I grab his wet hair, tighten my fists, and hold him to me.

"You're an animal," I breathe.

He thrusts two fingers inside me as his tongue lashes my clit. I'm slowly losing control between the slipping and probing. I can't slow down the pleasure coiling in my lower belly. Wes doesn't relent until I come on his mouth, quaking with ecstasy, hissing and wincing at the pain in my ribs, but not giving a fuck. My body is on fire. My veins thrum his name. I'm not even sure I know my own anymore.

In a daze, feeling so good, I whine when he turns off the water. But he wraps a towel around me, once again the serious scholar who's all about business. He swipes his wet hair, wraps a towel around his waist, and then offers his hand to help me out of the shower.

Such a gentleman.

I pout. "We're done?"

He grins and scoops me up, one strong arm beneath my thighs and the other bracing my back. Then he kisses my nose. "Not even close, you insufferable minx."

Something flickers in his eyes, and then it's gone. I don't have a chance to query it because he makes me pick up the relic and walks me out.

The room he takes us to is modest but neat. Clean bed. Dry. Warm. Wes places me gently on the covers and unwraps my towel. His brows knit together as he checks me over. His fingers—the same fingers that were deep inside me, demanding and harsh—are now gentle on my wounded thigh like I'm made of glass.

"You're not bleeding," he confirms. "I don't think you need stitches."

He mumbles about finding balm from the first aid kit to rub on me, but I'm done with this part. I want Wes.

I reach for him as he's climbing off and connect with his arm. He pauses and glances at me. He's about to pat and mollify me so that he can continue with his ministrations, but I shake my head.

"Kiss me," I say.

"You should rest, love."

"You should fuck me first."

His lips part. His cheeks flush with color.

"Does my filthy mouth scandalize you, Mr. Wesley?" I poke.

He sputters a little.

"Do we need to coax the devil out again?"

"He was always there, love. Just repressed."

He comes back to me. I thread my fingers into his hair and pull him down until our lips meet. I kiss him the way he deserves. I use my whole body, only wincing when my ribs twist the wrong way. He braces himself over me, trying not to lower his weight. Even when I'm begging to be used, he still tries to keep me from pain.

My throat closes up. My eyes burn. He pulls back just enough to see that I'm okay, and then he shows me what it feels like to be worshipped. He kisses over my body, lingers on the parts he loves, and promises them he'll return. He respects the areas that are sore and learns every inch. I've never felt more cherished. More seen. There is nothing on my body he turns away from. Not the scars. Not the stretch marks. Not the bruises.

He kisses his way back to my mouth. My fingers trail down his abdomen to where I stabbed him, to remind myself it's truly healed. Eventually, he captures my hand and gives me a look that says, *Enough with the reminiscing.*

Then he slides my hand to the base of his shaft. He gives me control.

I don't stroke. I take my time tasting him, starting at his jaw, licking down that tendon on his neck. He tilts his head back and submits to me. I go slow, tease, taunt... just as he did with me. I kiss everywhere around his groin except where he wants it.

"Love," he grunts. "You're killing me."

I grin against his lower abdomen and find a vein leading south. I lick down the line until I feel the rough texture of his pubic hair, trace over it and discover his erection. His breath hitches, and he thrusts up, chasing my lips as I skate past.

"Thea," he begs, voice a rasp of need.

"Yes?"

"Open your sweet, sinning mouth and suck my cock." He pants. "Please."

"Thought you'd never ask."

I take him into my mouth, swirl my tongue over the blunt head, and lick in the groove. Then I push down until his tip hits the back of my throat and goes further. He releases a string of curse words and struggles to hold still. His hand is on my head, his hips flexing.

"Sweet mother, you're—*Christ*. Fuck me."

He's shuddering with sensation. Gasping and digging his fingers into my hair. I suck him hard, drag off, then go down deep again. He gasps again. Then roughly pulls me off him with wild, dark eyes.

"I can't," he pants. "It's too good."

I wipe my lips with a smirk. "Then this is going to feel better."

"What?"

I straddle him and slide his tip against my entrance.

"Thea," he groans at the sensation.

"Keep saying my name, Wes. But don't hold back."

He grips my hips. With short, sharp thrusts, he works himself in. He stretches me, and it's so perfect, so right.

"God, you feel so good inside me, Wes," I breathe.

He rolls on top, then pushes inside me to the hilt. He does it watching my face, hunting for more of my response to him. My eyes flutter, and I struggle to breathe.

"Wes," I whimper.

"Keep saying my name, love."

He pulls out, and my body weeps. It must show on my face because he's still bewitched by what he sees. He knows I have no control now. I'm his puppet. He grinds his hips in circles, changing his angle to hit deeper, to stimulate my clit with his pubic bone, to wring what he wills from me.

"You're mine," he says, voice hoarse.

My eyes open and see anguish on his face.

"What's wrong?"

"I don't want to share you." He frowns and thrusts hard, a curl to his upper lip as if he's going into battle. But it's just me. We don't fight anymore. We only play. My hands slide down his back. I try to soothe him, but his eyes are almost manic as he drives in and out of me.

"If you're to remain a Sinner," he croaks. "Your body is for me."

The proclamation hurts him to say.

"Babe," I rock into him. "If another man tries to show me his dick, I'll cut it from his body."

Air expels from his mouth, and he hangs his head until his forehead meets mine.

It takes him a moment to gather his emotions. He tries to speak once. Twice.

"I shouldn't be happy with that, but fuck it, cut the bastard's todger off. Whoever he is. Castrate him if he touches you."

I know he needs this from me. I cup his jaw and claim his mouth with mine. My kiss is gentle and loving. It's the part of me that wants this to last forever. Something in his body language is more than passion. It's the need of a man who doesn't want to be alone... ever again. I hold his hand against my heart, letting him feel it beating for him. Then I slide our hands to where we join, allowing him to feel the slick evidence of how he makes me feel.

We kiss until his body starts moving again. Slow thrusts become hard. Wild. Our foreheads mash together as our hips clash.

"I'm coming," I gasp as he keeps me on the edge and brings himself to the same place. We fall together. He buries his face in my neck and releases a long, shuddering groan of satisfaction. While he catches his breath, his hand moves down my sweat-slicked front, absently caressing my belly.

It strikes a chord in me.

"I'm on contraception," I whisper hesitantly. "But one day, I don't have to be."

His eyes meet mine with hope. "Thea, I want that. I want babysitters complaining about kids that don't sleep. I want midnight walks with a puppy that shits itself when he's excited. I want you in my bed every night."

I close my eyes and savor the sound of dreams coming true.

"Hey," he murmurs. "Love, I'm sorry if that's too real for you too soon, I—"

"Wes, I want it too." I open my eyes. Tears leak from the sides. "I've always wanted it but haven't been…. I've been forced into this life. A family was never an option for me. But now… you make it seem possible."

"Because it bloody is," he growls and wipes my tears. "I'll make it happen for us."

Doubts flicker over me. I glance at the relic, still glowing softly by the wall. It's the first of five. "We might not get a chance."

He pinches my jaw. "You worry about saving the world, and I'll worry about us."

"But."

"No buts." He smirks. "Don't overthink it, love."

"Touché." I laugh and roll my eyes. "Is this going to be one of those things where we spend the rest of our lives trying to have the last word?"

"Absolutely."

Twenty-Nine

I don't think I've ever felt as content as I do now, lying in the dark with Thea in my arms, on a stranger's bed in a strange house. We've been asleep for hours, but the sun is coming, and I've never been good at ignoring it.

It comes with responsibilities and harsh realities. More nightmares wait in the wings for each of our dreams coming true last night. Pestilence is in Prue. I fell in love with a Sinner. Vepar was after me because I was the first to mend the cracks.

But being the first implies there are more, which means I have a responsibility. My mind turns to Zeke, Cisco, and Dom. We work well together because we don't ask questions about our checkered pasts. We know what we must and don't talk about the rest. But what will they say when I return with Thea like this? What will they think when I tell them I'm only the first?

We're supposed to dismantle this organization.

But now we know the coming apocalypse is real. We can't be separate. I hope they'll understand. I hope that as I remain dedicated to the team, no one will have problems with my feelings for Thea. The Reverend Mother might be another question. Their operatives are meant to be isolated and ready for any mission. Thea promised to leave the seduction part of her role behind, but will the others think that's fair? And then there's the part about the guilt she needs to purge with pain. I don't want that for her either. I don't want her to kill because they tell her to.

My Thea is a romantic at heart. I see it in her eyes when we talk about our future together.

Maybe the Sisterhood still needs to go. But only in a sense there's no more forced killing. It needs to exist in a way that these women are left happy and whole.

But Pestilence is here, and it's undoubtedly inside Prudence. Even if we defeat the horseman—woman—it might be too late for any of us.

Thea stirs in my arms. I nuzzle her neck, inhaling her scent.

"Did the alarm go off?" she mumbles.

"Not yet."

She makes cute little sounds and squirms until she's fully awake. I can't believe I'll wake up with this for the rest of my life. It feels too good to be true, but she wants what I want. I smooth my palm over her hips, slide my hand to her stomach and trace my finger around her belly button. She rewards me with a little moan and rolls to face me. Just enough light comes through the window that I can make out her beautiful face. Well, the blurry outline of her face. My glasses are on the bedside table.

She's as blind as me—she removed her contact lenses before sleeping. Now she's rubbing her eyes with her fists. A smile tips my lips, and I pull her hand down.

"You'll get sore eyes."

"Yes, boss."

I snort.

"Why are you awake?" she asks, her expression serious. "Did you sleep?"

"Yes." But a part of me couldn't sink into oblivion knowing how close we came to losing everything. I kept thinking Vepar would find us or someone else will. It's a given that another demon will take Vepar's place, but whether they continue to hunt me or one of the others is the question.

A thought strikes me. A demon took Zeke's sister. What if he's been targeted from the start like I was?

Thea smooths my frown. "You're very scowly for someone who slept well."

"I said I slept," I reply. "Not how well."

A glint in her eyes replaces the concern as her hand moves south down my abdomen. "I can make you feel better."

My lashes flutter as she strokes my cock, coaxing it to life. My nerves seize with pleasure. I can't function when she does this to me. I'm instantly hard. Suddenly there's nothing I want more than the comfort between her thighs. I roll on top of her, careful not to drop my weight on her ribs. She opens her thighs, and I push in. We take it slow, enjoying our pleasure until the alarm goes off on her cell phone, and then we finish at a grueling pace. Neither is willing to leave this room until we finish what we started.

Later, when we're dressed and carrying our bags to the garage, she stops and says, "You know I meant it when I said I chose you."

I smile. "I know."

"I really want you to believe me. Even if I didn't stab you —sorry about that, by the way—I would have used the staff on you to stop what Vepar did, and I would have still saved you, even if the relic only had a single use."

Guilt flashes in her eyes, and I know why she's brought this up again. It's not because she thinks I don't believe her. This declaration is more than an affirmation of our love. We're about to return home and face the loved ones we put second. I spent months working on a plan to get the broken manuscript to the Sinners so I could follow them to the relics. For Zeke.

"It's good that we chose each other," I affirm. "I believe that."

"Even if the relic doesn't work on Zeke or Prue?"

I open the door to the garage. "I don't know, but I'll never regret it."

A swishing sound startles inside, and we freeze. Someone is in here.

Thea clenches the staff. I wish I had a knife or arcane card, but I don't want to move suddenly. We scan the gloomy, dusty space for signs of life. Thea gestures for me to go one way around the car. I take a hammer from a box of tools and move to one side while she goes to the other. Her sharp gasp of surprise sends my pulse skyrocketing. I glance over, ready to attack the danger to her, but she's crouched or fallen. I can't see her over the car.

"Thea!" I jog to her side.

I find her on the ground, dragging a little squirming black creature from beneath the car.

"Look," she coos as she adjusts her package. "Have you ever seen anything like him?"

After confirming she's unhurt, I finally look at the creature in her arms. Its body is long like a Daschund but not a dog—scales shimmer in strange iridescent colors on its smooth dark skin. A transparent gray, papery frill decorates the spine on the length of its back and tail. Big, liquid eyes full of fear glimmer at her. It whimpers from deep in its throat like a dolphin caught in a shark net.

"What the bloody hell is that?" I blink.

She inspects it further, checking its clawed paws and sharp teeth inside its mouth. "It kind of looks like those demonic fish minions, but... it's not so grotesque. It's cute. It's even cuter than that puppy." Her smile drops. She groans and looks at me with wide eyes. "Oh no."

"What?"

"Oh nooo."

"Thea, what?"

"I think I healed one of them. I remember having compassion for it. It just looked so sad! It didn't burst into water but was thrown across the street. It must have healed into this, followed us to the car, and crawled in. Or it found our scent across London and came here."

"That thing can track us?"

"Shh." She scowls and hugs it to her. "You hurt his feelings and don't call him a thing. What's wrong with you? You love puppies."

"It's not a puppy," I grumble.

"He needs a name."

"Thea," I warn, seeing where this is going.

"Hmm. You look like a Squishy. Or a Flynn because of your fins."

"Thea, you can't take a demon home."

"Ex-demon," she corrects. "Or maybe Jinx because you knocked over all the paint in the garage. Yeah, I see the red paw prints, buddy, and it's how I knew to look under the car."

"We have to go." I open the car door.

"We can't leave Jinx here. He's my responsibility. I made him this."

"You sure it's a he?"

"Oh, shit." She lifts the animal's frilly tail and gasps. "It's a girl!"

I toss my backpack onto the back seat, then look at her. She gives me big liquid eyes, just like the demon puppy. But she's not wrong. She made it, and we can't leave something like that running around the streets of London. And I did wish for a puppy with her.

Christ.

"I guess we can work out what it is at the abbey. Just don't let the pilot see."

She grins and jumps into the car, taking my spot in the passenger seat. "You can drive."

"Really?" Yesterday she refused to let me get behind the wheel. "I see. I'm replaced already."

She rubs the little critter on the belly and then coos as its long tongue lolls from its mouth.

"Impossible," she says without looking up. "You're irreplaceable."

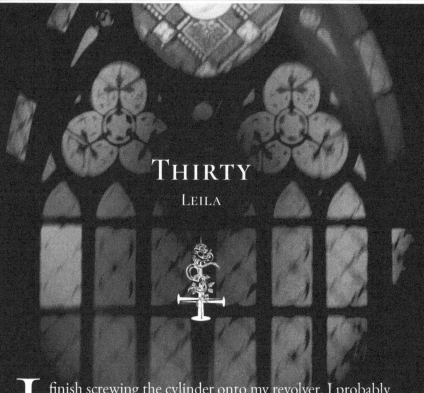

THIRTY
LEILA

I finish screwing the cylinder onto my revolver. I probably don't need to clean it as often as I do, but it's a habit that keeps my fingers and mind busy. It's either that or becoming like Prue and working myself to exhaustion from exercising. With everything happening right now, I need routine more than ever, and the old gun can take it.

The smell of oil is strong in this tiny cell. I hope if my roommate returns early from her mission, the smell will encourage her to find another place to sleep.

I need my space.

I need...

My thoughts shift to the newcomers. To Zeke. I can't believe he doesn't recognize me. Or maybe I'm worth nothing to him. Fucking asshole.

He was my only friend at the group home for orphans, and then he made me think he was dead.

My alarm pings on my cell phone. It's my turn to take watch by Prue's bedside. It's not a pretty sight. I want to help my colleague, but I was never really close to her. Not that I'm close with the others, but Prue and I never got along. She didn't like my dry attitude. I wish I wasn't this insensitive, but years of this sinning life have weighed on me.

Prue is old enough to know why I was brought to the abbey. She probably heard rumors of fires at my foster care homes—of no one adopting me because of things mysteriously burning around me. She put two-and-two together.

A knock comes at the door.

"They're back!" shouts Tawny and opens the door.

I scowl at her intrusion. Why does everyone think they have a right to come in without an invitation? Her blond hair is unwashed, and she has dark circles under her eyes. Of all of us who remained, she stayed by Prue's bed the most. When she catches my expression, she asks, "You okay?"

"I'm fine."

"But if you're not, you know I—"

"I said, I'm fine, Tawny."

"Okay, okay. I got it." She gives me the side-eye but doesn't push. "I'll meet you downstairs."

After she leaves, I gather my things. Thea and Wesley left a few days ago to find a holy relic they hoped would help Prue, and I honestly didn't believe it existed. The manuscript they based their intel on was so vague, and if it weren't for the strange Sight this gospel gives us girls, I would have told them not to waste their time.

But apparently, it was a success. Yippee.

I hurry into the hallway but crash into Zeke. We're a tangle of limbs and confusion.

"You fucking kidding me?" I shove him away.

He stumbles back, a smirk on his handsome lips. It's been decades, but he still looks the same—better. Adulthood has turned all his soft lines hard, but it's also made him a forgetful asshole. I use my shoulder to punch him out of the way.

"Psycho," he grumbles and grabs his arm.

I spin. "As if you can't take it."

He's a dirty street fighter. His nose has been broken. Little scars over his eyebrows, ears, jaw, and cheekbones are precisely the kind you get from brawling. And I know how he got the slash beneath his chin firsthand.

My words have the opposite effect than I intended. His hazel eyes sparkle with a challenge.

"But I can give a lot more," he drawls suggestively.

"You're revolting."

"You love it."

"I want to puke."

"You want to fuck me."

"I want to murder you." My shriek erupts from my heart, shocking him with its intensity.

"What's your problem?" His brows lower.

"My problem? Are you serious?"

"Yeah, your problem." He shoves my shoulder with two fingers.

The explosion of anger in my body evaporates. I still. My

mind empties to the killing calm all Sinners have. With slow, deliberate movements, I glance at where he still touches me. Then I slowly return my gaze to his face.

I never noticed his eyes were jaundiced before. He quickly looks away, shoves his hands in his torn jeans pockets, and jogs down the stairs.

"If you're spoiling for a fight, Zeke," I shout after him. "I'm your huckleberry."

He pauses halfway down the steps.

"Go on," the matron says, her voice deep and husky. "Go join the others."

She shoves me into the group home's courtyard and then leaves. I hug Mr. Snuggles tightly and look over his fluffy bear head to inspect my new home. The slate courtyard has high walls, a few straggly trees in pots, and a lingering sense of hopelessness. Three boys and one girl kick around a ball, taking turns to play piggy in the middle. Right now, the piggy is a boy with a limp. They're all older than me—big kids.

Hugging Mr. Snuggles, I shuffle forward. Maybe these will be different than the others. Maybe they won't care about the fires.

A red-haired boy notices me first. "Oh, what do we have here?"

"Fresh meat," says another.

Before I know it, I'm the new piggy, and they're using Mr. Snuggles as the ball. Tears streak down my face as I jump to intercept, but it's useless. I'm eight, and they must be twelve or older—all lifers, all too wretched to find a forever home.

Compared to them, I'm weak. But I don't let it stop me. I snarl, hiss, scratch, and kick shins until one of them grabs my arms and holds me, preparing me for punishment. I buck and struggle.

"Hey!"

Everyone looks to the entrance. Another big kid is there. He's scarier than the others. Dark floppy hair, angry eyes, fists clenched and ready to fight. He stalks toward us, and I almost pee my pants. But he doesn't come at me. He shoves the redhead hard enough he falls on his ass.

"You wanna pick on someone, Puck? I'm your huckleberry."

My eyes widen as a brawl starts. They all jump on the newcomer, but he's tougher and stronger. They eventually scatter, limping away with black eyes and swollen lips. The new guy stoops to pick up Mr. Snuggles and wipes a bleeding cut on his chin with his shoulder so he doesn't soil my toy when he dusts it off.

I startle when he hands Mr. Snuggles to me, then bare my teeth and hiss.

He laughs. "You're a real wildcat, huh?"

Zeke's knuckles go white on the railing. He faces me with a peaky complexion but says nothing.

I'm fucking done. If he wants to be a jerk about it, the least he can do is own up to it.

"Wh-what did you say?" he gapes.

"You heard me." I jog down, passing him without another look.

"Wildcat?"

My heart clenches at his old nickname for me. It's more

ingrained into my soul than the old Tombstone movie refer-
ences he spouted during our imaginary forays into the Wild
West. He was always Doc Holliday, and I was a lot of people.
Sometimes a damsel, sometimes a villain, but mostly Wyatt
Earp.

None of it matters now except to serve as a warning—
always guard your heart, especially from those closest to you.
They have the most power to break it.

Thirty-One

Thea

Wesley and I head straight to the infirmary at the abbey. The flight here was fraught with tension and worry. We couldn't relax, and it had nothing to do with Jinx scampering about the cabin, getting into mischief, and chewing on the leather. It also had nothing to do with the stolen artifact in my hands, and how we managed to sneak it on the jet and out of the country.

It's all to do with the things we've learned. Wes and I compared notes on the gospel, and my hunch about the blank pages was correct. He'd never seen some of the words written on them. So they're new and meant only for us Sinners. It will take a long time before we can translate everything.

As we hurry through the corridors, I can't help but notice how the abbey feels different. The air is different. The smells are different. Or maybe it's just me who's changed.

The relic warms in my hand as we cross the threshold to the infirmary. It must sense the demonic energy vibrating off the walls. Two steps in, I stop. Sunlight glaring from the window paints the scene of a horror movie.

In the corner, surrounded by Sinners and Saints, Prue is *floating*. Straps anchor her bowed body to the bed. She thrashes, bucks, and throws something wet from her damp hair and face. Probably a mix of sweat and vomit from the stench amongst the disinfectant.

Everyone is here from both teams except the Monsignor.

Zeke suddenly blocks my path. The desperate look in his eyes freaks me out. I've never seen him so wild.

"It will work for more than one," Wesley tells him. "Let her through."

For a moment, I think Zeke will fight me for the relic, but Wesley steps around me with Jinx in his arms and whispers something to Zeke.

His face crumples in relief. I might even see tears in his eyes.

"I'll come back," I promise, then rush to Prue's bedside.

"Thank God," the Rev says upon seeing me. She's sitting on a chair, holding her rosary beads to her lips.

Father Angelotti stands at the foot of the bed, holding his Bible toward Prue and praying. The tired man shoots me a look of relief. As I look around the bed, everyone has the same expression.

Their faith gives me the courage to take charge. Prue hisses and screams as the staff nears her, but I continue my healing thoughts. The staff heats and fires up, glowing brightly. It wants to help. But something is wrong. Prue's body suddenly drops to the bed. She surveys us and cackles like this is all a game. Iridescent scales roll beneath her sores and rotting flesh. Something moves inside her body. Something alien. It wants to break through.

"That won't kill me." The taunt from her lips is otherworldly and profound. "I am too strong. A prince of hell."

"No," Father Angelotti replies, his face stern as he wraps his rosary around his Bible, ensuring the crucifix faces the demon. "You are Loimós Leviathan."

Shock enters the demon's expression. Then the unmistakable pallor of fear. They must have waited for me to arrive before using the power of the name. I see why. Now the demon is desperate. It bucks inside Prue's body, thrashes, and moves with unnatural strength. A giant invisible hand grips her spine and flops her up and down like a ragdoll.

It becomes glaringly apparent that whatever came before this was an act. This is real. Leather straps creak as they strain. Chaos erupts.

"Hold her down," Mercy barks, renewing her grip on Prue's shoulder. Leila takes another. Raven grabs a leg, and Tawny holds Prue's head between her hands. The Saint mumbles something to Father, hands him a vial of holy water, then takes the other leg. Wesley gives Jinx to Zeke and joins in, holding down any part of Prue he can grasp.

Halogen lights flicker. Bulbs burst. I hold the relic to Prue's body and think healing thoughts, but it's still not helping. Wesley was right. I might have to obliterate the demon—as I did with Vepar... but that won't save Prue.

"I can't do anything until the demon is out," I shout. "Otherwise, Prue might die."

"I think she's dying anyway," the Reverend Mother says quietly.

Prue's body contorts with a succession of wet cracks... from the inside.

"Help her, Thea," Tawny cries. "Help her now."

"But—"

"Now!" she barks, eyes blazing.

Demon Prue's manic laughter escalates. She snaps the restraint on her left wrist and swings at Mercy. Father Angelotti lunges and intercepts. The strain of keeping Prue's fist from connecting with Mercy turns his face red. But he never once falters with his prayers.

Wesley turns to me. "You said the relic works with your thoughts, and if you match what Cisco says, perhaps you will combine powers."

Father nods without breaking his flow. His words are in Latin, but I understand every single one of them. With both hands on the staff, I keep pressing it to Prue's body and join Father.

She stops struggling. Her back lands on the bed again, and she stills. The thing inside her is watching us through black eyes.

"You won't kill me," it rasps. "I'll only take the Stony One's place. And then I'll find a way out."

"Stony One," Wesley mumbles thoughtfully.

The next part happens in slow motion. I don't think I'll ever forget the horror for the rest of my life. I increase the force of the relic. The light glows blindingly, just like when I healed Wes. Father pushes his rosary-wrapped Bible onto Prue's chest while dousing her with holy water. Prue's mouth gapes open, revealing sharp piranha-like fangs. Wesley shouts for us to stop, but I hear him through water as I arrive at the same conclusion.

Stony One.

Sakhr.

Prison.

We've been duped. But it's too late.

Out of Prue's unhinged demonic mouth, a masculine hand appears. I'm too horrified to move. Is this a hallucination? Is it real? No—I glance around the bed—only those with the Sight are as stunned as me. But they're still afraid. Something is happening. When I look back at Prue, a man has climbed out of her mouth.

An entire man.

He rolls over her body and drops to the floor between Mercy and Dom. They're both so alarmed they step aside.

The muscular, naked man with dark hair rises and faces the Saint.

"Perfect," he drawls, cracks his neck, closes his eyes, and releases a low, breathy grunt. He shakes out his limbs like he's about to race with Olympians. A dark, tailored suit now covers his body... a mirror image of the one Dominic wears.

Asmodeus.

Black demonic eyes meet mine, and he smirks. "In the tawdry flesh."

THIRTY-TWO

THEA

We've somehow released Asmodeus—the Stony One—from a prison we didn't know he was in. And from the smug look on his face, this is what he had planned all along. My mind whirls back to the summoning. When he appeared, he'd stretched like he'd been crouched forever.

I swing the staff at his head. Holy power thrums up my arms, charging me with electricity. "I'll send you right back, asshole."

He stops the staff from hitting his head with two fingers, then swats it aside like an annoying fly. A slow smile stretches his obscenely beautiful lips.

"Unless you wish to release Pestilence, I suggest not. That prison only has room for one. And I've been in there for centuries. Who would you rather—one of the horsemen or me?"

"I don't understand," Tawny mumbles. "How did we...?"

"Well, dove, it's like this." He turns to her, his words sharp as razors. "Remember that old lover who scorned me, and I killed every one of her husbands for seven marriages? Well, she made a deal with an archangel, and he gave her that staff. You can either use that thing on me, take your chances that it has enough juice to do the job again, or use it on your friends."

Gurgling at the bed steals my attention. Prue looks like herself, but she's choking on blood. It bubbles from her mouth as her eyes dart about the bed, trying but failing to focus on us.

"I held on as long as I could," she coughs.

I rush to her side. "We know, Prue. You did good. You did so good."

Asmodeus slinks back to watch. I don't have time for him. None of us do. Blood spits and oozes from Prue's mouth. She reaches for me. "I kept it inside as long as I could. I didn't give up."

I grab her hand and blink away the tears. The girls are touching her now, all struggling to hide emotion.

"I'm going to heal you, okay?" I wipe her sweaty face with my hand. Her pupils are pinholes of pain, and every bone in her body must be broken. "I'm going to make this okay."

"No," she grits out, wincing and shaking her head. "No more."

"But Prue—"

"*No!*" Her nostrils flare as she summons the strength to

speak. "I'm done, Thelma. My ride is over. Elvis has left the building. Let me go."

Open your eyes. Witness his death. Give his life meaning.

The memory slams into my chest, squeezing my heart. Tears burn my eyes as Father starts her last rights.

"Shut up!" I scream at him. "Shut the fuck up."

The Rev is in tears, praying. I look around the group, aghast. They've all accepted Prue's death already.

"No," I croak. "We're not letting this happen. Girls. You know our fate. She's one of us!" I press the staff to Prue's chest. It responds to me. Prue doesn't want it. I sense the rejection like a slap to the face. But I can't let her go to hell. I can't let her soul be tortured for eternity because I failed to follow my calling. Maybe if I'd accepted Team Saint's help earlier, none of this would have happened.

"Babe," I say to Prue, voice trembling. "There's plenty more of this ride to enjoy. It's not time yet. Trust me. Come on."

Prue's eyes defocus. "I did good. I held on."

"I know," I choke. "You did."

"So long..." She gurgles. Her eyes widen, and she seizes in agony—blood streams from her eyes, lips, and ears.

"Shh," I hold her as she suffers a seizure. "You're safe. You're one of us. We protect our own." I know I can find a way if I have enough time. This relic will work. I just need to calm my mind. Maybe—

"Don't overthink it, Thea."

My heart clenches. It's not Wesley's voice. Not a poor attempt at humor.

No, it was Prue who whispered the words. Prue, who first said them to me decades ago.

The lights dim and flicker in the room. The temperature cools. Something is coming. Something unholy. Death? From his quiet spot, Asmodeus glances around, sensing the same thing. Then his demon black eyes latch onto me. Talons distend from his stained black fingertips. In the span of a blink, he pushes in and whispers something to Prue. She nods, and then he reaches inside her chest and squeezes her heart until it stops.

The viper attacks. Tawny launches at Asmodeus so fast that he can't block her. But his lips twist into a parody of a smile. He captures her face between his hands and kisses her. She thrashes and digs her nails into his cheek. Blood wells through claw marks, but he doesn't remove his lips from hers.

We break free of the spell grief has cast on us. Every Sinner kicks into action. We launch to rescue our sister but grab air. The prince of hell evades us like we're moving in jelly, but he casually steps to the side and gives Tawny a wink.

"Why?" she shouts.

A dark look flashes in his eyes. "Revenge."

Then his visage shimmers, and he disappears.

Leila runs to the spot he vacated.

"Nothing. He's gone."

I turn back to Prue. Raven puts her fingers on Prue's lifeless eyelids and closes them. It feels as though Asmodeus squeezed my heart, not Prue's. What good is an archangel's power if it can't beat free will? I know she wanted this. But she didn't know what we know. She didn't know about the gospel.

Maybe if...

Rage builds inside me. The pressure is a kettle about to blow. I can barely breathe from the heat stampeding through my blood. What the fuck are we doing here? Why are we wasting our lives this way?

Wesley touches my back, and I crumple. Everything rushes out of me in an anguished sob of sorrow. I cry so loud and hard that I feel like the heavens open. My fist tightens around the staff. I pour all my grief and fear into it, and I demand the angel who gave this staff his power to listen to me.

"Take Prue," I urge through sobs. "She's suffered enough, sacrificed everything! Don't you dare leave her for the darkness, or I swear to the Holy Mother I will find a way up there and make you pay."

When my words die, the silence is deafening. My sisters look at me, wide and bleary-eyed. The men fear me. The Reverend Mother still holds Prue's lifeless hand, and nothing has changed.

Nothing except the relic heating in my hands, glowing without permission. The light grows, but that's all it does. It feels like an acknowledgment of some kind—I hope. I pray. And then I look at Prue's face and gasp.

"Can anyone else see that?" Raven mumbles.

"Is she smiling?" Tawny sobs.

"Love, I'm sorry, but I don't see a smile," Wesley says softly.

It's just us five Sinners with the Sight who see. I don't know what it means. But then the oddest thing happens. A bird lands on the windowsill closest to the bed. At first, I fear it's a crow, but it's too small.

"A mockingbird." I laugh through my tears, dazed.

Elvis has left the building, but the mockingbird is not dead. It pecks twice on the glass, looks straight at me, winks, then flies away.

"It winked," I mumble. "I swear to God it winked."

"Does that mean she's in Heaven?" Leila asks, her voice trembling.

"It has to be," Mercy replies. "What else would it mean?"

"Wherever she is... she's free." I look at the relic with reverence, a little ashamed of my previous threat. *If that was your doing, thank you.* It pulses in response.

Movement in my peripheral catches my attention. Zeke is standing back from us all, his hands in his pockets, his jaw set, his eyes bleak. Jinx has made herself comfortable around his neck. While everyone is still occupied with their emotions, I walk to him and quietly touch the relic to his arm. I wish him well.

The light glows. It sparks bright. Maybe I should have waited until we had privacy for this next bit. But I don't say what I'm doing, nor does Zeke. If he's healed, or why he was sick in the first place, is his story to tell. From the suspicious looks cast our way after the light fades, I know it won't be long before he has to tell it.

The little ex-demon crawls from him and leaps onto me. Jinx makes those little dolphin sounds and then settles around my neck.

Wesley is suddenly by my side. He squeezes my arm with gratitude. I check Zeke to see if he's okay, but he's already walking out of the infirmary, hands in pockets, shoulders hunched.

"You have explaining to do," The Rev says as she covers Prue with a sheet. "And as soon as we make the proper arrangements for Sister Prudence, we will convene in the archives."

Wesley puts his arm around my shoulders and kisses my head. "Come on, love, let's get cleaned up first."

Most in the room follow us out. Father is dead on his feet, and Dominic helps him walk. There is much to discuss, but we all need a break—a chance to catch our breaths and work out how we will deal with Asmodeus. We stopped Pestilence, but did we stop the apocalypse?

And then there's the gospel. Wesley can't hide what he's done from the Entity forever. I'm not even sure if Father and the Saint know.

Angry shouts filter down the corridor from the dining hall.

"That's not right." I frown.

Mercy pushes past me with Raven. Leila has her gun out, aimed, and ready.

"What's wrong?" Wesley asks.

"No one should be talking," I point out. "Everyone who lives here has taken a vow of silence." I glance behind me, where the others still gather. "We're the only ones who haven't."

We jog into the hall and find a war zone. The long benches are upturned. Mess is everywhere. Food. Drinks. Plates. Cups. Nuns hurl cooking utensils and food at each other. One has brandished a knife, and from the look of the torn strips in her opponent's robes, she's already had a good slash.

"You cut me!" the nun shouts, astonished.

"Because you fucking bumped me first!" the other replies.

My eyes widen. Oh shit, it's Sister Margaret. She's almost unrecognizable with that look of murder on her face. Her eyes are full of hate and a lust for revenge. One Magpie is pressed against the stainless-steel cooler door in the kitchen, and another is beating her up with a frying pan.

But that's not the worst of it.

A dreadful sight watches over the dining hall. The Monsignor has been crucified—nailed to the wall by carving knives through his palms and feet. Above his head, written in dripping blood, are the words: Ezekiel 18:4.

There's so much blood. Too much for the old man to have survived. Cisco and Dom rush to him—to check, but it's too late. The Monsignor is dead.

Someone whistling a tune draws our attention to a

window. Outside, a man in a black suit strolls across mani-cured lawns toward the gates. He vanishes.

One thought pierces the chaos. He did this. He created a battle in the most unlikely of places.

"Leviathan was a horseman. A prince of hell," I say.

Wesley's expression turns grim. "Asmodeus must be War."

Epilogue

A lone woman drags her blistered feet through a city street in the pouring rain. She struggles to breathe through a rattling cough. Her bell slips from her hand. The message board hanging over her shoulders is heavy. Around her, denizens hug their coats against the coming storm. Someone bumps her but keeps walking.

She falls to her knees.
No one stops to help.
No one blinks.

Another person bumps into her. She topples forward, face landing hard on the wet concrete. A chalk message is legible on her signboard only for seconds before the rain bleeds it away.

The age of sin has arrived.

**Read the SPICY BONUS EPILOGUE featuring that
steamy fantasy Wesley has about the library.**
https://geni.us/tsats-bonus

**DON'T MISS OUT - ORDER THE NEXT BOOK, THE
SINNER AND THE GUNSLINGER NOW.**

DID YOU KNOW...

The Sinners first appeared in *The Deadly Seven Series.*
It's a complete Fated Mate Paranormal Romance series
featuring the genetically modified heroes you met in this book
and their siblings. Like Marvel, but make it Spicy!

Get more on Patreon

Become an official Guardian Angel and Support Lana as she creates

From bonus epilogues, short stories (as voted monthly by the patrons) NSFW Art and behind the scenes, plus discounts on Lana's website. Four tiers to choose from including exclusive limited book and merch boxes.

Patreon Angels get **early access** to all releases in ARC ebook format plus all audiobooks free as they release.

patreon.com/lanacreates

Also by Lana Pecherczyk

The Deadlyverse

The Deadly Seven

(Paranormal/Sci-Fi Romance)

The Deadly Seven Box Set Books 1-3

Sinner (prequel origins novella)

Envy

Greed

Wrath

Sloth

Gluttony

Lust

Pride

Despair

The Sinner Sisterhood

The Sinner and the Scholar

The Sinner and the Gunslinger

FAE GUARDIANS WORLD

Fae Guardians Series

(Fantasy/Paranormal Romance)

Season of the Wolf Trilogy

The Longing of Lone Wolves

The Solace of Sharp Claws

Of Kisses & Wishes Novella (free for subscribers)

The Dreams of Broken Kings

Season of the Vampire Trilogy

The Secrets in Shadow and Blood

A Labyrinth of Fangs and Thorns

A Symphony of Savage Hearts

Season of the Elf Trilogy

A Song of Sky and Sacrifice

A Crown of Cruel Lies

CPSIA information can be obtained
at www.ICGtesting.com
Printed in the USA
LVHW030541010623
748371LV00006B/841